Terror's Temptress

Dublin Falls Archangel's Warriors MC

Ciara St. James

Ciara St James Publishing

Copyright © 2020 Ciara St. James

All rights reserved

The characters and events portrayed in this book are fictitious. Any similarity to real persons, living or dead, is coincidental and not intended by the author.

No part of this book may be reproduced, or stored in a retrieval system, or transmitted in any form or by any means, electronic, mechanical, photocopying, recording, or otherwise, without express written permission of the publisher.

ISBN-13: 9798637209286

Library of Congress Control Number: 2018675309
Printed in the United States of America

Cover Photographer- Taylor Alexander Photography-
www.tayloralexander.com
Graphic Designer- Niki Ellis Designs, LLC
Models- Chantel and Cody Mackie

Foreword

Disclaimer: Warning: This book contains sexually explicit scenes. It is intended for audiences 18+. There may be graphic description of sex acts some may find disturbing. There may also be descriptions of physical violence, torture or abuse. Some strong themes are found in this series. While the characters may not be conventional, they all believe in true love and commitment. The book is a HEA with some twists and turns along the way.

Archangel's Warriors MC: Brothers by choice, not blood. Born to ride until they die. All they wanted was to ride free until lightning strikes them without warning. Consumed by desire, surrounded by danger, they find the "one" who will consume, enchant, frustrate and ultimately love them. They only see each other. When Archangel's Warriors find the "One", they don't back down, they don't ever stray and they will do anything to protect their women, even kill for them. Their women are strong, feisty, and dangerous. They are each other's every fantasy come to life. The sex is hotter than anything they've ever known. Those who stalk their club or threaten their women had better beware!

Terror was the president of the Dublin Falls Archangel's Warriors MC. He wasn't looking for a woman. He could have any woman he wanted at any time. Until one night after a dangerous mission, Harlow unexpectedly walks into his life. She was tough, beautiful, sexy, deadly and the daughter of another chapter president. The club has an enemy stalking them already. And now she enters his life with her own enemy. He plans to win her for himself, but first he'll have to keep her father from killing him and their enemies from taking her away from him. Because he's found he can't live without his Temptress.

Dublin Falls Chapter

Declan Moran (Terror)- President
Grayson Sumner (Savage)- Vice President
Dominic Vaughn (Menace)- Enforcer
Chase Romero (Ranger)- Sergeant at Arms
Jaxon Quinn (Viper)- Treasurer
Slade Devereaux (Blaze)- Secretary
Logan Priest (Steel)- Road Captain
Mason Durand (Hammer)
James Johnson (Tiny)
Talon Adair (Ghost)
Galen Duchene (Smoke)
Dane Michaelson (Hawk)

Contents

Title Page	1
Copyright	2
Dedication	3
Foreword	5
Dublin Falls Chapter	7
Chapter 1: Terror	11
Chapter 2: Terror	24
Chapter 3: Harlow	33
Chapter 4: Terror	40
Chapter 5: Harlow	46
Chapter 6: Terror	51
Chapter 7: Harlow	58
Chapter 8: Terror	62
Chapter 9: Harlow	70
Chapter 10: Terror	78
Chapter 11: Harlow	90
Chapter 12: Terror	95
Chapter 13: Harlow	107

Chapter 14: Terror	116
Chapter 15: Harlow	122
Chapter 16: Terror	127
Chapter 17: Terror	139
Chapter 18: Harlow	156
Chapter 19: Terror	162
Chapter 20: Harlow	174
Chapter 21: Terror	180
Chapter 22: Harlow	190
Chapter 23: Terror	196
Chapter 24: Harlow	203
Chapter 25: Terror	210
Chapter 26: Harlow	222
Chapter 27: Terror	229
Chapter 28: Harlow	240
Chapter 29: Terror	246
Chapter 30: Harlow	253
Chapter 31: Terror	257
Chapter 32: Harlow	267
Epilogue:	275
About The Author	283
Books In This Series	285

Chapter 1: Terror

The cool evening air blew through my hair as I rode my Harley down the dark highway with my brothers. It was a great night for a ride. The hot June day had cooled off and the scent of night was in the air. Out here, the stars were bright with no town lights to hide them. It was a perfect Tennessee night. This was one of the greatest joys of riding. A sense of freedom, the wind in your face and the feel of power between your legs. I'd found nothing that compared to this feeling. I knew all my brothers felt the same way. Too bad we weren't out for a simple joy ride together.

Tonight was all about business, serious and dangerous business. We were having a meeting with the Satan's Bastards MC. They were a rival motorcycle club. Any kind of contact with the Bastards was never good or welcome. However, we needed to determine what their plans were and why they were trying to move into Warriors' territory. As President of the Dublin Falls' Archangel's Warriors MC, I had to protect not only my brothers and their families, but the territory we claimed as ours. The other Warriors territories were at risk from the Bastards, if we didn't push them back.

For several months, the Bastards had been trying to push into our area. They kept having confrontations with us. Until little things that were more annoying than anything. But we knew it would get worse. I knew they wanted what our club had and would do anything to get it. Which really didn't make sense. The Warriors were a totally different club than the Bastard's. Whereas the Bastards made their money from everything illegal: running guns, drugs, and prostitution, the Warriors made our money through legitimate businesses: garages, bars, tattoo parlors and construction companies to name a few. However, we made those businesses into very lucrative ones. Our territory was a huge roadblock in the supply routes for the Bastards' drugs and guns, as well as limited their prostitution business. We refused to allow their kind of shit in or near our town. Period.

This meeting was one I had tried to set up for months without success, when things first started to heat up with the Bastards. Not to say that things weren't always uneasy between us. There were scrimmages and such several times a year, but not like what had been happening for the last year. I'd asked repeatedly to meet with them, only to be put off. Then suddenly, Grinder, the Bastards' President, had reached out yesterday completely out of the blue asking for a meet. Each of us agreed to bring to the meet ourselves and nine others from each of our clubs. I didn't trust them to not use this as an opportunity to hit our clubhouse or one of our businesses. So, in order to ensure both were protected in our absence, I asked some of the Hunters Creek brothers to ride along with us and others to stay behind to help guard the businesses and clubhouse in Dublin Falls.

A lot had changed over the fifteen years since I had joined the Warriors. For one, we hadn't always been legitimate, like we were now. I had worked hard since becoming president six years ago, to make the club thrive and maintain our new legit status. At thirty-four years old, I had been with the Warriors close to half of my life. I knew nothing else I wanted to do. I had started hanging around them when I was sixteen. It was the old president, Deuce, who had taken a liking to me. He convinced me to sign up and go to the military as soon as I graduated high school. A lot of the members had served. So, at seventeen I went off to boot camp with the Army then straight into Ranger school after that. I would come home and work with the club when I had leave as a prospect, even while still on active duty. I got patched in at nineteen and finally left the Army at twenty-three. I didn't regret my time in the Army and knew that it helped me to mature. Which I think was what Deuce wanted to happen.

The fact that we were now legitimate didn't mean we wouldn't take care of business any way we needed to when necessary. This was my family and I trusted and protected them just as they did me. We always had each other's backs no matter what. Brotherhood was a key thing that made us such a strong group. We might get into arguments and even fights, but at the end of the day, we were always family, and no one could fuck with that and get away with it.

Along for the ride from the Hunters Creek chapter, was their President, Bull. Bull had been around and seen just about everything. He had been a Warrior for close to thirty years. In his fifteen years as president in Hunters Creek, he'd lived through all the changes we underwent as a club, to move out of the outlaw life and into a legit one. We'd done several rides together over the last several years and both chapters welcomed any chance to ride, party and if needed, fight together.

Bull was the one to offer his club members as extra 'insurance' against shady dealings from the Satan's

Bastards. One of his suggestions was that we include an eleventh person to act as a sniper, who would sit in a concealed position during the meeting. This was to ensure everything went as planned. As long as the Bastards did nothing underhanded, they would never need to know the Warriors had brought an insurance policy. However, we were positive the Bastards wouldn't stick to the ten-man total restriction and wanted to be prepared.

    The meeting place Grinder had insisted on ended up being held at an old farmhouse in the middle of nowhere. It sat roughly in between all three clubs' current territories and therefore, was technically neutral territory. Each club was no more than three hours from this farmhouse. With Hunters Creek being the closest, at just two hours away. The Dublin Falls chapter had met and rallied at our own clubhouse with Hunters Creek, but would go back to the Hunters Creek club after this meeting. We figured we'd have a lot to talk about and I welcomed everyone's thoughts and ideas. I knew this wouldn't only end up impacting my club, but the other Warriors' chapters as well.

    Bull rode to my right and to my left was my own VP, Savage. Behind us came Bull's VP, Tank- my Sergeant at Arms, Ranger- and my enforcer, Menace, beside Bull's enforcer, Payne. The remainder of our group consisted of my Treasurer, Viper, and Secretary, Blaze, and finally a senior patched member of Bull's club, Joker. The Hunter's Creek sniper, Demon, had been sent out earlier in the day straight from Bull's clubhouse. This was to allow him time to get set up, well in advance of the meeting time. This was to ensure that the Bastards wouldn't see him getting into position. Because of this, once the plan was settled upon, everyone had gone radio silent with Demon.

The only way the silence was to be broken was, if there was a life-or-death situation arise. While all of us were excellent shots and many were prior military in several cases, Demon had been a sniper in the Marine Corps. This made him a natural choice to be overwatch for us. An overwatch was usually a sniper or other elite marksman who covered the team from afar.

I thought more about the Warriors time as an outlaw club like the Bastards in the past. Ten years ago, the club started to finally see that kind of life just ended with you dead or in prison. We all wanted to live free and ride, but also, be able to do so as long as possible. This was when we took the steps in all our chapters to give up our one percenter patches and invested efforts into legitimate businesses. It wasn't without fallout. There were several members who left, because they didn't want to give up the loads of cash that could be made. We'd wished them well and had no hard feelings. The rest of us took the cut in pay for the better chance of living to a ripe old age. It was our responsibility to keep our club and Dublin Falls protected from the kinds of things the Satan's Bastards were doing. Even when we had been into the illegal stuff, we'd kept it out of our towns. It had mainly consisted of guns, protection, and some illegal gambling. We never did drugs or prostitution.

Up ahead, I saw the landmark Grinder had told me to look for. An old oak tree that was almost split in half. He'd said it'd been hit years ago by a lightning strike. We made the right hand turn off the highway onto an old dirt road and followed it a mile or so back in the trees. The road was overgrown and had potholes everywhere. We had to go slow and be careful not to lay down one of our bikes. There were trees lining each side of the road, which definitely didn't sit well with any of us. Everyone was hyper-alert to a possible ambush. As we cleared the final clump of trees, I gave a sigh of relief and looked ahead at the farmhouse we were told would be there.

The house had seen better days that was for sure. Its peeling paint and sagging front porch told the story of long-time neglect. Shutters half hung off the windows and some of those windows were nothing but open holes, where the glass had been broken out. In the front yard, was an old truck up on blocks with weeds and grass growing all around it. Other junk was scattered around the rest of the front yard. Off to the right, was an old dilapidated barn surrounded by small hills covered in scattered brush. To the left of the farmyard, were more trees making up a small forest. That was a good place for an ambush as well. The trees were most likely where Demon would have set up his post. Hopefully, our side had better firepower than the other MC, since there was no way the Bastards hadn't set someone or several people up in the barn or brush.

I pulled my bike to within a few feet of the front porch and my brothers pulled in behind me, making sure to fan out. Everyone had their eyes sweeping the whole yard, the surrounding hills, the trees, and the barn looking for signs of the Bastards. After a final scan, we turned off our bikes and swung off of them to stand waiting. The door to the farmhouse swung open and out stepped Grinder and his VP, Spider. I didn't know the names of the other members who followed them out onto the porch, but they totaled ten just as my group did. I stepped forward to meet Grinder by walking part way to the porch steps. I made sure to keep enough distance between us in case I had to go for cover.

"Grinder, well, we're all here it looks like. Our time is valuable. Let's get this meeting started. What exactly did you want to discuss with us? I assume it has to pertain to Warriors' territory. But I'm curious, why now? We've been asking for a meeting for almost a year. I have to wonder why have you and your club been trying to push so hard into our territory? It makes no sense when we have nothing to compete over when it comes to earning our incomes," I stated bluntly. There was no need to beat around the bush. Get straight to it, so we could get this over with as fast as possible. Grinder swaggered a little closer to the top step with an oily smirk on his pocked face. I'd love to wipe that look off his damn ugly face with my fist, but I kept my cool. There was no way anyone could trust him or his club. The knot in my stomach tightened just a bit more. Yeah, this wasn't going to end well. My warning bells were going off. They had been since the call yesterday. I took a quick look around again. I felt the hairs on the back of my neck stand up.

"Well Terror, we wanted to talk to you about running our supply lines through Dublin Falls. We need your territory opened up, so we can run our businesses better. You're smack in the middle of our supply lines out of Tennessee into North Carolina. Having to go around you is costing us time and money. You've been less than accommodating over the years to allow us through there. We want to get this worked out, so we can get this changed and our new routes started within the next couple of weeks." Grinder said with a cunning look on his face.

I laughed humorously. "You think we're here to discuss allowing you to run your shit through our territory? What would ever make you think for even an instant, that we're going to allow this to happen? We haven't been allowing you in our territory for years, even though your club always wants to push for it. Why would we do it now? If that's what you wanted to talk about, this is going to be a very short discussion and a total waste of our time."

Grinder glanced back at his guys and shuffled his feet a bit before he stepped slightly to the right. This brought him another foot closer to me. "We believe we can change your mind. We're willing to give your club a five percent cut of all the profits from those supply lines. Call it an appreciation fee for allowing us unlimited and protected access through Dublin Falls to Cherokee, North Carolina. In return, we'll no longer interfere with any of your legit businesses. You do your thing and we'll do ours. You guys don't deal in guns, drugs or girls, so it shouldn't be an issue, if we do our businesses in and around Dublin Falls."

"That's where you're wrong, Grinder." I told him. "We do have an issue with it. We want the people in our territory to be able to live free of that poison you keep wanting to peddle, as well as the guns you want to put in the hands of little thugs and wannabe gang bangers. Our families and everyone else in our territory deserve to be able to walk down the street without worrying that they'll be shot. Or that their kids will be sold that shit. And no one wants to see poor women being forced to sell themselves, so you can make another buck. So, I would say we have a really big issue."

Grinders' men all edged a little closer to him. It was obvious from their faces that they didn't like what they were hearing. The oily smirk on Grinder's face turned into a sneer. What was he thinking? That he could bribe us with a little percentage of the profit, and we'd be okay with this plan? It made no sense. While I'd been talking, causing most of the attention to be on me, my brothers had slowly shifted further apart. I knew they each had already chosen their target when the shit hit the fan just like I had. Because shit was going to definitely go down tonight. I knew it and Grinder knew it.

"The Warriors will let us run our lines through your territory or you aren't going to like the consequences. We've increased needs and those needs have to be met. We'll make sure you give us what we want, Terror. One way or another it's going to happen. It's your choice on whether it is the easy way or the hard way." He'd barely finished speaking when Spider, his VP, pulled his gun from his right hip holster and took a shot at Savage. I guess Grinder's "easy way or hard way" remark was the signal for the Bastards to try and take us out. Unluckily for him, Savage was a much quicker and accurate shot. Spider's shot went wide while Savage's shot took him in the right upper chest, causing Spider to yell out and drop his gun. The night was suddenly filled with the loud reverberation of gunshots coming from several directions.

Ducking quickly, after firing off my first shot, me and some of my brothers took shelter behind the old truck in the yard. My shot had taken down a Bastard with a gut shot. A few of my other brothers scattered behind the pieces of junk laying out in the front yard. Grinder and his boys were spraying the yard with bullets, trying to get back into the house, so they could shoot from cover. I assumed it would be out the front windows and door of the farmhouse. I took a peek around the truck and a shot came whizzing by my head as I shot at another Bastard. I ducked back around the front end of the truck. The engine block made an effective shield to stop a bullet, unlike the body of the truck. Just after I took my shot, another shot was heard ringing out across the farmyard. It was definitely the crack of a high-powered rifle and sounded like it was coming from the trees to our left. One of the Bastards hit the ground quickly, followed by another and neither of them got back up. It looked like Demon had entered the firefight. I'd guessed right as to where he'd set up.

A few shots were heard coming from the barn, confirming the suspicion that the Bastards had put some extra men there. However, more shots rang out from the trees. More cries could be heard from those in the barn and the surrounding brush. Demon was obviously out there using a high-powered night vision scope to see into the dark windows and door of the barn. They'd thought they were safe since it was dark in there.

By now, several of the Bastards had made it back through the door of the farmhouse, including Grinder. Scattered around the yard, I could see three Bastard's down for the count. While I knew a few others in the house had taken some hits. One of those in the house had to be Spider, since I didn't see him in the yard or lying on the porch. By my calculations on shots and shouts from the barn and the farmhouse, Grinder had brought maybe ten extra guys with him to our one extra man. However, they weren't able to wipe out the Warriors like they'd planned. Bad surprise for them but good for us. Thank God we'd brought our very own Demon.

More gun shots were exchanged between us and the Bastards. I decided the only way to end this quickly and reduce the chance of casualties on our side, was to go after the Bastards in the house now. Demon could keep the ones in the barn and brush busy. Otherwise, they could hold up in there for a long while and the advantage we had would be lost. While things were still a little crazy and they were off balance, we needed to strike. I signaled for Menace to go to the right side and Viper to go to the left side of the house. The remainder of the Warriors would keep the Bastards in the house busy and distracted with suppressive firing. Once they were in motion, I followed Menace during a long volley of bullets laid down by our brothers.

As I rounded the side of the house to the backside, I saw Menace and Viper had both made it to either side of the back door. They'd barely got into position on the back porch with their backs to the wall, when two Bastards came barreling out the door. They were probably thinking to do the same flanking maneuver we'd just performed. Menace and Viper were crouched down in the dark shadows and were able to get up behind each of them. They quickly and silently slit their throats. I knew they'd used their knives rather than guns, since we didn't want to chance alerting the Bastards inside, that we were coming in behind them. Easing the bodies out of the way, they went through the door. Menace went left into what looked to be the dining room door, while Viper went right into the kitchen. I went straight through the door and down a short hallway. From these three spots, we could see the whole front living room. The remaining seven Bastards were scattered around the room. They were all facing the front shooting out the windows and door. They had no idea we were there.

Menace quickly took aim at the man closest to the front door and shot him in the head, while Viper shot the one directly to his left beside the far window. I took my shot at one of the men standing off to the other side of the front door. After the shots rang out and the bodies fell, the other four Bastards swung around in shock and surprise. Two of the Bastards fired their guns, but were hasty and only grazed Menace along his right bicep and completely missed Viper. Both of those men went down as well. The two remaining Bastards decided to try and make a run for it. But apparently, they were either very rattled or just plain stupid. Because rather than going toward the three of us to get to the back door, they went out the front door. My other brothers were waiting, and we could hear the shots as they took them out.

After all the shooting had stopped, Bull and Tank made their way into the house to join us. We cleared the rest of it, while the other Warriors swept the barn and hills surrounding it. Since Demon had obviously been in the trees, we decided not to check there. He would've handled those ones. No one else was found, but once the whole house and area was searched, it was determined that Grinder and Spider weren't there. They must've slipped away right after going back into the house. Before our flanking maneuver had started. It figured they'd leave their men and run. Nothing but a couple of cowards.

"Well goddamn it. I'd hoped we would've gotten Grinder and Spider. Though I shouldn't be surprised they slithered away." I swore. "Let's get this mess cleaned up and back to Bull's clubhouse to have church." Church is what we called having a meeting of any kind in the MC. We broke up to start the cleanup process. We had several hours before this night would be over and we could relax.

While the Warriors were cleaning up anything that might identify them as being the ones there with the Bastards, no one saw the lone figure up in the trees to the left of the farmhouse packing up. Climbing down a tall tree, the dark figure started a long trek back to a bike. It was hidden in some trees over a mile east of the farmhouse. The shooter thought it was time to get back to the clubhouse, and be ready for questions when the rest of the group made it back. Bull and the guys would want to review all the details of this evening. In the whirlwind of cleanup, no one questioned why Demon didn't join them to help.

Chapter 2: Terror

Bull, me, and the guys all pulled through the gates of the Hunters Creek clubhouse four hours later. We'd cleaned up the farmhouse and disposed of the bodies where they wouldn't be found. Once we'd done that, we'd made the ride back in record time. I was ready to sit back, have a beer and relax. There was a lot of planning to do. This was definitely not the last we'd hear from the Bastards about this. They'd almost been decimated, but I knew they'd eventually come back. Everyone would have to be on the alert. They'd been up to something more than the usual shit. I couldn't see the few remaining ones letting it go and walking away forever.

Everyone eased off their rides and stretched, before tromping through the door of the clubhouse. Inside the main common room, the remainder of the Hunters Creek brothers sat around the bar having a drink. A couple were over at the pool table shooting a game. Two were playing a game of darts. The buzz of conversations came to a halt and the room became dead silent, as all eyes swung our way. All of them had worried and curious looks on their faces.

I could see them checking us out to see if we were all here and if there was any damage to us. Lucky for us, only minor wounds were sustained. We would get those patched up. Everyone had done a quick field assessment and a preliminary patch job at the farmhouse. Bull stepped forward and yelled for the prospect behind the bar to get us all a shot of whiskey and a beer. He went to the table sitting closest to the right of the bar and pulled out a chair. Me and the rest of the group, who had fought tonight joined him.

After looking around to be sure no one but patched members and prospects were around, I spoke up to the group. "So, what do you guys think of the little chat we had tonight? Not sure what they're playing at, other than thinking they could take some or all of us out. We all know that we aren't out of the woods with them by a long shot, but I have to say, I'm totally grateful we had Demon covering our backs." The other guys from Dublin Falls shouted their agreement. Just as we finished cheering about our luck, I saw Demon come out of the back hall where I knew Bull's office and some of the bedrooms were located. He had his right arm all bandaged up and in a sling.

I was stunned. Before I could say a word, Bull saw him and jumped up to go over to him. "Demon, what the hell happened? How'd one of them get you? I didn't think with the way they were shooting, that any of the shots even came close to your spot in the trees." I saw Demon look at Bull and grimace. I could tell he wasn't looking forward to answering those questions Bull had just thrown out at him. I just wasn't sure why, so I waited along with the rest of the brothers to hear what he had to say.

"Yeah, Pres you're correct, no one got close to me. I didn't get shot by any of them. As a matter of fact, I wasn't even there tonight." At this revelation everyone startled and looked at each other in confusion. He gave a deep sigh. "I laid down my fucking bike earlier today, when I was heading out to the farmhouse to get set up.

A car decided to pass me in my lane and pushed me onto the berm. I hit loose gravel or some shit. I went down before I even knew what was happening. I slid about forty fucking feet on my damn arm. It tore me up pretty good. Enough to make me worry I wouldn't be able to cover you guys at my hundred percent best." He gave a disgusted grunt.

"I thought about coming back to the Dublin Falls' clubhouse, but knew everyone would've already left to get set for the meet. Also, we'd all agreed to not communicate unless it was life and death. Even though I went down and fucked up my arm, it wasn't life or death. I knew I needed to get you covered and I had no time to come up with a different plan. I did the only thing I could, I brought in the other best shooter we have to cover your asses. There was no reason to change up the meeting. Now, I knew you weren't going to be happy about it, but that was my call and I stand by it. You were covered and that's what matters."

Bull had been looking at Demon with a furled brow at first, but as he continued with his explanation, I saw a light of understanding start to show in Bull's eyes. It was followed by a look of gathering anger. That wasn't good. "Tell me you didn't do what I think you did, Demon? Tell me that you didn't fucking do it, so I don't have to kill you right here and now." Bull snarled. I looked at those sitting at the table with me and shrugged at their looks of confusion. I had no idea what Demon or Bull were talking about. If Demon had substituted another sniper, it was something we would've liked to have known in advance. But I understood why he couldn't tell us. Everything had ended up fine, and so whomever he chose had gotten the job done. What was the big deal?

Demon looked at Bull slowly nodding. "Yeah, I did. You may want to kill me, but that was the most logical choice. You know this was the only way to go. And I was able to get back here, since it was closer, set it up and still get you the coverage you needed in time." Bull cursed and had just stepped up, raising his hand to take Demon by the throat, when a voice rang out.

"Stop that bullshit, right now! You know the call Demon made was the best and only one to make in this circumstance. There's no need to be choking the life out of him for making it. If he hadn't done it, some of you wouldn't be standing here right now. And delaying this meeting after trying to get it for months wouldn't have helped either."

The voice was a female one and rather husky too. I swung around to look toward where the voice was coming from. It was near the door to the parking lot of the clubhouse. As some of the guys parted, I saw the speaker. The breath actually left my body in a gasp. It felt like someone had hit me with lightning and rammed a fist into my gut at the same time. Standing there was the most stunningly beautiful woman I'd ever seen.

Now, I've seen many gorgeous women in my time and have slept with many of them. However, not a single one had ever had an impact like this on me. She was tall for a woman. I would say around five foot nine or so, at best guess. While that would allow her to look a lot of men in the eye, when up against my own six foot five, she would still only come to my chin. She had striking deep auburn hair that hung in a tight braid over her right shoulder, which hung down to almost her waist. I imagined when it was released from the braid, her hair would hang past her ass. Out of nowhere an image popped into my mind. It was of her naked on her hands and knees with my hand grabbing that thick, gorgeous hair. I was pulling it to tilt her head back while I fucked her hard and deep from behind. I felt my cock stir at the thought. I shifted in my chair.

Her face was a pale oval with the smoothest skin I'd ever seen. I'd heard of people saying someone had skin like porcelain, but had never understood what they meant, not until right now. Her face was topped by high cheekbones and completed by her startling eyes. Those eyes were surrounded by thick, dark lashes which set off their violet color. Who'd ever heard of violet eyes? But her beauty didn't stop there. Her body was just as gorgeous as her hair and face. She had generous, high breasts that looked to be more than a handful, even in my big hands. Below her chest, her ribs tapered down to a small, tucked in waist which flared out to generous hips. She had an hourglass shape. Those hips begged a man to grab them and hold on tight. Finally, came her legs which looked like they went on for miles.

I knew without a doubt that I wanted to see her naked and be between those legs soon. My cock was begging to see what she'd feel like wrapped around it. I knew she'd be tight and hot when I sunk deep into her. I grew harder. Now this was a woman I could ride all night and come back for more. Thank God I was sitting down, and the table hid the erection she was giving me. I wasn't a religious man, but I found myself praying she wasn't an old lady to anyone in the club. If she was, I might just die. This wasn't something I'd ever felt. I could have any woman I wanted. I had them frequently and always was adding new ones. I'd never found myself hungering after one to the point, that I didn't know what I would do if I couldn't have her. She had me off balance in a heartbeat.

All of these thoughts passed through my mind in a matter of moments. Once the initial jolt passed, I noticed how she was dressed. She wasn't dressed like a club bunny or a skanky barfly. She was dressed head to toe in black. She had on a tight, long sleeved tee shirt that was tucked into a pair of cargo pants with loads of pockets. A sturdy utility belt rested around her small waist and it held what appeared to be a knife, a flashlight, magazines for a gun, and other equipment. Her pants ended tucked into a pair of black combat boots.

I looked at my guys and saw the same looks of confusion I felt. Who was this chick in the clubhouse? Everyone but patched members and prospects had been told to stay clear tonight until after church. The other thought in my mind was, why was she dressed like that? I saw her glance at Demon with a smile and I found I didn't like that at all. I wanted to go over and knock his teeth down his throat, especially when I saw him smile back.

She switched her gaze back to Bull, as he swung away from Demon and started to stomp toward her. His face looked like thunder. I found myself standing up from the table and stepping forward as if to protect her. I thought to myself, *what the hell am I doing*? Bull began to shout. "You had no goddamn reason to get involved in this, Harley." She didn't step back or look afraid. In fact, she stepped up to Bull and looked him straight in the eye. Then she opened her mouth and rattled my mind even more than she already had.

"Now you know Demon made the best call based upon the situation and the time constraints. There was no other option unless you wanted to reschedule, and I don't think that was something anyone wanted. He made the call and we made it work."

I looked at Bull and then the rest of the brothers. What was she talking about "we made it work?" Bull groaned and dropped down on a stool at the bar. He gave a weary sigh. Before he said a word, the prospect behind the bar handed him a cold beer. He took a large swallow and then stated. "Goddamn it, Harley, you shouldn't have had any hand in club business. This is for brothers to handle." He glared over at Demon again.

Demon looked his president in the eye. "You know if there'd been any other option, I would've taken it. But there wasn't, and I knew we didn't want to chance trying to get them to agree to meet again. We've tried for months to get this under control. Also, we all know there was no one else you could trust to help if I wasn't available."

I'd had enough. I wanted to know what in the hell they were talking about? What 'help' had she given us tonight? "Bull, what the hell are these two talking about? What help did she give us tonight that Demon wasn't able to give us?" I glanced over at the woman he called Harley, and saw she was now staring at me.

Bull looked from me, to Harley and then around to all of the Dublin Falls' brothers. It was obvious from the looks on their faces, the Hunters Creek crew knew what was going on and who this woman was. But Bull needed to clue me and my crew in on what was up. He cleared his throat and looked a bit disconcerted. Since when was Bull ever hesitant or nervous? "What they mean is, with Demon out of commission, they substituted the next best shooter in the Hunters Creek club to take his place."

I looked at Bull and shrugged. "Yeah, I got that, but what does she have to do with that substitution and why would Demon involve her in any of this?" Before Bull could answer, Harley walked over to the table and faced me, since I'd sat back down. She looked even more beautiful up this close, and I felt an urge to reach out and touch her soft looking skin. She glared down at me and floored me.

"Why Demon dared to involve a mere woman in your big, bad plans for tonight, is because I'm the backup sniper who covered your big, macho asses. Believe it or not, I'm the only person as good, if not better, than Demon to get the job done." She finished with a smirk on her face. I stared at her dumbfounded. Had she said what I thought she'd just said? She was our overwatch tonight?

I glanced at Bull and saw him watching me with a worried look on his face. "Bull, is she serious? Who in the hell is this chick? And even if she's as great of a shot as she seems to think she is, what would make Demon or anyone for that matter, think she could handle an actual firefight?"

Bull looked at her then met my eyes. "She's dead serious, Terror. Who she is, is my daughter, Harlow or Harley, as we call her? Demon and I not only think, but know she could handle an actual firefight. She's done so before on more than one occasion." I felt my mouth fall open and I saw that my guys were just as stunned and sitting there with their mouths gaping open too. I had no idea what to think. Once the surprise wore off a bit, I responded without thinking.

"Since when did we vote to patch women into the club, and then allow them to go out on runs and participate in fights?" I knew as it left my mouth that I sounded like a sexist pig, but the thought of her or any woman in a situation where they could've been harmed made me crazy. It was our job to protect women and children. Call me a caveman if you want, I just felt like this was our duty as men.

    I saw Harlow's back snap straight and she scowled at me. I found I liked that pissed look on her face. It made me want to see if I could kiss it off or better yet, fuck it off. She spit her next words out between her gritted teeth. "No, the club didn't vote to allow women to patch in. It's still too damn scary to do that, since you big boys wouldn't be able to handle it. That might mean someone would have to take away your man cards. And yes, women can be in firefights as you mentioned, especially when said woman has been shooting since she was five years old and was trained as a motherfucking U.S. Marine sniper, you jackass! Hoorah!" Once she finished slamming me with those words, she swung around on her heels and stomped out of the common room and down the hall. Presenting me with a view of her equally sexy ass.

Chapter 3: Harlow

I felt the anger burning through my body. Goddamn sexist Neanderthal! What century did he think we're living in? Same damn shit I had to listen to in the Corps from most of the guys. I noticed not one of those assholes had even bothered to thank me for covering their asses tonight. I was just so tired of this kind of shit. I'd been home for three months and felt lost. Even though I loved the club, it didn't feel like I fit into it. When I was younger, I'd always felt I had a place and I was comfortable with it. Now, I just felt out of sync.

When I mustered out of the Corps, I thought I'd be able to just step into my old life with a few adjustments. But being back at the club, I felt I had no true place or purpose. Yes, I was the princess for the Hunters Creek chapter, since my father was its president and a founding member. But all that got me was a bunch of smothering, alpha males trying to babysit me. I hadn't needed a babysitter since I was ten years old. Before going to the Marines, I'd been used to my father not allowing me to go anywhere without at least a prospect following me. I'd understood the need to watch over their families. I even understood it now, especially with this Bastard thing going on. But the other women and children were the ones who needed that protection. I was more than able to take care of myself and he kept doing the same thing to me. I'd survived in the Marines without a babysitter.

Though to be honest, if he had been able to get away with sending one with me, he most likely would've.

Overprotective was my dad to a T. He hadn't wanted me to go into the service, but it was his fault I did. Him and the guys had sparked that desire in me when I was just a kid. My mom died when I was five, so I had been raised by a bunch of men. They sure didn't do tea parties, play with dolls, or do dress up. They had treated me like a boy, and that consisted of shooting, self-defense training, and knife handling to name a few, and it had thrilled me. Also, I saw how patriotic they were and wanted to serve like so many of them had. In the end, he hadn't been able to talk me out of it.

I made it to the end of the hall where my dad's room was at the clubhouse. He had the best set up in the whole place. His room had its own bath with a large sitting area set up with a couch, television, and sound system. The couch could pull out into a bed when needed. It was really a small suite. I didn't have my own room in the clubhouse, but had crashed here in his room many times when a party went late, or I was just too damn exhausted to drive. All the guys in the club had a room at the clubhouse they could crash in. Some of the guys lived here full time and others only once in a while. My father had a house, which was where I'd been living while deciding where I was going to finally settle down. He wanted me here in Hunters Creek, but I wasn't sure this was where I wanted to be.

I opened his bedroom door and then slammed it behind me, before going to the dresser in the corner. I always kept some clothes here at the clubhouse, since I never knew when I may need to stay over or might get dirty. I hated to sleep in dirty clothes or have to wear them again the next day. I'd had enough of that while in the Marines and over in the sandbox. I needed to have a bath every day and clean clothes, or it drove me nuts. Just one of my girly quirks. Over there, I couldn't do that, but here I could and did. I pulled out a tee shirt, shorts, and new underclothing. A hot shower was a must right now. Maybe it would help me calm down. Why I was letting Terror's words piss me off so much was a mystery. I was used to the club and most men thinking like him. Yeah, it pissed me off, but I could usually ignore it for a good while.

After getting the shower as hot as I could stand it, I stepped under the pounding spray. I took out my hair band and unraveled my braid. It felt good to let it loose. It was making my head hurt after being braided for so long. As I lathered my hair, my thoughts turned to Terror again. I had heard my dad speak of him over the years, and knew him and the guys in Hunters Creek all respected Terror. However, I'd never been around when Terror and his bunch had come to Hunters Creek in the past. When I was a kid, dad had kept me away from the clubhouse when there were other clubs there. After joining the Corps, I'd never been home on leave when one visited to be able to meet them.

It was a shame he was such a Neanderthal. Because when he had stood up in the bar, he'd commanded the room without saying a word and made my heart race. I'd felt myself get wet. That was nothing I'd ever had happen to me. I didn't react to guys no matter how good looking or buff they were. I could see them and appreciate their nice bodies or fine looks, but it had never actually resulted in me having a physical reaction like this! Terror had turned me on, big time.

Physically he was a huge, imposing man. Not that he was fat, but he was just heavily muscled all over. His shoulders were broad, and his biceps bulged in his shirt stressing the seams and looked like they were the size of my thighs. You could see the cut and definition in the muscles of his arms under the gorgeous tattoos he had running down both arms. He had full sleeves from what I could tell. I hadn't had time to look to see what they were, but they were colorful and suited him. His chest was deep and tapered down to a trim waist. I had no doubt he had at least a six pack under that shirt. I was curious to see if he had a mouthwatering 'V', called an Adonis belt, leading down to his package. I bet he did. Thoughts of that and his cock had the wetness between my legs coming back. What was wrong with me? His legs looked like tree trunks and he towered over me. At five foot nine inches, I was used to not having to look up very far to a lot of men, and down at many others, but he made me really have to crane my neck. I actually felt petite when compared to him.

As if his body wasn't enough, his face was stunning. He had a head full of long, thick wavy hair that he'd pulled back into a man bun. Not many men could pull off the man bun, but he could. That hair was coal black and I had felt my hands itch to take his hair down and run my fingers through it. I bet it was soft. His jaw was strong and square, though his mustache and goatee covered part of his jaw. This along with his slashing cheekbones and deep blue eyes made him breathtaking. He had a scar that ran down from his right cheek bone to his jaw. I wondered where he had gotten it. The scar did nothing to distract from his good looks.

This reaction I was having was making me nervous. It wasn't as if the club was full of fat, ugly men. Most were six foot or more, very fit with bulging muscles, tattoos, and to die for faces. But to me, they were all brothers or uncles. The thought of trying to kiss one of them, let alone do anything sexual with any of them, made my stomach queasy. Yuck! Terror made my stomach quiver, but in a whole different way.

Great! Just my luck. The one man to catch my eye ever in my whole twenty-four years and he had to be a chauvinistic, Neanderthal, alpha male biker! I knew the type since I grew up with them and had served with many of them. They still thought women needed to be protected and couldn't do it themselves. Some even thought a woman should just do as she was told. The kind of woman who did everything to please her man and never opened her mouth to voice an opinion or thought. That was definitely, not me. Oh well, there went that fantasy. No way Terror would want a woman like me, a foul mouthed, ass kicking, free opinion spouting bitch. And I couldn't see myself with a man, who didn't think I had a brain or was useful for anything other than sex.

As I finished my shower and was drying off, I heard a knock on the door. I knew my reprieve from dad and the club was over. Hurrying to get my clothes on, I opened the door while brushing out my long, wet hair. It was a chore to do, at any time, but if I let it dry first, it would be a beast to tame. My hair tended to get a bit wild and when it was down it hit at just the bottom of my ass cheeks. Even though it was a chore, I refused to cut it, even when I had been in the heat and sand of the Middle East. I felt it was one thing I really had, that reminded me of my mom. Looking up, I saw my dad standing there.

"Harley, baby, you know you shouldn't have left

the bar like that. I'm not sure why you got so ticked off, but we need to discuss tonight. The guys need to know of anything you saw or heard before we got there or during the fight. I gave you time to get over your tantrum. Now get your ass out there and let's get this over with." He growled. Dad's normal was to growl, so I wasn't too worried he was totally pissed at me.

"Look dad, I respect the hell out of you and the guys, but I couldn't stand there and feel like, because I don't have a dick, I'm useless! I did what I did to help all of you and to be sure everyone made it back. Yes, I can understand it was a shock to them, especially if no one knew you have a daughter, who had been a Marine sniper. But you know how remarks like that put my back up. I just couldn't shrug it off like I typically do. I put up with it for six years every day and I don't want to have to put up with it here too. I know all of you are super protective, but this shit of keeping the women at home, unaware, is nonsense. There are women out there who can take the crap that goes on and even be of help, if you ever tried to listen. Being unaware makes us vulnerable. I'm not saying every woman can go do what I did tonight, but they can help in a number of ways. This thinking you guys seem to have, that you have to protect us and do it by keeping everything under wraps, is why I could never be an old lady. I couldn't live with being treated like I am brainless and useless."

As I started to walk past my dad, I saw Terror leaning against the doorway to the room. He was staring at me with a look on his face that I couldn't figure out. As I got to the door, I expected him to step aside to let me pass. He didn't. Instead, he took a step toward me. This put him in my personal space, and I felt my heart start to speed up. He looked me up and down then said. "Look Harlow, I didn't mean to imply since you're a woman that you couldn't do the job. We were surprised and had no idea who you were and how you could be involved. We'd like you to come out and tell us what you saw. Any and all insight is needed and appreciated. And for the record, I don't think since you're a woman that you're brainless or useless. Also, I have to say that I for one am very, very happy you don't have a dick babe." He said with a smirk.

With this said, he turned and started down the hall and back to the bar. I looked at my dad to find he had a scowl on his face. I decided to follow Terror back to the common room and get this over with. Once I told them my story, they could all go into church and decide what the next steps would be. Based upon tonight, it looked like the Warriors were going to be busy.

Chapter 4: Terror

Damn, that gorgeous ass as she stomped away could almost bring me to my knees. It was perfect just like the rest of her. It was heart shaped and she had enough to give a man more than a handful to latch onto with both hands. I could imagine spanking that ass and making her like it. Where are these thoughts coming from? She was Bull's daughter for Christ's sake! There's no way he would let a brother tap that and I wasn't looking for a relationship. Right? So, I guess I should let these thoughts die. But my mind kept thinking those kinds of things.

I turned to look at Bull and the rest of the guys. Like me, I could see the others from my chapter staring at her retreating ass. Their eyes all held deep appreciation. A growl welled up in my throat out of nowhere. I didn't like any of them looking at her. *She was mine!* What the hell was wrong with me? We all had shared women before. The club bunnies were there for all the guys and many of them took on more than one of us at a time. My brothers, Hammer and Steel, preferred to be with the same woman at the same time. I'd never cared if one of my brothers wanted the same woman as I did. This had been a crazy night. Maybe I was more tired and rattled than I realized. That had to be the reason for these thoughts going through my mind. I never felt possessive of a woman.

Clearing his throat, Bull sat back down at our table and Demon took a seat as well. Bull started off the conversation. "Okay, yes Harley is my daughter. Though I am pissed that Demon brought her into this." He threw a dirty look at Demon, who just grinned and shrugged. "She was the only logical choice and she was more than capable of handling any situation that was thrown at us. She isn't lying about being a Marine sniper and having been in firefights before. Since the military changed its stance on women in combat roles, she was one of the first they tried out in the role of a sniper. She's been shooting with me and most of the club members since she was little. She excelled in basic training and they couldn't wait to have her as a sniper once she graduated boot camp."

"She got out after serving six years a couple of months ago. She's seen a lot over in the sandbox and unfortunately, it consisted of several firefights. She was excellent at her job and they didn't want to let her go. However, she said she'd had enough and got out when her enlistment was up. No one was in danger tonight by her taking Demon's place, I can assure you. I just don't want her to be in these types of situations if it can be avoided."

Once he stopped talking, Demon spoke up. "Bull, none of us want to put Harley or any woman into a dangerous position, but this was the only way to go. We couldn't afford to leave you without coverage, and she can handle herself. Do you think I would put her in that kind of position if I thought otherwise? I would die protecting her and you know it." I saw his face and he was dead serious. What was going on there? Were the two of them in a relationship together?

I hadn't heard Demon had taken an old lady, but by the look on his face it appeared as if he definitely loved and cared about her. This thought made a new knot clench in my stomach. "I know," Bull sighed. "I just hate to have her around any of this. Though we're a legit club, shit still goes down and we've always protected our women and children from as much of it as we can. However, I realize that times are different, and we have to change our ways some, even if I hate it."

During the break in their conversation, I spoke up. "I get that she had no choice but to cover us, however, I agree with Bull that keeping women out of this is what I would do too. Do you think she's calm enough to come back out and fill us in on what she saw before we got there and during the fight? She had a whole different view of the scene than any of us. We have to be prepared and in order to do that, we need all the help and information we can get." Though I made it sound like I just wanted her to tell us what she saw, that wasn't the real reason. I wanted her back out there, so I could see if she caused the same sensations as she had the first time.

Bull took his time finishing his beer before getting up from his chair to start down the long hall. After he was out of sight, I decided I'd go down and be sure to back up his request that she come speak to us. Yeah, right. I just wanted to lay eyes on her before the rest of the guys did. As I stood, I saw Savage look at Menace and they both smirked and grinned at me. I flipped them off as I walked off down the same hallway, which just caused the dicks to laugh at me. At the end of the hall, I could see Bull standing inside of an open door. As I got closer, I could hear Harlow speaking.

"Look dad, I respect the hell out of you and the guys, but I couldn't stand there and feel like, because I don't have a dick, I am useless! I did what I did to help all of you and to be sure everyone made it back. Yes, I can understand it was a shock to them, especially if no one knew you have a daughter who had been a Marine sniper. But you know how remarks like that put my back up. I just couldn't shrug it off like I typically do. I put up with it for six years every day and I don't want to have to put up with it here too. I know all of you are super protective, but this shit of keeping the women at home, unaware, is nonsense. There are women out there who can take the crap that goes on, and even be of help if you ever try to listen. Being unaware makes us vulnerable. I'm not saying every woman can go do what I did tonight, but they can help in a number of ways. This thinking you guys seem to have, that you have to protect us and do it by keeping everything under wraps, is why I could never be an old lady. I couldn't live with being treated like I am brainless and useless."

Out of her whole speech, the only things that I really heard was her remark about not having a dick and never being an old lady. I knew I was personally grateful she didn't have a dick, since I didn't swing that way. And the no old lady remark at least let me know that she and Demon weren't seriously hooked up. Sitting there for the last half hour, seeing her and hearing her dad talk about her, made me realize that there may be reasons why brothers decided to take an old lady. I'd never thought about doing it, but I had never had a reaction like I did to her either. Just hearing her voice now, made a shiver move up my spine. I knew she was special, and I was going to have to decide if she was special enough to pursue a relationship with, for the first time in my life. Or stay with my usual hit it and quit it ladies, like I normally did. Because no matter what happened, there was no way in hell Bull or his club would allow a brother to play fast and loose with their princess. That's why I was confused about what her exact relationship was with Demon.

I came up further behind Bull and caught sight of her. She was in a tee shirt and a pair of tight shorts with her hair hanging wet and I had never seen anything so sexy in my life. Again, I felt my cock stirring, so I tried to distract us both by making conversation. "Look Harlow, I didn't mean to imply since you're a woman that you couldn't do the job. We were surprised and had no idea who you were and how you could be involved. We'd like you to come out and tell us what you saw. Any and all insight is needed and appreciated. And for the record, I don't think since you are a woman that you are brainless or useless. Also, I have to say that I for one am very, very happy you don't have a dick babe." On that last note I gave her a smirk. I wanted her to know I was interested. The look of shock on her face was exactly what I wanted.

I turned and left to go back to the bar. Hopefully she'd come along with Bull. We still needed to have church tonight, relax and party a bit. I knew the guys were looking forward to some down time with this chapter and getting a taste of the club bunnies the Hunters Creek chapter had to offer. Something new to look forward to for everyone. But now, I didn't find myself looking forward to it like I would have. As I entered the bar, I saw the prospect was busy filling orders for shots and beer at the bar. Everyone either stood or sat around in small groups chatting. I retook my seat.

I had just taken a drink of my beer, when everyone got silent. Glancing over my shoulder, I saw Bull and his daughter enter the room. She was dressed in the outfit I had just seen her in, and I didn't like the looks in my guys' eyes at all. Her tattoos on her arms and legs were visible which added to her attractiveness. She should have put some clothes on. Ones which would've covered her from head to toe. I guess we'd be getting her input on tonight after all. Now, all I had to do was keep my cock under control and not kill my brothers for the looks they were giving her. I would be putting a stop to their dirty thoughts, in a hurry. If anyone got Harlow Williams, it was going to be me.

Chapter 5: Harlow

I admit, when Terror made his comment and then left the room, I was stunned. First of all, he left me just breathless in general and then to hear his comment and have him call me babe, was another blow. Yeah, it wasn't unusual for the guys to call me babe. It was just the way they spoke. But the tone and way he said it, made me wonder why it sounded different coming from him. And by the look on dad's face, he was thinking the same thing. I was used to his overprotective scowl. Terror would most likely be getting a warning from dad.

My dad had warned all the guys in his chapter that I was off limits as soon as I started developing at thirteen. He continued to give the same lecture to all new prospects when they came on board, except now, he had the other patched members saying it too. Ugh! If I was ever interested in a biker, I sure as hell wouldn't be able to get one, since dad and the guys scared everyone off. Not that I was looking for a quick lay, which is what these guys always went for. They tended to go for quantity, not quality. It would just be nice to have the option, if I ever decided I wanted it.

With a sigh, I quickly threw my hair up in a ponytail and gestured for my dad to lead the way. I was tired and wanted to get this over with so I could go to bed. I knew all of them had to be tired as well and they still had church tonight. As I followed dad down the hall and back to the bar, I thought about the evening. There was something off about it and I couldn't put my finger on it. I wanted to hear what the guys thought. As I entered the room, everyone got silent and looked at me. Good thing I was a confident woman, otherwise I would've been intimidated. All these big, strong alpha males were staring at me. I took one of the two seats open at the table where Terror sat. My dad took the other one.

    I decided to jump right in and get this show on the road. The silence was a little unnerving. "Okay, so let me get you up to speed on what I saw, before you all got there and during the firefight. It wasn't much. I rolled in around thirteen hundred. I stashed my bike a mile or so off to the east, just in case they'd gotten someone there early as well. I hiked in to check out the layout. I decided they were most likely to set up extra guys in the barn thinking they'd have more cover, so I took to the trees. The place was mostly dead except for a prospect or two milling around. They were oblivious and not really paying attention like they should've, so it was easy to sneak in. Once I got set up in my tree, I scoped the whole area. Nothing unusual stood out. Then a couple of vehicles came and started to unload the Bastards about an hour and a half before the meet time. You had agreed to ten men total for each club. They brought twenty. Five of those extra men were placed in the house and the remainder went into the barn. I couldn't hear much of what they were saying, but it was obvious they were pleased."

    "I have to be honest, I wanted to start taking them out then, but knew there was no way I could, and still get away before one of them figured out where I was. Anyway, they wondered around a bit until about forty-five minutes before you were due to show. Then they all went and took their various places. A couple of them got close to the tree I was set up in, during their wandering, and I was able to hear them talking. One of them was wondering if you would bring extra guys too? He asked if they should be looking around for them? Their president, Grinder, walked up while they were talking. He knocked that idea down thankfully or they might have found me."

"He just sneered and said you were all too damn honest and boy scouts to ever do something like that. He went on to say this was what made you all weak and easy to push out. One of the guys remarked, they had to either get you to agree to the proposal, or out of the way, or there'd be trouble for them." After hearing this, the guys all started to murmur and curse. I kept going. "After all of you came, you know how it went down. The only thing is, I don't think just getting routes through Dublin Falls is what they're after. I have nothing concrete, but my gut is saying, they have a bigger agenda."

"What makes you say that, darlin,"? The one identified as Menace on his cut, asked. I saw Terror give him a glare. What in the world was that all about? I decided to ignore them.

"Because, why now, babe? They've been pushing in aggressively for almost a year. They could've called a meeting, just like this a long time ago and pulled this shit. Why didn't they? What made now the time to do it? There's more at stake here than a sudden urge to expand. What caused the sudden urgency to move their products? And it sounds like they have increased their business lines production. How are they getting more guns, drugs, and women to sell? Do they have a partner? Why would there be problems for them, if they didn't get you to agree or eliminate them? I think maybe more than just the Bastards MC is involved." I told him. This caused the guys to get restless and start talking even more.

I saw my dad and Terror exchanging looks. They were doing that communicating without words thing. I recognized it. You developed that with people you worked day in and day out with for a long time. I had it with the guys in my unit when I was in the Corps. It came from living and almost dying together on more than one occasion. Also, I knew from some of the remarks made in the past by my dad, a lot of these guys like his own, were prior military men. Even though this macho man environment made me crazy, it was also the one I had been born into. To be honest, it was the one I usually was most at ease in, because I knew how to navigate it. Go figure. I wasn't into chick drama.

Terror stood up and walked around the table to stand beside me. His approach made butterflies come alive in my stomach. I had the urge to reach out and lay my hand on his thigh. What I did was look up into his eyes, so that I wouldn't be looking at his crotch, which was at my eye level. He smiled and placed his hand on my right shoulder. "Thanks for the back up tonight. We did appreciate it and know that without it, some of us wouldn't have made it back. We're going to go into church, but if you think of anything else, let us know." His thumb was rubbing back and forth on my shoulder. God, that simple touch made me want to shiver. Why?

He started to walk off toward the room where dad and the guys held church. As everyone else rose to follow, Demon came around the table and gave me a quick peck on the mouth. He was the only one who did that. The other guys would kiss me, but it was always on the cheek.

"Thanks, babe." He said. "You were awesome tonight

and you saved all their asses." He gave me a wink and ran his forefinger down my cheek. I smiled at him. I loved Demon so much. He was the older brother I never had, and we always got each other. As he headed to church, I saw Terror looking back at us. He had an angry scowl on his face. Why was he glaring at us like that? I was too tired to worry about him and his moods. I was going to get me a drink and relax. I motioned to Ace, the prospect, behind the bar. He nodded. He knew what I liked. I sat down to wait and see if they had anything else to ask me after church. Then I planned to crash for the rest of the night.

Chapter 6: Terror

What the fuck was that shit? As we all were headed to church, I looked back and saw fucking Demon kissing Harlow on the lips and caressing her face. Was I wrong? Was there something between them? Well, if there was, I'd find out. If she wasn't his old lady, then she was fair game and I'd decided as we listened to her talk, that she was going to be mine. Even if I had to beat every other guy in the Hunters Creek chapter and my own down. I'd already given Menace his warning with that look, when he called her darlin'. Of course, all the bastard did was grin at me. He was an asshole. He was my best friend and knew me too well. He knew that darlin' remark would rile me up.

Everyone filed into the room and took a seat at the huge wooden table in the center of the room. Bull took his spot at its head. The last one in closed the door then Bull pounded his gavel to get the meeting underway. He nodded to me, so I took point to get the conversation rolling.

I repeated for those who hadn't been at the meeting, what Grinder had said and what the firefight had been like. Once they were all informed, I continued. "Alright, it looks like things went the way we expected. This was just the Bastards way of trying to wipe a chunk of us out. We knew they wouldn't stick to the allotted number, so I'm very thankful we had Harlow covering us. I agree with Harlow. It is very likely there's more than just the

Bastards wanting to run through our territory. We know they've always run their business around us then down through Cherokee. So, why all of a sudden are they pushing to get us out of the way? It has to be a partner. Maybe another MC or the cartel. Are they dealing in other things they didn't deal in before? We need to figure out who we're up against and fast."

Demon spoke up. "I know I wasn't there, but based on what you just told us and Harley's gut, I have to agree. I'm afraid we should expect things to heat up. I wouldn't put it past them to target not just us, but also our families and even people in the community. We can't watch everyone, but we need to have eyes on our businesses and make sure our families are watched. I know it hasn't really affected us here in Hunters Creek, however I still think we should be on alert."

"I agree with Demon. We'll make sure to tighten things here, but also, I think we should be sure to send some of our guys to Dublin Falls for a bit. In addition, it may be worthwhile to see if any nomads are available to come help out until this thing is resolved." Bull added. "Even with extra help, you guys will be spread a little thin. First order of business is to get schedules set for covering the businesses. Second, make sure none of the women and children in the Tennessee chapters go out unescorted."

"Fuck!" Said Joker. "Who is going to tell Harley she can't go anywhere without a shadow? I know it isn't going to be me, and when someone does, please let me know ahead of time. I plan to leave the fucking country. But I promise to come back for that brother's funeral." He laughed. All the Hunters Creek brothers laughed along with him. I heard several of them agree they wanted to go with him too. Apparently, she lived up to her red hair and was a handful.

I decided to add onto the conversation. "I would welcome extra hands from both this chapter and the nomads. The good thing is our compound is almost impenetrable, so if we need to lock it down, we can keep everyone safe. I don't know if they'll start anything over here, but better safe than sorry. Escorts for the women and kids is the way to go. I know it may be inconvenient, but surely they'll understand why it's needed, even your daughter, Bull."

"Oh, she'll understand the need for women and kids to be watched. We don't have old ladies either but some have extended family here. She'll just not think she should need it. I can guarantee you. She's going to want to help in the protecting part. I don't want her to be exposed to any violence. However, I think it could be helpful in keeping her here." He stated with a frown on his face.

"What do you mean, help keep her here?" I asked. Was he thinking she was wanting to go somewhere else? I didn't like that thought. I wanted her to stay where I could find her. Preferably somewhere I could see her daily, such as in Dublin Falls. Now, why had this specific thought popped into my head? But once it did, I couldn't forget it.

Bull slouched down a little in his chair and rubbed his forehead with his hand. It looked like he had a headache. The guys around the table were all looking at him. "She hasn't been able to settle since she got out of the Marines. I know she's been trying to fit back into life here and figure out where she stands. But I can see that she truly doesn't feel good in her skin. I saw some websites on the computer at the house. She was looking at jobs and rental property in other parts of Tennessee. I'm afraid if she doesn't have something to focus on, she'll decide to move away. That's something none of us want." He sighed.

At this, all of his guys began to mutter and get restless. I could see the worry on their faces. They didn't like the thought of their princess leaving the club. I didn't like the thought either. Demon had a more pained look on his face. I wasn't sure if he was worried as a brother or as something more. It had better be just as a brother. He sat up straighter and cleared his throat. The murmuring died down.

"I don't want her to think I've broken her trust, but you're right about her not feeling like she fits. She told me she's been thinking maybe a change to a new place would help with her discontent. I tried to tell her it's only been three months since she got out, but I think there's more to it. From a few comments she made one night when she was drinking, I believe there was more behind her leaving the Corps. More than she was just ready to get out. Someone pushed her to decide to do it. I have no idea who or why, but I feel it from what she said and didn't say to me." Demon said.

His revelation caused the whole room to tense. Bull jumped up from his chair and came storming around the table to stand next to Demon. He was glaring at him again. I have to say Demon didn't flinch this time either, and he stared back at Bull with a passive expression on his face. "What the hell are you talking about? You knew she was thinking of leaving, and you said nothing to me! And you think there's someone who caused her to get out of the Corps. Didn't you think I needed to know this? Fuck Demon, I know what your relationship with Harley is, but this isn't something you keep from me. This affects all of us." Bull bellowed at him.

"I know, and I was planning to talk to you about it. She just mentioned the idea of moving a couple of days ago to me. You know I'm the last one who wants that to happen. But our relationship is very important as well. I want to be sure not to have her think she can't confide in me. As for a person making her leave the military, I just have a feeling and she wouldn't tell me anything else, even when I asked her."

Again, what was his relationship with Harlow? That thought kept teasing my mind. Both Bull and Demon had now alluded to there being one and I hated the thought, even more each time it came to mind. I knew I wanted her and if they were in a serious relationship, I wouldn't push in on a brother that way. I needed to find out what their status was. This raised the thought of sitting down soon, to feel out Bull on what he would think of his daughter having a relationship with me. Shaking off those thoughts, I tuned back into the conversation. Business first, then Harlow.

"We need to find out who has her worried. If there was someone, it had to be bad because she isn't easily intimidated. Also, we have to keep her close. With all this going down with the Bastards, she has to stay where we can keep an eye on her. I wonder if there's something we could do to let her help, while still keeping her protected?" Bull looked thoughtful.

An idea popped into my head. I wasn't sure if Bull would go for it, but it would get her away from Hunters Creek. In addition, it would give her something helpful to do, while keeping her protected and had the added benefit of getting her closer to me. It was worth a try. I coughed to get the attention of the guys.

"What would you think about her coming to Dublin Falls for a while? Yes, it places her closer to where things may be hotter, but our compound is super secure. We can get her to help out Tiny's old lady, Sherry. Sherry has been organizing the new clubhouse since the renovation. Doing things like making sure everything gets fitted out from the decorating, to supplies and such. She spends most of her time at the clubhouse. So, Harlow would be watched, without it being noticeable. When Sherry is offsite, she's usually setting up our charity events or getting supplies for the clubhouse. She always has a prospect with her to use for labor. Additionally, several of us have houses inside the compound, so this would give her a safe place to stay at night. We'd only have to deal with the instances when she wants to go out alone. It's likely we could sell her on the idea, she would need an escort since she isn't familiar with the area. Finally, if there's someone she's worried about from the Marines and this person comes looking for her, she wouldn't be here to be found."

I saw Bull and Demon nodding along with a few other brothers from his chapter. My guys were looking at me with speculation. They had to be wondering why I was trying to get her to our compound. Yeah, Sherry would probably welcome help, but it wasn't like she couldn't handle it by herself. She was resourceful and used to working at the various businesses we had. Though, looking at Menace and his smirk, I think he had some thoughts on why I was trying to get her to Dublin Falls. I took a deep breath and waited to see what Bull had to say.

After about five minutes of mulling it over, he looked up at me. "I think overall it's a good idea. I don't like the fact it puts her closer to the issue with the Bastards. But your compound is more secure than this one, with all the upgrades you recently made and your houses being inside the walls. And your thoughts on helping Sherry sounds like it would be a good distraction. I definitely like the idea, if someone comes looking for her, that they wouldn't know to look there. Now, the hard part will be selling Harley on the idea."

Once he finished sharing his thoughts, everyone seemed more relaxed around the table. Knowing we'd discussed all we could, for now, I made a suggestion. "I think we should conclude the meeting until we know more."

Bull nodded. "I agree, meeting adjourned," as he knocked the gavel once on the table. The brothers all stood and filed out of the room. Now to do the convincing part.

Chapter 7: Harlow

They'd been in church for an hour. I wondered if they were coming to any conclusions and itched to be in there with them. Not that this would happen. It was still boys only in motorcycle clubs. I wasn't sure if it was due to them being a bunch of chauvinists, or they were that protective of women. Though I had to admit, my dad had taught me to ride a motorcycle when I got old enough. He and the guys had taught me all about defense before I ever went to the Marines. I'd just decided to get another drink from Ace, when they began to file back into the common room. There were some looks of consternation, plus a few odd looks thrown my way. Not sure what those were about. At the tail end of the group came dad and Terror.

Terror. I wondered where he got his road name and what his real name was. Dad got his because he was built like a bull, though I always told him it was because he was bullheaded. I looked at Terror closer and tried to figure out what it was about him that had captured my attention. It had to be more than his good looks. I liked the confidence he seemed to exude, even though it irritated me too. I'd been around confident and good-looking men all my life. It was probably best to ignore these unusual feelings. He wouldn't be someone to get serious with anyway, and I wasn't built to be a 'hit it and quit it' kind of girl.

As they started to push up to the bar and shout

their drink orders to Ace, the front door opened and in came the few family members of patched brothers and some of the club bunnies. I knew the families would only stay a little bit to see their men were okay. The bunnies would stay longer and then the party would begin. For now, it appeared the bunnies would help serve some food they'd helped make earlier. However, when the sex started, I'd be leaving. Dad never wanted me around when it did, and I never liked to stay anyway. Not that I hadn't seen shit, just not if I could help it.

    The free-flowing sex mentality wasn't my thing. I couldn't see myself having sex with someone just for the hell of it. I saw Demon coming my way and I had to smile. He came up and slung his arm around my shoulder, drawing me in for a hug and a kiss on the forehead. "How're you doing. Sweetheart." He asked with a look of concern. Before I could answer, movement caught my eye. I saw Terror standing at the end of the bar looking our way again. He had a frown on his face, and he looked ticked off.

    "I'm doing great, sexy. Did you get the whole world solved in there? I really think there's more to this than anyone thought. So, will Dublin Falls or all of us be going on lock down?" I had to ask. It seemed likely we would at some point. Also, I knew as close as Demon and I were, he wouldn't tell me more than he should. He was still a patched member and knew the rules. Though it'd been known for some guys with old ladies in some clubs to let them in on more details, but never all of them. It was supposed to be for our protection, in case something went wrong. I think when mom was alive, dad used to tell her more. Before he could answer me, dad and Terror came over to join us. Terror came up on my right to stand with his shoulder brushing mine. The contact made my nerves sizzle.

Dad grunted which drew my attention away from Terror. "Harley honey, we wanted to ask you for a big favor. While we were in church, it came up that the Dublin Falls chapter needs some help. We thought of you. I know you've been trying to keep busy and this would help to serve a couple of purposes. They've recently renovated their compound and it still needs a lot of work getting it organized and squared away. One of the brothers, Tiny, has his old lady doing most of that, but she's only one person. We wanted to see if you would be willing to go over to Dublin Falls for a while, to help her out with all of that. They'll be having her not go out without an escort, just to be safe and I told them you would be able to help with protection by being with her as well. Right now, she's the only old lady they have in their chapter."

After dad finished, I saw him glance at Demon and Terror. He was up to something. However, the idea of getting away for a bit sounded appealing. I needed to clear my head about where to go next with my life. Also, I liked to be useful, busy and it sounded like they might have a lot to do. Lastly, the idea of being able to protect rather than be protected sounded good too. However, I was surprised dad would even suggest it. "Sure, I could go over for a few weeks and help. If they let me know where it's best to stay in town, I can set up a hotel room and get things arranged. How soon do they want me to come?" I asked as my mind began to plan.

Terror replied rather than dad. "There's no need to set up a hotel room, we have plenty of room in one of the houses inside the compound. Our chapter is different than here. Those who have houses have them all inside the compound walls. It makes it real convenient to get to the clubhouse and to our garage, which is right there as well. We can get you set up and if you could come right away, that would be wonderful."

I mulled it over and then told him. "I'll need a day or two to get things squared away here. How about I come over on Tuesday? That gives you time to get set as well. I'll drive over and get there in the afternoon if this works for you." Just as I finished, dad spoke up.

"Sounds good. I have to run over for another meeting soon, so I'll be there some of the time. Demon can go with you since he knows where the compound is. We'll be sending over a few of our guys to help them out as well. Probably by the end of next week. It'll take you a little bit to get familiar with their town, so it'll be best if you have a guide when you go out." I nodded that would be fine.

Suddenly, I heard the music volume increase. I realized the laughter was getting louder. I saw the ones with families, escorting them out for the evening. They'd had the chance to see everyone was safe. I guess the fun was about to start. Time for me to say goodnight. I turned toward dad. "I'm planning to crash here tonight in your room, and by the sounds of it, this is my cue to head out." I gave dad and Demon a quick kiss on the cheek. I turned to Terror. "Goodnight Terror. I'll see you in a couple of days." With that said, I headed down the hall to my dad's room.

Chapter 8: Terror

I watched Harlow leave the room. I felt my gut tighten more, as I thought of that kiss, she'd just given Demon. Fuck! What was up with all the touching between those two? He'd gone straight to her after church and kissed her again a second time. Now she gave him a kiss. Maybe they did have something going, but if so, why had he agreed to her coming over to Dublin Falls for a while? Maybe I needed to have a word with Demon and feel him out.

I turned back toward Demon and Bull as Bull stated. "Whew, that was easier than I thought. Now we just have to see how long we can keep her busy and over there. How about you two join me for a drink?" He indicated a table to the left of us. Before we moved off to sit down, I took the opportunity to ask. "Could I talk to you for a minute outside, Demon?" Bull looked a little surprised. Demon just smiled and nodded yes. I led the way out to the parking lot and around to the side of the building.

"What's up?" Demon asked once we made it to a secluded spot.

"Man, I need to ask you something. I'm not real sure how to ask this, so I'm just going to ask it straight out." He nodded for me to continue. "What's your relationship with Harlow? It looks like you're both super close. I'm surprised you would be agreeable to her coming to stay with us for a while and putting her closer to the Bastards."

Hopefully it sounded just curious and concerned to him. "I don't want to cause you two any trouble." I added to play up the concern for a fellow brother angle. In reality, it was me needing to make sure she wasn't involved with him. I wanted her, and it was a need growing stronger every minute.

Demon paused, looking down at the ground for a minute with a look of deep concentration on his face. Shit. Then he looked back up at me. "My relationship with Harley? You want to know what it is? I can tell you my relationship with her is a deep one. I can tell you I love her and would do anything for her." My heart dropped when he said this. Fuck, I knew it. They were in a relationship. He continued. "She's a beautiful, courageous, and unique woman who I'm proud to have in my life. I'd do anything to protect her. I know she feels the same way about me. She's like a little sister to me. I grew up in this club and have been around her since she was a kid. We have a great bond. Is this what you wanted to hear? Maybe you want to know if there's anyone else she's close to or in a relationship with?"

Before I could reply, he continued. "I'm not dumb. I saw the looks you've been giving her tonight. I saw the interest in your eyes. And no, she's not in a relationship with anyone. But I'm going to tell you straight up, you need to forget starting anything with her. She's not some easy pussy like the club bunnies or the barflies. She isn't made that way, and neither Bull nor any of the Hunters Creek brothers would allow her to be used like one. I won't let her be used like that. She's a woman a man goes after, only when he's looking to have a serious relationship." As he spoke, his expression became more and more dark.

I stepped closer to Demon and decided to lay it out to him. "I honestly don't know what this is, Demon. I've never in a million years felt close to anything like what I've been feeling tonight. However, I do know without you saying it, that she's not a 'hit it and quit it' kind of woman. I know she'd never even think about being that way. And I know Bull wouldn't stand for it, especially with a brother. I've never been in a long-term relationship. I've been happy to get some for the night and then move on. You know there's never a lack of pussy to be had for a biker. But she's getting to me in a way I've never had happen. I want to see where this goes. I know in order to do that. I have to be willing to commit to being with one woman. The goal has to be things go all the way." I told him uncomfortably. Guys didn't talk about feelings or relationships. That was a chick thing, but I knew I had to have someone on my side. I hoped Demon could be that someone.

Demon raked his hand through his hair and blew out a loud breath. "Look Terror, I have all kinds of respect for you, man. I would do anything for a brother. But I won't let Harley get hurt. She's special and we love her. I can tell you, if you fuck with her, every brother in this chapter will have your ass. You won't just have me and Bull to worry about coming after you. Brother, think long and hard before you make a move like this. Really be sure you want to try for a long-haul relationship with only one woman. Because if you decide to go this route, it can only be with the intent to make her your old lady. Nothing else is acceptable."

In the past, anyone talking to me about finding an old lady had sent me running in the opposite direction. I knew a few brothers in our affiliate clubs had them. Some even seemed to be happy, like Tiny in my club. I knew I never thought I would be one contemplating it. But just after a couple of hours knowing her, my gut and mind were pushing me to go after her with everything I had. To snatch her up before someone else got her. The thought of her with someone else made me feel furious. It made me want to kill whoever it was. To take her somewhere, where no one could take her away from me. This was insanity! But my mind and definitely my cock agreed. She needed to be with me. For her, I could go the distance.

"Demon, I know she's special, and she's not just a piece of ass. All you have to do is look at her and it's written all over her. I have this overwhelming need to have her near me. I want the chance to make her mine. I just wanted to be sure she's not already involved. If it was some guy, then yeah, I'd just go after her. But if she was with another brother, I'd never try to take her away from him. Hell, to be honest, with the way I'm feeling, that may not have even deterred me from going after her. This plan for her to come to Dublin Falls is going to give me a chance to get to know her. But also, I want to be sure she's protected. Though the Bastards haven't stirred shit here with you guys yet, it's likely only a matter of time until they do. I have to know she's safe, and I want her where I can ensure she is."

Demon slowly nodded his head. "Okay, I'll have your back. Just don't hurt her, whatever you do. And I can tell you one thing right now, she'll not ever tolerate sharing her man with another woman. So, if you plan on continuing to play with the club bunnies and barflies, then forget it. She'll leave your ass in a heartbeat and never look at you again. There's none of this 'what happens on the road or at the clubhouse stays there' bullshit.

She's seen that happen and has made it loudly clear, she'd never put up with it. Believe me, there are many guys who would gladly step into the role of being her man, if she indicated she wanted them."

The thought of others wanting her didn't surprise me, but I wanted to ask him who they were. What guys in the Hunters Creek chapter wanted Harlow? I knew I had a lot of work to do, to get things in place before she came to Dublin Falls in a couple of days. Until then, I needed to spend some time tonight with all the guys. I clapped him on the shoulder, and we headed back into the clubhouse. In the short time we'd been outside, things had gotten even louder. The music was cranked up more and the club bunnies were out in full force rubbing up against several of the guys. I knew all of us had been happy at the thought of new pussy tonight. But after seeing Harlow, I found I didn't have that urge anymore. We both headed over to where Bull was sitting. He looked up with a concerned look on his face. "Everything okay, boys?" He asked us.

"Everything is great, Bull. Just a couple of things I wanted to ask Demon. Now, is there anything we need to do specifically to get ready for Harlow to come over to our clubhouse? I'll talk to Tiny so he's in the loop on why she's there. That way he can help direct Sherry. I wish we had an idea what the Bastards will do next."

Bull took a drink of his beer and then sat it on the table. "There's nothing special you need to set up for Harley. As long as she has a secure place to sleep at night, that's all she'll need. She's likely to want to use some of your facilities other women might not use." I gave him a confused look. What facilities was he referring to? He grinned. "She'll most likely want to use that tricked out gym and the shooting range, if you don't mind. She's used to working out almost daily and practices her marksmanship frequently."

I laughed. "She's welcome to any of the facilities she wants to use. It might be fun to see her in action. She can help critique our new remodel and give us input. FYI, we're thinking of building more houses for some of the guys on the compound. The guys with old ladies already have them, which is just Tiny right now. Plus, I have mine. Hammer and Steel have one they share, even though they don't have an old lady. Now some of the other guys are thinking they might like a place of their own. It sure keeps the construction part of the business busy on top of the commercial and residential work we're doing. You might think about doing something like this here." He got a considering look on his face.

As we continued to talk about club expansion and how the different businesses were doing for both of our chapters, a tall blond club bunny came slinking up. At first, I thought she was coming over to Demon, but she passed him and came up to me. She had a heated look in her eyes. She was definitely looking for a companion for the evening. She had a decent body which was on display in her itty-bitty shorts which were so short, the cheeks of her ass hung out. She had a cropped top on showing her toned belly and it was cut super low with her ample cleavage spilling out. She was one I would've taken a ride with gladly any other time, but I found she did nothing for me tonight. I was wanting a certain redheaded beauty.

She ran her hand up my arm and leaned her body into mine, so she could rub her tits on my arm. I felt a bit disgusted. I didn't want her touching me. "How about we go and have a little fun, handsome?" She purred. I pulled my arm away from her claws.

"Sorry, not tonight. Why don't you go and see if one of my brothers is available? I know one of them would love to keep you company." I told her. She looked stunned. I didn't think she'd ever been turned down. I wanted to laugh at her expression Well, surprise sweetheart, I'd never turned it down either. She frowned and then stomped off. I saw Bull looking at me with a surprised look, while Demon was giving me an appraising look. There was no way I was going to touch her and throw away a chance with Harlow.

After drinking with them for another hour or so, I decided to call it an evening and bid them goodnight. My brothers were in good hands I could see. As I went down the hall to the room Bull had given me to use for the evening, I couldn't stop thinking about Harlow. What I wouldn't give to be going to bed with her tonight. The thought just made my cock grow hard again. I needed to keep my mind off her and get some sleep.

After a hot shower, I crawled in bed naked and tried to sleep. But her image wouldn't leave my mind. I found myself thinking about her beautiful face, that gorgeous body and those full, pouty lips. God, I could imagine those lips wrapped tight around my cock. They'd be stretched to take as much as I could give her. Her mouth would be so tight and wet. I'd feed her my thick cock inch by inch and watch her swallow it down. Just the thought of her mouth on my cock had me standing at attention. I was never going to get any sleep with those thoughts running around in my head and a stiff one tenting the sheets. I needed to get some relief. I grasped my cock and started to stroke it up and down. As I thought of her tight, luscious mouth, I tightened my grip more. I groaned at the sensation. I knew she'd feel so good, so tight, and so wet.

As my fantasy continued to run through my mind, I started to stroke faster and faster. When I'd stroke up to the sensitive head, I'd squeeze it just a little harder. I was panting and groaning at the sensation. Just as I got to the part in my fantasy of me filling her sweet mouth with my thick cum, the tingling in my low back increased and shot to my groin. I came shooting my real load all over my belly. I came hard in long thick ropes of cum. Jesus Christ! I hadn't come like this since I was a teen. Just the thought of her, got me off better than any woman I'd been with. What would it be like to have her for real? After my heart settled a little, I got cleaned up and settled down for the night. Only a couple of days and then my pursuit would begin. Look out Harlow, I'm coming for you. The temptress would be mine.

Chapter 9: Harlow

Today was my first day in Dublin Falls. This morning I'd gotten the last of my things packed and started out on the three-hour drive to the Dublin Falls compound. Terror had sent two of his guys to escort me and dad was sending Demon. Not sure why they thought it was necessary to send more than Demon. He would have sufficed, but they were insistent, so I followed behind the two from the Falls. Demon followed behind my car on his bike. It was a great day for a drive as the weather was clear and the temp was comfortable in the eighties. It would've been even better, if I'd been on a bike too. But I couldn't haul my stuff on my bike, so the car it was. For most of the drive, I sang along to the radio with the windows down. When we pulled into Dublin Falls, we passed through the middle of it to the other side of town. About five miles outside the limits, the two Dublin Falls' guys, Hammer and Ghost, turned left into two steel gates that were topped with razor wire.

From what I could see, extending from the gates were walls made of cement blocks. They stood around twelve feet high and were topped with razor wire as well. The prospect at the gate opened them after seeing Ghost and Hammer. I followed them slowly into the parking lot, outside of what I assumed was the clubhouse. It was huge and looked like it might have been a warehouse in the past. I pulled my jeep into a spot beside some of the bikes. I got out of the car and walked over to Hammer and Ghost. Demon came up to join us. I saw a few guys outside what looked like a garage that was across from the clubhouse looking at us. I gave them a smile, turned, and followed the guys inside.

Inside there were a few more guys. A couple were at the bar and another three were playing darts. All of them stopped talking when we came through the door. I felt their stares drill into me. Did no one tell them I was coming? As I looked around, I noticed Terror coming from a hallway to the right. He was headed straight for us. I felt my heart jump. He was even more gorgeous than I recalled. Had it only been two days since I saw him? Why did he cause me to feel this way? Too bad he was off limits, because he's the one man, I could see myself going after. But he'd be like all the rest, out for a good time. He'd want to hit it, if I was lucky, a couple of times then go. If I wanted meaningless sex, I could get it from anywhere and almost anyone. No thank you. Not for this woman.

Terror came up and smiled. "Hello Harlow, I hope the drive was a good one. Glad you could come and help us out." He placed his hand on my arm and wrapped his fingers around it. I usually didn't like people I wasn't used to touching me. But his touch only made me feel warm and tingly. He then moved his hand to my low back and turned toward the rear of the common room. "Let me introduce you really quick to Tiny and his old lady, Sherry. You'll be mostly helping Sherry get the damn place in shape," he stated.

Out of a back room, came the biggest man I had ever seen. He had to be close to seven feet tall and as big as a mountain. He had his arm wrapped around a pretty brunette who looked to be in her mid to late twenties. He came forward and stopped in front of us. He nodded at me when Terror confirmed this was Tiny. Sherry was less reserved. She smiled and actually hugged me.

"Hi Harlow, I'm so glad to meet you. I can't tell you how nice it'll be to have help with this and to have another woman around all this testosterone." Sherry teased. I liked her smile and friendliness. I thought we'd get along just fine.

"No worries, Sherry. I have no doubt we can knock this out. As for the testosterone, believe me I'm used to it. Between growing up in the MC and being in the Marines, I am a testosterone expert." I joked with her.

As Sherry and I were chatting and joking, I heard Terror greet Demon while Tiny stood silent and somewhat menacing beside Sherry. I could tell he was trying to decide if I was someone he could trust around his wife. He threw off protective vibes for everyone to feel. I hoped what he saw reassured him, because he would be a terrifying guy to have as an enemy. He gave Demon a quick hand shake. Terror gestured for all of us to sit at a nearby table. Once seated, the prospect behind the bar came over to ask what we wanted to drink. No surprise, all the guys said beer. Sherry asked for a Coke and I decided to have the same. It was a little too early for me to drink, plus I never was one who drank very often anyway.

I felt Terror looking at me. When I looked up, he had a look in his eyes. It was intense and rather heated. What was that about? He held my gaze for a moment then ran his eyes from my head down to where the tabletop began and back up again. His lips quirked up into a naughty smirk. Wow! That one look made my whole-body tingle. Why, oh why, did he have to be the one to trip my non-existent libido to the 'on' position? I looked him back in the eyes and raised my eyebrows, as I shook my head no. He needed to know. I wasn't going to be the next plaything for his short-term amusement. Unfortunately. Damn him, all he did was smile broader and wink! Cocky fucker!

I decided the best course was to ignore him and talk to Sherry. If he kept it up, I'd have to shut him down hard. "Sherry, do you have a plan you're working through step-by-step or is it more of a tackle what grabs your attention one, to get this place in shape?" She laughed.

"A little of both. I have a list of what all needs to be accomplished, but I have no order I am tackling them in. Whatever takes my fancy next is what I work on. I think it drives Terror crazy, since he's a much more disciplined soul, but in the end, everything will get done. If there's something he wants prioritized, he lets me know." Sherry responded with a smile at Terror.

"Well, I'm here to help however I can. I have to admit, I tend to be more of an organized plan kind of girl myself, but I can adapt when needed. I know it's already afternoon, but do you want to get started today on anything or wait until tomorrow?"

"No, we can wait until tomorrow. I know Terror has asked everyone to come over after work to meet you. Also, you'll want to get settled in. I think tomorrow we'll work on the kids' room. I've ordered lots of things for it and most have come, so maybe we can get it set up." I was surprised to hear they had a kids' room in the clubhouse? I'd never heard of anyone putting one in, even though lots of clubs had members with children. Before I could ask, Sherry continued. "We already have the outside play area put together, this is more for when the kids can't go outside due to the weather, if we happen to go on a lockdown or have a party."

"Does this chapter have a lot of kids?" I asked her. As far as I knew no one had an old lady except Tiny. Though that didn't preclude them form having kids. I was curious as to why a club would think of doing something like this.

"No kids yet, but as the members start finding their old ladies, we anticipate this to change." Terror said with a gleam in his eye. Was he thinking of having kids? If so, I'd be surprised.

"Yeah, then I thought we could work on this common room next to get it all freshly painted and new furniture situated." Sherry added.

"My dad mentioned you'd done remodeling here. Was it just cosmetics or was there additions added? From the little I see. This room doesn't need a lot." I replied. I was now curious to know what they had changed or added. Before Sherry could answer, the door opened and in came three more brothers. They were all chatting, but when they saw us sitting at the table, they became silent. I saw them look at each other, exchange amused looks, then came over to us. One I recalled seeing at our clubhouse, Menace I believe, spoke up first.

"Well, hello, beautiful. So glad to see you here. Hope to get to spend some time with you while you're with us." He said with a twinkle in his eye. I heard what sounded like a growl come from Terror. Looking at him, I could see he was less than happy and was glaring at Menace. However, it didn't seem to faze Menace. All he did was chuckle

I could tell Menace was a natural flirt. He flirted with women like he breathed. I could deal with his kind of flirting. His type was fun to joke around with. I gave him a wink and spoke. "So glad to be here now handsome." I definitely heard Terror growl this time. His face had a look of thunder on it. Interesting. Before anything else could be said, the other two with him both smiled and introduced themselves as Smoke and Hawk.

No sooner had they pulled up chairs and called out their orders to the prospect, Kade, than the door opened again. What I thought had to be the remainder of the members came in. There was Savage, Viper, Blaze, Ranger, and Steel. They had all been on the run a couple of nights ago. I didn't see any other women yet. I was curious who out of this bunch had girlfriends. All the guys were very welcoming and flirtatious, but that was a typical biker for you. I'd grown up with this. It made me feel comfortable. I didn't ever take their comments to heart. They were just guys. Though I caught more than one look from Terror directed at them, that looked less than nice. Surely, he wasn't upset with them for being a little flirty?

We'd been sitting and talking for maybe a half hour when through the door came some club bunnies. Now, I usually ignored them at home. I knew they served a purpose for all the single guys and if this was what the girls wanted to do, fine by me. If this was the life they wanted, then it was their call. What I couldn't stand was if I saw one going after one of the guys who was taken. I'd seen it happen a time or two in other clubs we associated with, and suffice to say, I was never silent about my opinion. There were three of them who came in, two blondes and a brunette. They all made a beeline to the tables where we were sitting. The tallest blond came right up and leaned into Terror. She had a smirk on her face and was rubbing herself against his shoulder. The other blond went over to Demon and the brunette went up to Savage.

The one hanging all over Demon didn't bother me a bit. He was a free agent and if he wanted to spend some time with her, that was his business. But if she thought he was her ticket to be an old lady, she was going to be disappointed. I knew my "brother" as I thought of Demon. He wouldn't ever make a woman his, if all his brothers had had a piece of her. He thought he wouldn't settle for just one woman, but I knew differently. One day he would meet the one and I couldn't wait to tell him, "I told you so". I heard her tell Demon her name was Jen.

The one hanging onto Savage I heard him call her Amber. It was the one practically attacking Terror who had my attention. For some reason, the sight of her with him made me angry. I didn't want her touching him. I wanted to grab her by the hair and throw her ass across the room. What was wrong with me? Obviously, with how familiar she was acting, he had "touched" her before and would again. And he was free to do so like the others. He wasn't encouraging her, but it still bothered me, so I decided I needed to take a breather. I stood up and pushed my chair back. Terror looked at me and asked me. "Where are you going?"

I looked at him and his bunny. "Out for some air, it's gotten a bit stuffy in here. I'd like to stretch my legs more after that long drive." As I turned to head for the door, I heard the girl hanging onto Terror ask.

"Who's that bitch and why's she here at our club?" This stopped me in my tracks. Oh, no way was I taking shit off of a club whore. Before he could answer her, I swung back around and stalked over to get in her face. She seemed surprised and leaned back against Terror. I leaned closer.

"This bitch is from the Hunters Creek chapter. I'd

watch running that mouth, if you want to keep all your teeth. Now you don't know me, so this time I'll let you keep your teeth. But call me a bitch again and see what happens." She was momentarily stunned then I saw the anger flash in her eyes.

"How dare you...," she didn't finish because Demon stood at the same time Terror did. Demon stared at her.

"I don't know how it is here, but in our chapter, whores don't mouth off to old ladies or our princess. So, I suggest you keep your mouth shut. She'll hand you your teeth if you keep it up. And you'll be lucky if that's all she does." Just as he finished telling her off, Terror got her attention.

"Laci, you don't come into this clubhouse running your mouth to anyone, but especially someone you don't know. Harlow is our guest for the next several weeks and I expect you and everyone else to be civil. If you can't, then you don't need to come back to the clubhouse. You need to know your fucking place." He growled.

Laci stuck out her bottom lip in a pout and said. "But Terror, honey, I just wanted to know who she is. Why's she here? We don't need any new girls here." I didn't know what Terror said to her in response, because I walked over to the door and outside. I really needed that air now. Her calling him honey confirmed they had more than just a once or twice kind of thing between them. It was disturbing me which only angered me. Why did I care if he was fucking that whore or anyone else? Maybe this wasn't a good idea after all. I needed to talk to Demon, but that could wait, for now I was going to walk around the compound.

Chapter 10: Terror

I thought things were going well, even if some of the guys had come onto Harlow. I gave them my best dirty look, but the bastards were trying to rile me. As I saw Laci, Amber, and Jen come in, I looked at Harlow. I knew some old ladies and princesses really hated the club bunnies.

She was looking at them with mild interest but no disgust. Before I knew it, I saw Jen over by Demon, Amber talking to Savage and damn it, Laci slinking up beside me. I was about to tell her to let go of me and get lost, when Harlow stood up from the table. I could tell she was now a little upset and then Laci opened her mouth. When Harlow got up in her face and told her off, I was so turned on. This was the kind of woman a man needed, especially the president of a MC. She knocked Laci back into her place big time. Laci had been stepping more and more out of her designated spot lately. I knew I was going to have to address it, but hadn't done it yet. Harlow just did it for me.

Harlow obviously could be tough when she needed to be, but also caring and loyal too. Demon beat me to warning Laci first about mouthing off to Harlow. After telling Laci to back off, my gut twisted a little when Harlow still went out the door. Pushing Laci away from me, I went to follow her out. As I rounded the table, Demon caught my arm.

"Listen man, let her go. She needs time to settle.

This chick mouthing off to her set her off and she'll want to cool down a bit. However, I'll tell you right now, if having her put the bunnies in their place when they step out of line is going to be a problem, send Harlow home. She'll not tolerate shit from them or them getting up in an old lady's face. It's a pet peeve of hers."

I considered what Demon said and then let him know my thoughts. "I have no problem at all with Harlow putting the bunnies in their place if they need it. And the only brother I have, who has an old lady is Tiny, and the bunnies know to stay clear of him. You know I want her to stay and why."

"Yeah, I know why you wanted her here. Just remember. If you want a relationship with Harley, having one of those whores rubbing on you or you going off with one of them, will make sure that never happens. I saw her eyes. She's confused by you and if she thinks you and a bunny have something still going on, she won't let you near her. You won't get a chance to see if there could be any kind of relationship between you two." He said with a sigh.

Fuck! Had I already blown it before I even had a chance with Harlow? I couldn't let that happen. I would have to be sure to warn all the whores to stay away from me and Harlow. Yes, I'd hooked up with Laci several times. It was purely for sexual release like any of my brothers. But I knew she liked to try and single me out and that wouldn't be happening. I think she hoped I'd see her as old lady material. That would never happen! Where once she could turn me on in a matter of moments, she didn't even make a blip on my radar now. She stirred nothing in me. My cock didn't even twitch, and in the past, she could always get it to rise. Harlow was the only one I wanted, and I'd do anything to get her.

If Laci had ruined my chances, I'd have her ass out of the club in a heartbeat. Nothing and no one were going to get in my way. Which reminded me, time to have church and let my brothers know where Harlow stood on the availability score. She was a beautiful woman and every one of them had shown a spark of interest. I was the only one who was going to be taking Harlow to bed. I nodded to Demon to let him know I heard him and understood. I whistled to get the room's attention and yelled. "Church in ten minutes." With this said, I headed to my office. I needed a couple of minutes to get my thoughts in order.

Ten minutes later found us all in church seated around the table. Demon had joined us. Everyone was chatting until I rapped the gavel on the table. This brought everyone to attention. "Okay guys, first thing, as you saw we have a guest for the next several weeks. Harlow is from the Hunters Creek chapter and she's Bull's daughter. She's here to help Sherry, but also so we can keep an eye on her. There's concern someone may come looking for her. However, if she's here and not in Hunters Creek, then they won't hopefully know where to find her."

Hammer looked up sharply. A look of concern was on all the guys' faces. Hammer asked the question first. "Who's after her? We need to know who to keep an eye out for in order to keep her safe."

Demon answered. "We believe it's someone she was in the Marines with. Harley got out three months ago. From something she said one night to me, we're concerned she got out due to someone in the Corps. Now, we don't know if someone will come around or not, but she seems more cautious than she usually is. We thought her coming here was a good idea."

They all had a look of surprise on their faces. Hawk asked what the others appeared to be thinking. "She was a Marine? You're fucking with us, aren't you?"

I shook my head. "No, we're not joking. She was a U.S. Marine, a sniper in fact. Her safety is a priority. You know what's going on with the Bastards and about our skirmish the other night. What some of you don't know is Harlow was part of that." I'd told the guys who had gone that night not to mention Harlow's involvement until we had church. Not sure why. A murmur went around the room. They were all surprised. We hadn't had church since we got back, so for several of them, this was news.

"No one saw her, but she was our sniper that night since Demon here was out of commission with his arm. Her and Sherry need to have someone with them every time they leave the compound. She'll be staying at my house while she's here." I informed them. That got even more looks and murmurs. "One final thing, she's off limits. Not a one of you better lay a hand on her or you will lose it." I saw Blaze look at Viper.

Viper looked over at me and asked. "Why's she off limits?" I stood and leaned forward at the head of the table.

"Because she's going to be mine, so hands the fuck off!" At this they all started laughing and Menace yelled. "

"Like that's a surprise. We saw how you acted when we came in. You looked like you wanted to piss on her to mark your territory." I flipped him the bird. Bastard. He was right. I did have the urge to mark her, so everyone would know she was mine and hands off. I had it bad.

"Laugh it up you, assholes. Just remember you've been warned. She's not up for grabs. One other thing, Bull is going to be sending over a few of his guys to beef up our chapter for a while. Demon is going to be one of them and the others will be making their way over here in the next few days. Are there any questions?" I asked before dismissing the meeting.

Menace nodded and added. "Hey man, just want to be clear on this Harlow chick. Are you claiming her off limits just for the duration she's with you? I mean, when you get tired of her, can she be with another brother?" I felt instant rage fill my veins. I saw the same rage fill Demon's eyes. Before he had the chance to say anything or get a hold of Menace, I came around the table getting right in Menace's face.

"What it means is she's mine, period. There will be no 'get her when I'm done' shit! She's mine and I plan on her staying that way. She's not some easy piece of ass you bang and then move on to the next one. She's a woman to ride the road with and I plan on her being on the back of my bike permanently. Does that answer your fucking question? Does anyone need it spelled out plainer? If so, we can continue this discussion outside."

Menace just smiled and laughed. "No man that's clear and what I thought, just wanted to be sure these other assholes understood you. No need for you or Demon over there to kill me. I didn't see old Bull being okay with his daughter being treated like a club bunny." The bastard just had to rile me. Fucker always knew how to push my buttons. But then I knew how to push him. One day I'd be paying him back for this.

I dismissed the meeting and we all filed out of the room. I was the last one out. I looked around for Harlow, but didn't see her anywhere. Sherry was over in the corner standing with Tiny, so I walked over to her. "Did Harlow come back in?" Sherry looked at me and then Tiny. She looked a bit worried.

"She walked outside right before you guys went into church and she hasn't come back. I was starting to worry about her and was going to go out and look for her when you all came out." She said hesitantly.

I'd turned to head for the door, when I saw Harlow come back in and she was looking around. Her gaze caught mine for a moment then she kept looking until I saw her eyes land on Demon. She didn't look happy and I wondered what she was thinking. Was she still upset over Laci? I started toward her as she started toward Demon. On the way, Viper stopped me to ask a question. When I turned back around, she was in an intense conversation with Demon. They were now alone in the far corner and she was even more upset looking than a minute ago. He had a frown on his face and was rubbing his hand up and down her arm like he was trying to soothe her. Time to find out what was wrong.

As I approached them, I heard her saying "I'll talk to dad tomorrow. I don't think it'll work." She looked up at that moment and saw me. She didn't look happy to see me. Fuck! I needed to get her to relax and talk to me. I wanted her to forget all about Laci. Thankfully, I didn't see Laci anywhere in the clubhouse.

"So, we're all done with church. How about we relax for a while and get some food going?" I suggested. Harlow just shook her head.

"I think I need to rest for a bit and settle in. Can you have someone show me where my room is so I can do that?" She asked. I got the feeling she wasn't really being honest about being tired. She just wanted to avoid me. I decided not to push her right now and I just nodded.

"Let me show you around a little so you know your way and the same for Demon. Then I'll show you to your rooms. Make sure to let me know if there's anything you need or want. I'll make sure you get it." I told her with a smile. She gave me a curt nod.

I showed them the clubhouse areas which consisted of the main room, kitchen, the massive playroom for the kids, the various bedrooms and my office on the first floor. On the second floor was mainly open space and storage. Downstairs was a big area set up as a gym with a wrestling ring and a big dorm like area. As we went around, I watched her face to see if I could get an idea what she thought of the compound. We'd finalized the remodel and I was very proud of the changes we'd made. It was more up to meeting our needs now. Also, I explained about the houses they would see on the compound as well. While we were looking around, I showed Demon his room. After the tour, Harlow gave me a questioning look. "Where is my room?" She asked with a frown.

I took her arm and started to lead her toward the front door as I explained. "You're going to be staying in a house and not here in the clubhouse. It'll be more private and comfortable for you. Let me show you." Demon met my eyes and gave a slight nod before heading over to sit with some of the guys. After hesitating a moment, Harlow followed me out the door.

"I don't want to put anyone out. I can easily stay in one of the rooms and from the looks of them they're very comfortable." She said.

I shook my head and told her, "you're not putting anyone out and we don't have women stay in the clubhouse as a rule." She seemed a little surprised then shrugged and continued to walk with me across to my house standing the farthest from the clubhouse and garage. It was a large two-story white house with the traditional black shutters and a red door. I had nothing to do with its style, since it had been the original house on the property when the club bought it several years ago. It was the oldest home, but also the largest and it was in excellent condition. There was a wraparound porch with several rockers and even a swing on it. I had to admit. I did like to sit out there some nights and enjoy the night. Sherry had helped with picking out some of the furnishings.

It had five bedrooms, four and a half baths as well as a home office and theater room. It was way more room than I needed, and I spent more nights at the clubhouse than in it. But with Harlow around that was going to change. I wanted my time with her to be private. I was hoping she liked it. I couldn't believe I was worrying about if a woman liked my house!

As we reached the steps, I couldn't stand it any longer and placed my hand on her arm. I acted like it was to help her up the stairs, since she had on high heeled boots. But the real reason was, I just wanted to touch her. She seemed to falter for a second then she continued up the steps with me. Reaching the front door, I opened it and gestured for her to go first. Walking into the entry, I could see she was surprised and if her expression was correct, she was appreciative of the house.

There was a large glass light fixture hanging in the entry. The stairs and floors were all polished dark wood. The original crown molding and baseboards were also in the same dark wood. When we had renovated the house, I tried to keep as much of the original woodwork as possible. I closed the door and faced her. Once she stopped looking around the entry and the hall leading off to the back of the house, she looked at me. "Tiny and Sherry's house is gorgeous. I can tell just looking at the outside and this entry. Are you sure they're okay with me staying here with them?"

I shook my head at her. "This isn't their house. They live in the smaller light blue house you saw just beyond the garage. This is my house. You'll be staying here." I told her as I watched to see her reaction. Trying not to let the pleasure I was feeling at the thought of her in my house, to show on my face. Her eyes grew big and then she started to shake her head no.

"I can't stay in your house, Terror. There's no need. Surely, if you don't want me in the clubhouse, I could get a room out in town. It's no big deal." She reassured me.

I stepped forward and grasped her hand. "Babe, you're not staying out in town. Your dad and I discussed this and there's no way that's going to work. You need to be close and available when Sherry needs you. And as for staying with Tiny and Sherry, there's no need. This house is huge and I'm rarely here. It needs someone to live in it. There's no inconvenience for me. I'll show you around and then you can take whichever of the bedrooms you want." I could see she was still not comfortable with this idea, but she didn't resist, so I showed her around.

I could tell when she saw the kitchen, she really liked it. Her eyes seemed to gleam, and she ran her hands across the granite counters and the stainless-steel appliances. It had more cabinets than one could ever need and a large walk-in pantry. There was a large farmer's sink in the island, which sat five people on stools and a six-burner gas stove top. Double ovens rounded out the kitchen. Sherry had insisted double ovens and the six burners were a must. There was a breakfast nook off to the side, open to the kitchen. It had a window seat and seated six people at the round table without the leaf in it.

The living room was open to the kitchen and breakfast area in an open concept. It had soft leather furniture with an oversized chair, sofa and loveseat. On one wall was a large sixty-inch television. On another was built in shelves on either side of a large fireplace covered in stone with a raised hearth. Taking her hand, I took her across the hall to show her my office on the first floor. I told her she could use the computer and the space any time she wanted. It faced the front of the house with two large windows. Two walls were floor to ceiling bookshelves.

Down the hall and off of the kitchen, was a large dining room that had never been used since I'd been here. It had a large dark wood table which could seat sixteen. The downstairs was finished off with a half bath and a large bedroom and bathroom suite. It could be used as a master suite, but I had one upstairs. The bathroom like all the bathrooms was tiled in stone and the shower walls in matching stone tiles. The counters were light marble.

I took her downstairs to see the theater room. It was decked out with the theater reclining seats and a huge screen. The guys were the ones who talked me into putting this in the house. I told her this and she laughed. Our final stop would be the upstairs where the remainder of the bedrooms and bathrooms, including the master and the laundry room were. The bedrooms up there were large but had minimal furniture. A couple had beds. The laundry room was large with a deep sink, cabinets, and counter space.

Our final stop was the master suite. It had huge walk-in closets and windows that overlooked the property. Between those windows were French doors which led out to a balcony. I had a king-size bed with large pillars on all four corners against one wall with matching nightstands and a large dresser. At the foot of the bed, was a sofa that faced the wall where another television hung. However, the master bath I had to say was my favorite. It had a massive standalone shower with the rain type showerhead and two others coming out each side of the shower walls. There was a big, deep garden tub which could hold two people easily. I could definitely see her in the shower and tub with me.

To be honest, I could see her in every room of the house and on every piece of furniture. Just being next to her and smelling her scent had me ready to throw her over my shoulder and toss her on the bed. That king size bed in the bedroom was testing my resolve to let her get to know me a little before seducing her. After finishing the tour, I invited her to choose which room she wanted. Secretly, I hoped she would say mine but no such luck. She ended up choosing the bedroom farthest from the master. That was okay, she wouldn't end up there for long if I had my way, and I always had my way.

I could tell she was feeling unsettled, so I decided to let her have a little time alone. "I'll send over your bags with Kade, the prospect, and let you settle in and rest. I'll come get you in a couple of hours for dinner. Sherry will want to get a chance to chat some more with you." I explained. I reluctantly left her and headed back to the clubhouse. I needed to see when Bull was coming down for sure. I knew I wouldn't touch her until I had a chance to tell him my intent. But make no mistake, Harlow Williams was going to be mine and soon. I had seen her eyes flare with heat and felt her body tense when I touched her. She wasn't immune to me.

Chapter 11: Harlow

Wow! Terror's house was gorgeous. I loved everything about it. It was like he had gotten in my head and created my dream house. The kitchen was to die for, and I loved to cook and bake. I could imagine what I could do with a kitchen like that. His whole house had overwhelmed me, but nothing like finding out it was his and he expected me to stay here. I didn't think I can stand it. Just being near him made my palms sweat and my heart race.

He was the sexist man I had ever laid eyes on and he kept making me feel things no man had ever made me feel. That was the big issue. How could I stand to live here and be around him? He was used to having any woman he wanted and then moving on to the next one. I could see myself falling for a guy for the first time in my life and he wasn't a "forever" kind of guy. Damn it! I needed to talk to dad and see if I could find a way out of staying here. If not, then I'd work night and day to get Sherry's project list finished and then get back to Hunters Creek as fast as possible.

Five minutes after he left, there was a knock at the door. When I opened it, I found Kade standing there with my bags. He was a young guy, probably about twenty I'd say with long blond hair and gray eyes. Like all the guys he was very good-looking. But he appeared to be trying not to make eye contact. Not sure why he would be shy around me or any woman. He had to be beating them off with a stick. I gave him a gentle smile and showed him which room to put my bags in. He quickly beat a retreat once he put them in there. Looking at the room I thought of Terror. I needed to get him off my mind, so I decided to take a bath and unpack.

Two hours later as I was sitting in the living room reading my emails on my laptop, the front door opened and in strolled Terror. He came over to stand beside me as I shut down. "Hey beautiful." He said. "Are you ready to head back over to the clubhouse? Everyone is wanting to get a chance to talk to you and get to know you better."

I was a little startled. Why would all of them be wanting to get to know me better? Must be because I was Bull's daughter. Oh well, I was starting to get hungry, so I stood to follow him out the door. Once on the porch, he reached out and took my hand and led me down the stairs. When we reached the bottom, I expected him to let my hand go, but he kept a hold of it and not just until we reached the clubhouse door. He walked in with my hand still clasped in his.

Inside, the crowd was all laughing and drinking. In the corner I could see Demon with a big grin on his face. He seemed to be enjoying himself. As we got further in the room, Sherry came up and latched onto my arm. "Come over here to our table and let's chat." She said excitedly. She led me to a table where Tiny was already sitting along with Menace and two others I hadn't met yet. As I went to pull out my chair to sit, Terror reached around and pulled it out for me. I was startled. Most guys weren't the gentleman type. As I sat, he asked me what I wanted to drink. I decided to try and relax, so I asked him for a rum and coke. He waved his hand to Kade, whom

I could see was attending bar again. Kade came over and Terror gave our drink orders while the rest of the table chimed in with their re-orders. The two guys I didn't know introduce themselves as Hawk and Smoke.

Once the drinks were served, Sherry and I began to discuss our plan for tomorrow and how we were going to organize our day. Suddenly, I felt Terror shift his chair closer to mine and then I felt his fingers stroke my back. I looked at him and saw him staring at me. His eyes had a predatory look in them. I felt like he was going to eat me alive. I had to be projecting my own fantasies onto him. Why would he be looking like that at me? Maybe I'd have to set him straight after all. I wasn't there to be one of his many quick lays. As we sat there, Hawk, Smoke, and Menace started to talk to me.

Hawk spoke first. "Harlow, we heard you were a Marine. Not only that, but a sniper and you covered the guys the other night when the meeting with the Bastards went down. Tell us this isn't true, and Demon and Terror were just pulling our legs." He said with a laugh. I smiled and shook my head.

"Sorry to disappoint you guys, Hawk, but I was a sniper in the Marines, and I did cover them the other night." I told them with a grin and deep satisfaction. It never got old to see the surprise on people's faces when they found out the Marine part and then the sniper on top of it. I saw all three of them and Tiny exchanging looks. Terror and Demon just looked amused and Sherry looked stunned.

"Come on." Smoke chimed in. "You can't be serious. No way the guys in the Corps could have stood to have a sexy, gorgeous woman like you distracting them all day. How did anyone get any work done?" He teased and winked? I felt a laugh bubbling up. Beside me I felt Terror shift closer. I looked over at him and he was giving Smoke one of those death looks. Before I could say anything to Smoke, Menace added his thoughts.

"How long did you serve and why did you get out? I'm surprised your dad let you enlist."

"I did six years and got out at the end of my enlistment three months ago." No way was I going to tell them the truth. That was something I planned to keep to myself and forget if I could. Demon spoke up.

"Bull didn't want her to go and if he'd been able to send one of us with her, he would have." That got a bark of laughter not only out of them, but others who had moved closer while we were talking. I had to laugh at that as well.

"Demon's right about that. Dad almost had a coronary when I told him I'd enlisted. When he found out they wanted to change my job after boot camp, he swore he was going to kill them all and bring me home. Of course, he was a Marine and he and the guys all raised me, so why they found it surprising I wanted to be one, made no sense to me."

Steel spoke up from his spot behind Hawk's chair where he had settled. "What were you going to do when you originally enlisted"? I grinned and told him.

"Oh, something much easier. I went in as an Arabic linguist." Everyone froze. They had stunned looks on their faces. Before anyone could say anything, Demon jumped back in.

"Once they saw how she could shoot, they decided to use her as a sniper, since they would be out nothing in the linguistic part. She already knew Arabic, so she became an official scout sniper, who happened to be able to also function as an interpreter unofficially. They got a twofer."

He said proudly. I was never sure who was prouder, my dad or Demon when people were told what I did. I always felt a little embarrassed when they told people.

One of the other guys asked. "How do you know Arabic?"

"I went to a private high school. They offered language classes in Arabic. On top of that I took classes at the local college, what the guys who had been over there had taught me. I picked it up quickly." They were all looking at me with more awe. I looked away from them as I squirmed in my seat. Terror caught my attention when I felt his breath on my right ear as he whispered.

"Don't be embarrassed sweetheart, that's fucking awesome and you should be proud of yourself. It just shows you have brains to go with all that beauty." A shiver moved down my spine. I so wanted to feel those lips on my skin. He was distracting me again. I gave him a brief nod. I decided to finish my drink. When I was done, I stood and made the excuse I was tired and wanted to turn in. They all tried to get me to stay but I told them another time.

Terror rose, insisting on walking me back to his house. There was an uneasy silence between us. I didn't know what to say. Once inside he insisted on escorting me to my bedroom door. I'd turned to thank him when he leaned forward and grazed his lips across mine. "Goodnight and sweet dreams, darlin'," He whispered hoarsely. Then he turned and left me there. Dear Lord, I think I just melted my panties. It was going to take me a long time to fall asleep tonight.

Chapter 12: Terror

Harlow had been here for three days and I was about to lose my fucking mind! Having her close, in my house and not being able to have her in my bed was making me crazy. I walked around with a permanent hard on straining my pants. All the guys thought she was great and kept flirting with her, just to see how much they could piss me off. This morning she was out with Sherry picking up more stuff for the clubhouse. Kade had gone with them to be their gopher slash bodyguard.

Bull and three more of his guys had shown up a little bit ago and we'd just finished discussing the last few days. Besides Demon, Bull had brought his prospect, Ace, and two patched members, Player and Slash. The four of them would be staying with us as extra help for the foreseeable future. With church out of the way, I told Bull I needed to talk to him alone. We strolled down the hall and into my office. Closing the door, he took a seat in front of my desk. "What's up? I can see something is on your mind, and it's not the Bastards."

I took a moment to calm my mind. I found myself nervous to tell him. I decided to cut to the chase. There was no sense in beating around the bush. Worst case scenario was he killed me. Clearing my throat, I began. "Well Bull, you know I respect you and would never do anything to earn your distrust or hurt the Warriors. This is my family and I only want to make it stronger. It's because of this, that I wanted to discuss this with you." He looked puzzled and concerned, so I hurried to continue. "It's about Harlow." He sat up straighter with a surprised look on his face. "I've found since I met her that I have these feelings for her. Ones I've never had before for a woman. As her father, I wanted you to know this. Straight up, I want to be with her. I know this is coming as a shock. You've never known me to want or be involved with a woman long-term. But before you say anything, let me get this all out. I know she's your daughter and your chapter's princess and I would never disrespect that. Also, I know she's not just some easy piece of ass that a guy spends a little time with and then moves on."

"She's one hundred percent a ride the road forever kind of woman. I've never wanted that. But after meeting Harlow, I've had a lot of thoughts and started thinking about what I want going forward. My ideas on being with one woman have changed. I want her and I'll do anything I can to have her. I just wanted you to know what's in the cards. Now, I haven't touched her since I hadn't spoken to you yet, but I plan to start my courtship of her after this. I want your approval to do so. But I have to be honest, if you say no, I don't think I can stop from trying to get her anyway. She's made to be my old lady, Bull. She just doesn't know it yet."

I could tell I had stunned him. He stood up and began to pace around my office. I was nervous about what he would say to such a bold declaration. But also, I knew I had to be completely honest and blunt as well. He was the kind of guy who liked all the cards laid out on the table. He came to a stop in front of my desk where he leaned forward.

"Listen Terror, you're a great brother, fellow president

and I respect you as well. But this is my daughter we're talking about. What's best for her is always what I'm going to want and will ensure she gets. You're right about her not being a hit it and go kind of woman. She's not one to hook up with a man for a period and then walk away. She's like her mom. A one-man woman and she expects it to last forever. Lastly, she's not ever going to be one to tolerate being an old lady, whose old man gets a piece on the side, while he expects her to look the other way. If that were to happen, not only would she walk and never return, but me and my chapter would kill you, if she didn't kill you first. You're used to having the bunnies and barflies at your beck and call. Now, if you get together with Harley, those all have to go away forever. It may be hard to get them to realize you are off limits. You have to be prepared for some fallout. And as her father, I won't let her be forced into something she doesn't want." He growled out the last part in warning.

 I had to set him straight, so he knew we were both on the same exact page. "Bull, I know she's a forever woman and that cheating is a deal breaker for her. I knew that from just meeting her. Plus, Demon warned me as well. If she decides she doesn't want me, I'll respect that, but I don't see that happening. She wants me, she just doesn't know yet she can trust me. I can see it in her eyes. I'll do everything in my power to make her happy and keep her safe. That includes keeping her safe from anyone inside or outside the club who might want to harm her. I just wanted you to know what I intended. I hope you're okay with a fellow Warrior being with your daughter. She's your princess, but I want to make her my queen."

 I could see the wheels moving inside his head. He was considering if what I was saying was the truth. I meant every damn word of it. There was no way I could walk away. She had to be mine and I was willing to do anything to make her see she was intended only for me. As I waited for him to respond to my last comments, my stomach cramped. What if he said no, then how could I change his mind? Finally, after several minutes of silence, he nodded his head. "Fine, I'll give you my blessing, but if I see it's going wrong, I'll step in and end this shit and you too, if I have to. But I'm curious, why did you talk to Demon about this before talking to me?"

I chuckled. "I wanted to see if there was anything between the two of them. They were always smiling and kissing each other. I wanted to be sure I wasn't going after a woman who was already a brother's old lady. He told me what their relationship was and then warned me about the same things you just did." He grinned.

"Yep, that's Demon. Those two have been best buddies forever. So, you'll have to be able to live with that too." I nodded my head in agreement and stood to shake his hand to seal the promise. Afterward he gave me a slap on the back, and we headed out the door. Out in the common room, I could see the rest of the guys were here. It was after five, so everyone was off work for the day and the weekend was about to start. Tonight, we had planned to have a barbeque and a small party. It would be good to have Harlow meet the hang-arounds, friends of the club and as much as I hated it, the club bunnies. A few had been around the last few days, but tonight all of them would show up. Once she was my old lady, she'd be in charge of them and they needed to know her place in the club.

About an hour later, in came Sherry and Harlow. Dragging in behind them was Kade. It looked like they had run him ragged today. Harlow saw her dad and ran right over to give him a big hug. He swept her up, swung her around in a circle and gave her a kiss. "How's my girl doing?" He asked her smiling. She smiled and told him

"Fine. Busy but fine." Once they had a chance to say hello, I walked up and got her attention.

"Harlow, we're going to have a barbeque tonight, why don't you take your dad to the house for a bit, so you can talk and rest from all that shopping today? Then in about an hour you both come back, and we can get the barbeque started. I want to check on a few things before the weekend gets going." She paused a moment and then nodded her head okay. I watched as she pulled her dad out the door. I wondered if he would try and get out of her if she felt anything for me and was willing to get into a relationship? Damn, I wish I could go listen, but I needed to get this settled.

After checking in with Sherry and the prospects, to check that we had everything we needed for tonight, I ran into Demon. He had a smirk on his face and a gleam in his eye when he looked at me. "So how did your talk go with Bull? I assume okay, since you're still breathing." He said with a shitty grin spreading across his face. I slapped him on the shoulder.

"It went fine and he's now just in a waiting mode to see what I do and if he needs to kill me or not." I half joked with him. He threw his head back and laughed.

"Oh, there'll be a fucking line to kill you if you fuck up. Just keep that in mind and know I can reach out and touch you from at least a mile away and you'll never know it's coming." He warned me. I gave him a nod to show I understood what he was saying. Now that I had spoken to Bull, my plan of seduction would commence. I knew she wasn't immune to me. She hadn't been able to hide her physical responses to my light touching or innocent kisses the last few days. She tempted me as no other ever had. She was my temptress and Temptress beware, Terror was on the loose and on the hunt.

I went into the kitchen and found the steaks and chicken were being organized for the barbeque. We would be waiting a few hours still before cooking them, so it gave everyone plenty of time to relax. I saw Sherry bring in some dishes from her house. I assumed she had made them when Harlow was over there yesterday. I threw an arm around her shoulders.

"Hey Sherry, what great stuff did you make us this time? You know we all love your cooking." I told her as I rubbed my stomach. She smiled and said.

"Oh, I made my usual baked beans with bacon you all love and coleslaw. However, Harlow was the one who knocked it out of the park. She's a machine in the kitchen and insisted on doing most of it." I was surprised. I guess I hadn't expected Harlow to cook.

"What did she make?"

Sherry laughed. "What didn't she make? She's a fantastic cook and I know because I sampled everything while she was making it. She made potato salad, some kind of street corn, a cheesy noodles recipe, several different pies. and a chocolate dessert that is to die for. When I tasted everything as she made it, I almost died and went to heaven. She said she would've made more, but didn't know exactly what everyone may or may not like." Just as she finished telling me what Harlow had made, Demon strolled in. He grinned. He must have overheard our conversation.

"Yeah, she's always the chief chef when we have

parties and barbecues. She can cook and bake something fierce. She's never made anything we didn't clamor for more of. She can cook ethnic food too. Thai, Middle Eastern, Italian, you name it, she can cook it." I was blown away. I guess it was kind of naive to think a modern woman wouldn't be able to cook or want to cook. Especially one who looked like her. As I turned, I saw Bull and Harlow come into the kitchen. I guess the hour had come and gone already. She handed Bull off to me.

"Take him so Sherry and I can get the rest of this food prepped. I've been told my homemade salsa and guacamole has to make an appearance, so I need to get those whipped together." She rolled her eyes at her dad with a teasing smile on her face. I grabbed Demon and Bull to get them out of the way. Before I left the kitchen, I told her.

"If you need anything, have Kade run to the store for you." She nodded and turned to the sink.

We went out to the grass area behind the clubhouse. Several of the guys were already there laughing and having a few drinks. We had horse shoe pits off to one side. The huge grills were already set up and ready to light when the time came. There were still a few hang-arounds and friends of the club we were expecting who hadn't arrived yet, but it was still early. I knew a few of the ladies with them would bring food as well. If we had a full party and not a family one like this, then the club bunnies were also expected to help cook. A little while later, I saw Harlow stroll out of the clubhouse headed toward my house. I caught up to her.

"You need anything?" She shook her head no and said she was just going to get changed. I thought the long skirt and blouse she had on was great, but maybe she wanted to be in something more comfortable. She had her hair up in a bun from running around all day with Sherry.

About thirty minutes later she came back out. I froze with a bottle of beer halfway to my mouth. She was in a pair of jeans that hugged her hips and ass like a glove. I wanted to peel those down those long ass legs of hers and unwrap her like a present. She had changed into a turquoise halter top with silver jewelry on her ears, wrists, and neck. Her eyes were lightly made up with makeup and her lips looked like she had slicked on some berry-colored gloss. She was wearing a pair of wedge shoes that gave her a couple more inches of height. To complete the vision, all that gorgeous red hair was down and hanging below her ass, swaying as she walked. This was the first time I'd seen her hair all the way down.

Now, the guys had gotten used to seeing her over the last several days, so they tended not to stare at her as much. But I saw almost every guy who was a hang-around or friend of the club stop dead and stare. Tongues were practically hanging out touching the ground. Even my guys did a double take. Time to be sure the new ones knew the score as well. I walked over to her and wrapped my arm around her waist. I bent down and placed a quick, soft kiss across her mouth. She froze and threw me a startled look. I whispered. "You look stunning as always, Temptress. Make sure you stay close to me tonight. I have the feeling I'm going to have to hurt some guys around here." She glanced around and then back at me. I could see she was taken back by the kiss and my comment. Good. I wanted her to know I wanted her and would protect her.

We walked over to her dad and some of the guys he was standing with. In the group was Sam and his wife, Julie. They were friends of the club and worked at our bar slash restaurant in town. She was a waitress and he was our main bartender slash assistant manager. Viper and Blaze were with them. Evan and Bobby, two hang-arounds, rounded out the group. Bobby was okay but Evan irritated me. His dad had always been a friend to the club, so he was allowed to associate by default. There was something I didn't like about him. Bobby was giving Harlow appreciative looks, but not being offensive about it. Evan was practically eye fucking her even after he saw me kiss her. He and I would be having a chat in a bit if he kept that shit up.

I made sure to keep my arm around her. She seemed to be a little stiff at first, but then eventually started to relax. As we kept talking, more people came to join our group. I made introductions to them. Harlow was very charming to all of them and shook everyone's hand. Except Evan. She merely nodded at him. She didn't like him either. While her and Julie were talking about some store in town with great clothes, I gestured to Evan to follow me, because I saw how he was still looking at her. He looked hesitant, but stepped away with me. I headed toward the garage. Once I got him out of earshot, I stopped.

"Evan, I have to give you fair warning. If you want to keep your face intact and still be allowed to come around the club, then you'd better stop eye fucking my woman. I'll have no problem putting you in the hospital and telling your daddy why. Show some fucking respect. Didn't the kiss and the holding onto her give away who she belongs to?" I growled out between my clenched teeth. He got a sullen look on his face before abruptly nodding. He hurried off to stand over by one of the fire pit areas. I saw he would glance at Harlow from time to time, but he stopped with the leering looks and stayed far away from her and me.

Once I rejoined our group, Viper leaned over and said quietly. "So, I see you told old Evan how it was. I wondered how long you were going to wait before putting an end to that shit. Of course, I was wondering if I was going to have to pull you, Bull, and Demon off of him all at the same time." I just grinned. I was trying to behave a little civilized, but in all honesty, I wanted to go all barbarian on him as soon as he looked at her.

"I think he's got the message now. Just keep an eye on him since I don't trust the little weasel." I told Viper. He gave me a chin lift in agreement. Everyone seemed to be settling in nicely. Someone put on some music and alcohol was flowing. I decided to get the grills going. Savage and Ranger stepped up to be the grill masters. They tended to be the ones who did our grilling since they liked to do it. The ladies all went inside to start organizing the other food. Not long after, they came out bringing the food and setting it up on the tables we had placed for this.

About forty minutes later, everything was ready to go. All the food was on the serving tables along with plates, utensils, and napkins. Everyone was in a line filling up their plates as high as possible. There was some mild elbowing and jostling to get ahead of each other, but it was all in fun. These guys loved their food.

In addition to the food made by Sherry and Harlow, it looked like someone made au gratin potatoes, a broccoli and cheese casserole, a mixed roasted vegetable dish with squash, zucchini, onions and mushrooms and a huge fruit salad. The pies Sherry had said Harlow made turned out to be a dozen total and were a mix of apple, cherry, black raspberry, and peach. The chocolate dessert was a layered dish of chocolate, whipped topping, nuts, something crumbled with chocolate shavings on top. By the end, everyone was groaning and complaining they couldn't move. I made sure to taste every single thing Harlow made and it was the best I'd ever tasted.

It looked like I had better up the workouts, if my woman could cook like this and did it very often. Hammer spoke up and asked which ladies fixed what. We found out the fruit salad, broccoli and cheese casserole and potatoes were brought by Julie. Another woman with one of the hang-around had brought the roasted vegetables and fruit salad. The guys knew Sherry's cooking, but seemed stunned to find out what Harlow could do. She laughed and asked them?

"How do you think my dad survived all these years? It sure wasn't due to his own cooking."

Hammer put his hand over his heart and begged Harlow. "Please marry me, you gorgeous woman. If you can cook like this and are single, then let me take you away on my iron steed." Everyone laughed and Harlow just shook her head at him and laughed too. I looked at him.

"You think about taking her away and I'll have to kill you. You're going to have to find another woman to cook for you." He just grinned more and went back to talking to Ghost.

As the sun set, we lit the firepits and pulled chairs up around the fires. I wanted to get Harlow closer, so when she went to take a seat, I pulled her down to sit on my lap. She looked at me with a questioning look on her face and leaned in.

"What are you doing Terror? First you kiss me and keep your arm around me all evening. Now this sitting on your lap thing. Why are you acting like this? I know it isn't because you're desperate for female companionship." I grinned at her.

"Well baby, I just wanted to make sure everyone knows who you were with and to not get any ideas." She got a funny look on her face and tried to stand up, but I pulled her back down.

"Come on, sit with me and later when we go to the house I'll explain. Just relax and enjoy." I told her. I could see she was considering what I said and debating what to do. Finally, she sighed and relaxed back onto my lap. Now, all I had to do was not get too excited. My cock wanted to be nudging up into that snug ass of hers. It was torture to have her on my lap for the next few hours. But it was a torture I'd take any day. Around eleven o'clock the party started breaking up. Tonight, had been more of a family friendly one, so there was no crazy sex happening anywhere and everywhere.

Bull stood and said he was going to call it a night. He hugged Harlow and shook my hand. Not long after, I helped her up and started to walk her toward the house. The closer we got, the more nervous she seemed to get. Now was the time to let my temptress in on what I wanted.

Chapter 13: Harlow

The party had been a really nice one. Everyone seemed to be like a great bunch of people overall. The food had been good, and everyone loved what I had made. I loved to cook for people and have them enjoy it. The guys back home always appreciated it, but they were also used to it. It was nice to get fresh opinions. The only thing tonight that really made me uncomfortable was Evan, the creep. He looked at me in a way that made me feel dirty. But he at least stayed away after Terror had spoken to him. I was curious to know what he'd said to him.

The party was breaking up and Terror was now escorting me to his house. I wondered if he was going back to the club house to enjoy the club bunnies. I figured they'd be slipping away with the guys about now. This was usually what happened at home after a party. I was feeling nervous; however, I wasn't sure why. Maybe because I didn't want him going back there and hooking up with Laci. But that made no sense. He could hook up with anyone he wanted. He wasn't mine. Though he'd been confusing me all night with that kiss, keeping an arm around me, and then having me sit on his lap at the firepit. What had all that and his remarks meant?

Terror's hand on my lower back seemed to be hot and burned through my top like a brand. The feel of just his hand made me shiver and warmth coil in my stomach. Once we got to the door, he opened it and walked inside with me. I expected him to say good night and leave, but he surprised me. He just closed the door behind us with a snap. He began to take off his boots. I slipped off my wedges.

I turned to give him an inquisitive look. "Aren't you going back to the clubhouse with the guys? I expect they're continuing the party. Please don't feel like you need to entertain me. I'm used to the goings on after a party. Hope you guys enjoy the rest of the night." I told him. He just looked at me and then smiled. His smile had a naughty look to it. What was he thinking? Then he responded.

"Oh, I'm exactly where I want to be this evening. You and I need to have a little talk. Let's go into the living room." He grasped my hand and led me there. Was he going to explain his behavior? He took me to the sofa and sat me there and then he took a seat right next to me. I turned so I was facing him and waited for him to speak. He just sat there looking at my face and then I saw his eyes look down the length of my body and back up. His eyes now had a burning look in them. Oh no, that didn't bode well for me. Before I could move away, he grasped my arm and pulled me closer. Our mouths were only inches apart. I could feel his warm breath on my face. Then he spoke and what he said left me speechless for a few moments.

"We need to talk about us. You have to know, since I laid eyes on you, I've wanted you. I've been trying to be patient and get to know you a little better, but I can't keep dancing around it. You asked outside what I was doing and why I was acting the way I was. The answer is, I was claiming you, so that all those guys out there knew you belonged to me and to keep their hands off. I already told my guys when you came a few days ago you were off limits, but there were new people here today who wouldn't have known that." He stated boldly.

After I got over being stunned at his audacity and bluntness, I felt a bit of anger. Who was he to decide I was his? Did he think that I would just fall into his hands and give him a little fun while I was here? First of all, I wasn't made that way and secondly, my dad would kill him. I had to set him straight. "Terror, I don't know where you get off in thinking you have the right to decide I'm yours and then lay it out to your club or anyone else? I say who I spend time with and I'm not willing to spend it as some biker's piece of ass. I know how this works. I've seen it all my life. You guys hook up for a bit and then when you get bored, you move on to the next one. I'm not like that. When I choose to be with a man, it will be because I plan on it working between us for the long haul. So hence, no bikers. Also, my dad would kill you for even trying that. I'm not sure why he didn't say anything to you tonight with the way you were acting to be honest."

He just smiled. "Harlow, do you think anything you just said, I didn't already know? I knew from the start you weren't someone who has a quick fling and then moves on. Also, I know your dad wouldn't put up with it, even if you were inclined to act that way. The reason he didn't say anything today about how I was acting is because I told him my plans."

"W-what do you mean he knows your plans? What did you tell him?" I stuttered.

"I told him that you were going to be mine. And it was going to be for the long haul. This isn't just some hit it and quit it situation. I told him I would do everything I can to protect you and make you happy. That's why he didn't say anything." Terror said with a bigger smirk on his face. What the hell? Didn't I get any say in this?

"Don't I get any say in who I'm with? Or do you think you and my dad decide, and I go along with it like a good little girl? What if I don't want you? What then? I'm just shit out of luck!" I yelled back. My temper was starting to take over. The fucking audacity of him and my dad! I felt my temperature rising and knew I had to get away from him quickly before I released it. When I got too angry, the rage only had two ways to get out: crying or fists flying. I didn't want to do either in front of him. I went to stand, but he grabbed my hand harder and pulled me toward him. I started to struggle to get away.

Before I could get loose or throw my first punch, he grabbed me behind the neck and pulled my mouth to his. As his lips touched mine, I tried to stay still and keep them closed. He was pressing his lips hard to mine and then started to lightly nibble on them. Then I felt him trace around my lips with his tongue. The sensations were wonderful and made me want to kiss him back, but I had to stay strong. It would do no good to encourage him. When I didn't return his kiss, he pressed his mouth to my jaw and ran his lips and tongue up it, then nibbled on my ear and licked just behind it. Who knew that could feel so good and make one so needy? I could feel my nipples getting hard in my bra. My panties were starting to get damp and that was just from a kiss! What could he do to me if I let him go further?

I decided I needed to end this before things got out of hand. When it came to him, I was weak. I pulled my head back, but he just followed me. Next thing I knew, he had me laid out on the sofa and he was stretched out over top of me. He had my hands pinned together and held in one of his over my head. I knew I could get away from him if I wanted. He stopped kissing me and looked into my eyes. I could see desire there and something else that I wasn't sure what it was. He nipped my lips again before he spoke.

"Baby, of course you get a say. But also, I know you have desire for me just like I have for you. I've seen it in your eyes. I've felt it when I touch you. And if your dad didn't think I was serious, him and Demon would have killed me already. They both have laid down the law about you. If you don't desire and want me too, then this goes nowhere. I would never force myself on you. But be honest with me, you do have some feelings for me, don't you?"

He was right, I did have feelings for him. I was just confused on what those were. I knew I desired him, but wasn't sure why. No man had ever made me feel like this. In fact, I'd felt for a long time I might be asexual. Women didn't attract me either. But one look at him and I felt it. He could make me hot with just a look and had me wanting to tear my clothes off. But could he be serious about wanting me long-term, or was this his way to justify being with me, so dad and Demon didn't kill him? I was surprised they would let a biker near me or any man for that matter. They had run off every guy I'd ever tried to date in the past.

"Terror, I can't say you don't make me feel something. But I don't think you're really a long-haul kind of guy. You're a biker who is used to having a different woman every night if you want. Easy pussy is thrown at you and you enjoy it. But I'm not someone who can be with a man and him also keep other women on the side. What happens when you get bored? You move on? You fuck other women when I'm not around but keep me, since you don't want to piss my dad off? I don't think so. So, yeah, I may feel desire for you, but I'm going to be smart and ignore it. You need to do the same." I told him.

He shook his head and kissed my lips again. This time he was even more aggressive, and he pushed his tongue for entry into my mouth. I sighed and slightly opened my lips. It was a mistake. His tongue took over my whole mouth. It dueled with mine, caressing along the sides of my tongue, and the roof of my mouth. Then he started to thrust his tongue into my mouth, mimicking what it would feel like if he was thrusting into my pussy. God, he was fucking my mouth and it was turning me on so much! My panties were now drenched. My breaths were coming in pants and my nipples were so hard, I thought they could cut through my clothes. Suddenly, I felt his hand under the bottom edge of my top. It went trailing up across my stomach until he reached my breast. There he paused, and then gently squeezed. I reared my hips up off the couch. When I did, my hips thrust into his and I could feel his hardness and desire. Before I could do anything, he pulled his mouth back from mine again.

He was panting as well, and his eyes were half closed with a slumberous look. They were blazing with passion. He actually made me breathless with a look. Could kissing and barely touching me cause him to feel like that? He laid his forehead on mine and growled lowly. "I have no fucking desire for anyone else but you, my Temptress. You're who I want, and I don't see this ever changing. You're all I've thought about since seeing you. I can't get you out of my mind. I see you and all I want to do is tear your clothes off and fuck you until we both can't move. But I don't' just want you for your body. I love just hearing you talk, listening to your thoughts and ideas and seeing how you are with my guys and others. I want to know everything about you and consume you. But I want you to consume me as well. I have no intention of using you and then moving on to someone else. I plan to keep you for at least the next hundred years, then we can decide after that. You're meant to be mine and only mine and I'll do whatever I have to make it happen."

With this said, he ran one hand back into my hair to hold me still for his kiss. His mouth was attacking mine again, while his other hand let go of mine and pulled up my shirt, before pulling down the cup of my bra on my left breast. His thumb was rubbing back and forth over my hard nipple. The sensation was wonderful. He pulled back from my mouth and started to trail more kisses down my jaw to my neck. From there he went across my chest kissing and sucking, until he reached where he had my breast in his hand. His tongue circled around my nipple. It was driving me wild. I wanted him to touch my nipple. He finally put me out of my misery, closed his mouth over that hard-little pebble and sucked. Lord! The feeling it gave me. He was sucking and then I felt his teeth lightly bite down on my nipple and tug on it. Instant lightning shot to my clit. Fuck, I couldn't think! He kept touching and kissing me. I was drowning in sensations and desire.

He moved over to my right breast freeing it from its cup. He gave it the same treatment he had the other. Then I felt his hands caressing down my ribs and along the waistband of my jeans. When he got to the snap, I felt it give. Was I going to really do this? I was nervous. I had no idea what I was doing. Even though I was twenty-four, I'd never had sex. There'd never been anyone I wanted to have it with. But he had been consuming my mind since the night I met him, and it seemed a long time ago rather than just a week. He was totally out of my league. I needed to let him know this. There was no way he wanted a woman who had no idea how to pleasure him back. I put my hand over his to stop him. When I did, he looked up at me. "What's wrong baby?" He asked softly.

"Terror, you need to know, I'm not going to be able to give you what you want. You're used to experienced women who know how to give you pleasure back. That's not me." I told him bluntly. He got a puzzled look on his face then I saw understanding dawn, followed by surprise.

"Are you telling me you haven't ever been with anyone before?" He asked incredulously. I squirmed and looked away from his eyes, but he grasped my chin and made me look back at him. Nodding my head yes, I said.

"Yes, that's what I'm telling you. So, I won't hold it against you for backing out on this. We'll just forget this little interlude happened." I mumbled back. I was so embarrassed. I could feel my cheeks burning. I hated to blush, but as a red-head I was used to it. Luckily, it took a lot to embarrass me, so it didn't happen often.

He let out a huge chuckle. His grin stretched ear to ear. How dare he laugh! This wasn't fucking funny! I shoved against his shoulders to get him off me, but he stayed in place. He grabbed my hands and held them both in one of his and pushed them to above my head again. Leaning down he kissed my lips then pulled back. The grin was still there.

"Fuck that! You think telling me you're a virgin is going to turn me off? It fucking makes me ecstatic! The fact no man has touched you makes me very happy. I've been hating the thought of any man knowing what it was like to be inside of you and wondering who I had to hunt down and kill. I have no doubt you can give me pleasure and I will enjoy like hell teaching you anything you don't know." He moaned.

With this said, he pulled me up off the sofa into his arms. I grabbed a hold of him, placing my arms around his neck and my legs around his waist to keep from falling. This caused my pussy to rub along his thick erection which I could feel behind his zipper. This made both of us moan and shudder. He turned and headed toward the stairs. He climbed them while kissing me the whole time. I wasn't sure how he could see where he was going, but the next thing I knew, I was being placed down on his huge bed. I guess tonight was going to end differently than I'd expected. Was I willing to risk this? Looking at his face and thinking of his words, I decided this was a risk I had to take. I may never feel this way again.

Chapter 14: Terror

Goddamn, this woman was driving me wild! How could she think just because she had never been with a man, I wouldn't want her? It fucking thrilled me. I'd only kissed her and touched her breasts and she had me hornier than I could ever recall being in my life. Once I got her naked and tasted the rest of her, I might just die, but I would die a very happy man. Placing her down on my bed, I took a moment to look at her. Her hair was a sexy mess. It spread out across my pillows like red fire. Her beautiful breasts were peeking out over top of her bra. They were all rosy and full. Her nipples were surrounded by the palest pink areola that I had ever seen. They begged to be sucked and played with more. I laid down on the bed beside her and leaned over, placing a quick kiss to her lips, before going back to her breasts.

I tugged off her top and bra. I went back to worshipping those beautiful, full breasts. I'd been right, they were more than a handful even for my large hands. I pinched her nipples between my thumb and forefinger. She moaned. I tugged on them with my fingers and then decided to add some teeth. I bit down gently and tugged over and over. Each time I did, she would squirm more and let out a breathy pant. Every once in a while, I would lick her nipple and flick it with my tongue.

After worshiping them for several minutes with my tongue, teeth and fingers, I trailed my hand back down to the waist of her jeans. This time she didn't stop me. I lowered the zipper. Once that was out of the way, I slipped my hand down the front of her jeans, under her panties to her pussy. Christ! She was so fucking wet, and her pussy was giving off so much heat. I could feel she was completely bare. I loved that. I had to see and taste her now! Pulling back, I grabbed her jeans and yanked them, along with her panties, down her legs and threw them to the floor.

Sliding down the bed, I got my first look at her pussy. Fuck she was so gorgeous! Her bare pussy looked like a flower with dark pink inner petals which begged to be touched and tasted. I put one of my hands at the top of her mound and used my thumb and forefinger to open her outer lips. Her inner lips glistened with her juices. I lowered my face and smelled her floral scent with its underlying musk. I licked her softly from her entrance up to her clit. She tasted wonderful! I dove back in and started to attack her pussy a little harder. I was starving for more of her taste. I needed more of her wonderful honey. I admit, I was a man who liked to eat pussy. Her pussy was the best I'd ever seen or tasted. I had a new addiction.

She let out a moan and raised her hips off the bed. I took this as a sign she was enjoying it and wanted me to continue. While I continued to lick her from back to front, I slid one of my fingers into her core. She was so tight! I slowly finger fucked her pussy while I sucked and licked that sweet thing. I made sure as I stroked in to hit her G-spot. She shuddered every time I did and got wetter. After several strokes, I added another finger. The tightness was still there, but she was slowly stretching to accommodate those fingers. I had to get her ready. My cock was on the large side in both length and girth, and I didn't want to hurt her more than it should from taking her cherry. I knew being a virgin there would be some pain, but I wanted to make it as little as possible. I wanted her to get pleasure from her first time.

I continued to pleasure her for several more minutes and I could tell she was getting close to an orgasm. Her breathing was labored, she had slipped her hands into my hair and was tugging on it and pushing me closer to her pussy. Also, I could hear her making low keening noises. If that left me in doubt, then the tightening of her inner muscles on my fingers would have been signal enough that she was close. I increased the pressure with my tongue on her hard, little clit while stroking my fingers faster and deeper into her pussy. Suddenly she froze, gave out a strangled scream, and her pussy clamped down hard on my fingers. I felt the rhythmic contractions of her muscles around my fingers. By this time, I had worked three fingers into her. Jesus, she was going to strangle my cock when I got in there, but it would be so worth it! She gushed more wetness over my fingers.

Once she came down from her high, I eased back and looked at her face. Her eyes were slumberous and a faint smile was on her lips. I stood up at the side of the bed. She looked at me questioningly until she saw my hands pull my t-shirt off. Once it was off, I unbuttoned and unzipped my jeans. My cock was being crushed in the tight confines of my jeans. I could feel the pre-cum oozing out on the head of my cock. I eased my jeans down to my ankles and then kicked them off. As I rose back to my full height, I saw she was checking out my body. Her eyes ran all over my chest and arms. Then she ran them down my belly until she finally came to my cock. I saw her eyes widen and a tinge of worry enter her eyes. I knew I was intimidating, but I knew we would fit together perfectly. Her pink tongue peaked out and she licked her bottom lip. Yeah, she might be a little worried, but she liked what she was seeing.

I eased back onto the bed over top of her. I placed another hard kiss to her lips and sunk my tongue into that hot mouth. Our tongues played together again. As I felt her relax, I eased her legs apart with my hand and settled between them. I had to have her now. But first I needed to ask her something important. Looking her in the eyes, I asked her. "Baby, are you on birth control?" She looked startled for a second and then nodded her head yes. Thank God! "Good, because I want to take you without a glove. I want nothing between us so I can feel all of you." She looked a little worried then. Before I could ask what was wrong, she spoke up.

"Terror, I don't think that's a good idea. I know you've been with a lot of other women and...." I broke in.

"Beautiful, yes I have been with other women, but I've never gone without a glove ever with a woman. And even though I always use a condom, I get tested regularly and did just a couple of weeks ago and I've not touched anyone since then. I'm clean and I know you are too. And darlin' one more thing. When we're together, especially in bed, I want you to call me by my real name. It's Declan, Declan Moran." Once it sank in what I said, she nodded.

"Okay, Declan."

I placed the head of my cock at her entrance and holding her gaze, slowly started to push into her body. She was so tight. Just the head was in and she was already squeezing me so much, it felt like she was strangling me. I could feel her working to relax, so I just held her gaze and stroked her face. As she relaxed more, I would ease in more, inch by inch. I finally got to where I could feel her barrier. I leaned up and gave her a kiss. As she relaxed into it and became distracted, I pushed through that thin membrane. She stiffened, crying out in pain. I held still murmuring words of reassurance until she relaxed, then I pushed all the way into the hilt.

She felt like nothing I had ever experienced. She was so wet, hot, and tight. My cock just wanted to fuck her hard and never stop. I pulled back and saw she didn't flinch, but slowly I eased back in again just to be sure the discomfort and pain were gone. Seeing she was okay and feeling the lust rising, I pulled back and thrust again just a little harder. Her hands were running through the hair on the back of my neck. She leaned up and placed kisses on my mouth and then on my chest. Suddenly, I felt her lick and then gently bite my nipple. It sent a bolt of fire through me and I couldn't hold back. I needed to fuck her harder and go deeper!

I started to move harder and deeper into her hot pussy. She lifted her legs and wrapped them around me. I felt myself losing control. I started to slam my cock into her harder and faster. Probably way harder and deeper than I should for her first time, but I couldn't stop. She tightened her legs around my waist, and raised her hips up to meet my downward thrusts. She was meeting me just as hard. I powered in and out of her over and over again. I couldn't think of anything else, but having her come for me and then me filling her with my cum.

I felt her nails gripping my shoulders and she was panting louder and harder. Sweat was dripping off my face and running down my back. I felt her start to tighten around me. She had to come before me. That was my goal.

She had to get pleasure from our first time, not just me. All of a sudden, her pussy clamped down and I could feel those muscles grasping me and trying to milk my cock. She gave a long, keening wail as she found her release.

I gritted my teeth and prolonged her orgasm until I felt her start to come down, then I gave one final hard thrust and let go. My cum blasted out of my cock like a volcano erupting. It just kept coming and her pussy kept milking my cock. I'd never come like this or felt so deeply satisfied after sex in my life! This meant something more. It was confirmation. This just wasn't sex. This is what other guys found when they said they found the one and were willing to never have another woman again. She was mine and I was never letting her go after this. I actually felt lightheaded when I finished splashing my cum all over the inner walls of her pussy.

After I caught my breath, I eased out of her and laid down beside her. I ran my hands through her hair and watched her beautiful face. She had her eyes closed and a smile on her lips. Giving her a quick kiss, I rose and went to the bathroom. Wetting a washcloth, I went back to the bed and washed between her legs and then wiped myself clean. I threw the washcloth toward the hamper in the corner and laid back down. I pulled her snug into my arms. Kissing her once more passionately on the lips, I told her softly.

"You're so fucking beautiful, and have no doubt, you can satisfy me, woman. Rest for a bit because I'm not done with you yet." She opened her eyes, smiled at me and then closed her eyes again. She snuggled closer to my chest. Her breathing evened out quickly, and I found I soon fell asleep too.

Chapter 15: Harlow

I felt myself surfacing from what felt like one of the greatest nights of sleep I'd ever had. As I became more aware, I felt Terror kissing my face. He had awoken me again last night to make love to me a second time. It was even more fantastic than the first time. And I hadn't thought I'd enjoy my first time, but he made sure I saw stars. Afterward he had made me get into a hot bath so I wouldn't be so sore. This had surprised me. I never imagined him even thinking of such a thing. Now that it was daylight, it was time to face what we had done. Did I feel guilty about it? No. Did I want to do it again? Yes. Would this work out? I hoped so. I slowly opened my eyes and saw he was looking down at me. A smile creased his face as he said to me.

"Good morning, baby." I smiled and told him.

"Good morning, Declan." I could feel he was aroused again, as I could feel his hard cock pressing into my thigh. I reached down and wrapped my hand around it. I couldn't reach all the way around him, but I did gently squeeze and stroke him. He moaned and kissed me again. Then I felt him take my hand away from his cock. What the hell? Didn't he want me to touch him? Was he already over it and now not interested? I felt insecurities start to take a hold. I pulled my hand away from his and rolled to get up from the bed. Before I got to the edge, he pulled me back into his chest.

"Don't you dare think I don't want you. I want you so much I can hardly breathe, but we have church in about fifteen minutes, and I don't want to rush making love to you. Also, since last night was your first time, I want to give you a chance to heal a little. So, I'm sacrificing my sanity and being a nice guy. But tonight, all bets are off. I'll definitely be getting more of you and you can touch me all you want," he whispered.

Hearing sincerity in his voice, I quit fighting to get away from him. I turned my head and placed a kiss on his mouth. He then let me go so I could get up off the bed. I headed to his bathroom. He followed close behind. When we got in there, he insisted I take another bath while he showered. He told me. "I'd love to have you shower with me, but then I'd never get to church on time, and it would be wrong if the president didn't show up for his own meeting." He grinned. Telling him I understood, he started to run my bath water while he jumped in the shower.

As he was washing up, I looked my fill at his body. I'd been right. His chest was super muscled, and his stomach did create a luscious 'V' below his six-pack abs. His cock, even soft, was large and so intriguing. In addition to the full sleeves of tattoos he had on his arms, his chest had tattoos over most of it as well, and on his back was the Archangel's emblem. It was a Celtic dagger with archangel wings on each side depicting two warrior helmets above the apex of the wings. The wings were a little tattered but still majestic. The top rocker had *Archangel's Warriors* written on it, while the bottom one denoted *Dublin Falls, TN*. I could feel myself getting turned on again.

I decided I needed to concentrate on getting my bath.

All too quickly, he was done and turning off his shower. He stepped out and dried off that magnificent body. I had to stare. When he was dry, he looked over and saw me staring. He winked, then smirked before he sauntered over. He bent down and laid a super-hot kiss with lots of tongue on me. Standing back up, he chuckled and walked off to the bedroom. I had to yell after him. "Tease!" I heard him roar out a laugh. A few minutes later he stuck his head in the bathroom door and said.

"I'll see you in a bit in the clubhouse. And woman, I'll show you a tease later." With those words he disappeared. I finished off my bath and then went down the hall to my room. There I spent a little bit of time fixing my hair into a long ponytail and applying just a smidge of makeup. Mostly it was a little pink to my pale cheeks with tinted balm on my lips and curling my lashes. I was lucky my lashes were naturally dark and long, so I usually didn't use mascara unless I was going out. From my closet, I pulled out a long summery dress. I hadn't worn one since I had been here, but today felt like a good day to wear one. It was in a bright, cerulean blue with small flowers all over it. It was sleeveless and had buttons that ran down the whole front of it. It formed a decent 'V' at the neck, which allowed some of my cleavage to show without being too daring.

On my feet I slipped on a pair of white sandals, and in my ears, I put gold dangling earrings. I then hurried down the stairs and out the front door. Closing it behind me, I looked toward the clubhouse. The front lot was filled with bikes. I walked over to the door and went in. Inside I could see Kade, once again at the bar. In the corner were a couple other prospects and I saw Sherry sitting on one of the couches. I walked over to join her.

"Hi Sherry, I hope you haven't been waiting long for me." I told her. She smiled and shook her head.

"No, it was a late-night last night, so we just got here not too long before church. I saw Terror come in with a big smile on his face. Is there something you want to tell me about last night?" She ribbed me. I just gave her a laugh.

"I plead the fifth." This made her burst out laughing. We chatted for a bit longer while we waited for the guys to get out of their weekly meeting. About forty-five minutes later the doors opened and the guys started to stream out. Terror was one of the last ones out with dad and Demon beside him. He looked around the room and when his eyes found me, he made a beeline straight for me. Reaching the couch, he bent down, grabbed me behind the neck and pulled me into a searing kiss. He didn't rush it and didn't seem to care he was doing it in front of everyone, including my dad and Demon. When he was done and raised back up, I just stared at him with my mouth gaping. He laughed and then sat down beside me throwing his arm around my shoulders along the back of the couch. Sherry gave me a smile and rose up to go to Tiny.

I decided to take a peek and see what my dad was doing. He was just standing there looking from Terror to me. He caught my eye and gave me his hard, probing stare. At least he wasn't pulling out his gun and shooting Terror. That had to be a plus, right? He grabbed Demon's arm and they both came toward us. Wonder what they were going to say? They both reached us and stood there looking down. I glanced at Terror.

Terror looked up and said casually. "Are you two going to join us or just stand there?" Dad gave him a long, hard look as well and then shook his head and grabbed a chair to pull closer. Demon found one and did the same. Sitting down dad looked back at Terror.

"I saw your claim loud and clear with that kiss and your behavior yesterday. I can see she seems to be okay with you claiming her. But let me be sure to remind you, if you hurt her in any way, there won't be enough of you found for them to do anything with." He growled.

Terror just smiled and nodded. He responded to dad with. "Your message was received loud and clear and I'll never do anything to hurt her. I'll keep her safe and happy. I understand this makes our relationship different, because I'm no longer only a fellow Warrior and president. I'm now your daughter's man as well. We'll have to separate the two as much as we can. I don't want to do anything to negatively affect the club."

Dad nodded his consent. Demon was silent. I couldn't tell for sure if he was okay with this or not. "Demon, what are you thinking? You're awful silent over there." I said to him. I was nervous. I wanted him to approve since I thought of him as my brother, however, he wouldn't deter me from being with Terror if he didn't approve. Neither would my dad.

Demon took a minute before he responded. "As long as he treats you like you're a princess and does nothing to hurt you, then I'm okay with it. But if he fucks up, it'll be a race to see who kills him first, your dad or me." He said quietly.

Terror nodded and told him. "I plan to treat her like a queen, so no worries." Well, I guess that hurdle was over with. Wonder what the rest of the day would bring?

Chapter 16: Terror

I was breathing a little easier. I was still worried what Bull would say about me being with Harlow. When I had started church today, I could see him and Demon watching me. They had to know something had gone down last night. So, when church was dismissed and I saw her in the common room, I decided to put it out there for everyone to see and know. I was glad they were rolling with it. I understood where they were coming from too. If I had a daughter or someone who I considered a sister and some guy hurt her, I would plant his ass deep. So, I took no offense to their threats. I relaxed more against Harlow and slowly rubbed up and down her arm with my free hand. We sat chatting about nothing in particular for a while.

I saw some of the guys heading in our direction. Once they stopped and were standing there, I asked them what was up. Menace was part of the group, and he spoke first. "Just want to be sure you were smart enough to lock this woman down. That kiss made it look that way, and Bull didn't kill you for doing it, so I think you must have." I looked at all of them and then nodded.

"Yes, she is officially mine and every on every one of you bastards better remember it. First fucker who doesn't, gets put down." I told them. All of them threw back their heads and laughed at me. Then they all started to congratulate us. Harlow looked a little overwhelmed with their approval.

Sherry came and gave her a hug. Tiny shook my hand. I got numerous slaps on the back. Harlow smiled at everyone and rested her hand on my leg. Damn, just that touch made me want to take her back to my bed right then, and ravish her. I swallowed down my desire and leaned over to her once everyone settled down. "We were planning to go on a ride today. Will you go with us?" I asked her quietly.

"As long as you're all okay with it. If you guys rather go alone, I understand. I don't want to interfere with your routine." She told me.

"Baby, I want you on the back of my bike and would love for you to go. Sherry will be going with Tiny. Let's get out of here and enjoy the day." She nodded her head yes and said.

"I'll go change my clothes and meet you back here in ten minutes." I helped her stand. I watched her all the way out the door. The guys started to break up and get ready for the ride. I knew it would probably be way over ten minutes, but I headed out to my bike after getting my gun. By the time everyone got out to the bikes and situated, ten minutes had lapsed. About that time, I saw her walking across the lot from my house. She had changed into jeans, riding boots, had a long sleeve t-shirt on, and was pulling on a leather jacket. She had put her hair in a braid. In her hand she carried a helmet, and leather riding gloves. My girl came prepared. Looking at her in that jacket, I knew I would have to order her a property cut right away. I wanted to see *Property of Terror* on her back.

She reached me and placed her hand on my left shoulder. She swung her leg over the bike and put her feet on the foot pegs. She slid forward until her groin pressed into my ass and she wrapped her arms around my middle. Damn that felt good! Her breasts were rubbing into my back. I pulled her just a bit closer. I started my bike followed by everyone else. Within minutes we were outside the gates and on the road. We'd decided in church to take highway 441 toward Maryville and see where we ended up. It was a great day. The sun was out, and it was hot but tolerable since the humidity wasn't high. We just motored along looking at the green trees and fields of flowers. This road was a nice one to ride on. A couple of hours later we stopped to stretch our legs and get a bite to eat in Sweetwater. There was a small diner there we'd stopped at before. It had decent food.

We walked into the diner. It was a little after lunch time, so it wasn't completely full. Everyone in the place of course looked at us and stopped eating. A young blond hostess came up and nervously told us to give her a few minutes to get some tables together. Viper and a few of the other guys followed her. She jumped but then when they started to help move the tables, she stepped back and let them. Once they had them situated, we all took a seat and she handed out the menus. A quick look had me deciding my order. I leaned over to Harlow. "Do you see anything that interests you," I ask her? She smiled and said she did.

About that time our waitress, who was older, probably in her early thirties, came over to take our orders. She was very flirty and when it came to taking my order, she leaned over my shoulder and bent down to ask me. "See anything you want, sugar?" She said close to my ear. Her cleavage was putting on a show by spilling over my shoulder. Now in the past, I would've taken what she was offering, but after having Harlow, she didn't interest me one bit. Before I could say a word, Harlow answered.

"Well, first you can get your tits out of my man's face and then fucking stop touching him. If you want to flirt with the single guys here, knock yourself out. But you keep flirting, eyeing and touching him, and I'll beat your ass down. Now, why don't you take our orders and move the hell along. Do you understand that, sugar?"

To say the waitress was surprised was an understatement. Her mouth was hanging open and her face went beet red. The guys were rolling in their chairs laughing and Harlow just stared the waitress down. She was totally serious. She had a hard, pissed look in her eyes. Apparently, my woman didn't like anyone trying to flirt with her man. That was fine with me. I had been about to tell the waitress to back off when Harlow did. I looked at Bull and Demon. They were the only ones not laughing and just calmly watching. I guess Harlow's remarks didn't surprise them.

The waitress, Beth, according to her name tag, stuttered and then stepped back from me. Not looking me in the eye, she asked for my order. Once I gave it to her, she asked Harlow, who calmly gave hers. After getting all the orders, Beth moved off to the kitchen. Several of the other customers had heard the exchange and were staring. But after she left, they got back to their meals.

I looked at Harlow, she was watching me with a raised brow. "What," she asked? I raised my hands and told her.

"Not a thing." She smiled and then responded to something Hawk asked her. I took time to look around the table. All the guys were nodding at me with respect on their faces. She had cemented her place even more. She wasn't afraid to speak her mind and I knew she'd be able to back up anything she threatened. Soon, our food was brought out. It was the same waitress, Beth, but she didn't flirt with anyone and was very professional. Once all of us were done eating, we hit the restrooms before getting back on the bikes and on our way.

We rode another hour before deciding to turn back. This was a long ride. It was going to total us being out about six hours. Thankfully I had a great seat with a very decent bitch seat on it. The ride back was just as peaceful and having Harlow on the back of my bike made it more wonderful. We made it back to the compound around dusk. Pulling into our places out front, Kade came outside. He walked over to my bike. Once I shut off the engine he spoke up.

"Hey Terror, there was someone who stopped by here while all of you were gone." I looked at him. He seemed a little uneasy.

"Who was it, Kade?" I asked. He looked from me to Harlow. I saw him swallow and then he said.

"It was a man looking for Ms. Harlow." At this I stiffened, and Harlow sat up straighter. She asked Kade.

"Did he leave a name?"

He nodded and said, "he said to tell you Cannon stopped by and he left me a number so you could reach him." At hearing this Harlow relaxed. Kade handed her a slip of paper. She swung off my bike. I remained there waiting for her to explain who this Cannon was. She met my glare.

"Terror, there's no need to get that look on your face. Cannon is one of my former team members. I'm not sure how he knew to come here and ask for me, but he knew I could be found at the Warriors' club in Hunters Creek. I'll have to call him to see what he wanted." I didn't like the thought of her talking to some guy from her unit. Honestly, I didn't like her talking to any man. I got off my bike and followed her. I led her to my office in the clubhouse, so she could make her call in private. However, I remained in the room. She just rolled her eyes and placed the call.

"Hey, Cannon I heard you were looking for me? How in the hell did you know to ask here instead of Hunters Creek?" She paused to listen to his response. "Really. Okay, we can meet tonight if you want." She looked at me when she said it. I gestured to her indicating here and she nodded. "How about you come back to the compound, say in an hour. We can meet and chat then since you said it's urgent. Looking forward to seeing you too. I'll see you then. Bye." She told him. When she hung up, she faced me with a frown on her face. "He said he found out from one of the prospects at dad's club where I was. He said he'd heard some bad news and wanted to tell me in person."

I didn't like the idea of her talking to him. But at least he'd be here where we could watch him. Just short of the sixty-minute mark, we heard a bike pulling up outside. In a couple of minutes, Eric, one of the other prospects, showed a man inside the common room. He was a solidly built guy who stood about six foot two and thickly muscled. His hair was dark blond, and his face was handsome. Harlow went to him and gave him a hug. Definitely didn't like that shit!

Pulling away she brought him over to me. "Terror this is Jack Cannon, he was in my unit in the Marines. Cannon, this is Terror, he's the president of the Dublin Fall's chapter of the Warriors." Before she could say more, I interrupted.

"Also, I'm Harlow's man." I told him. His eyes widened

a little and then he stuck out his hand to shake mine. After a couple of seconds, I gave him mine. He had a hard grip. Dropping his hand, I turned to Harlow. She just shook her head at me. She quickly presented him to Bull and Demon, but it appeared as if they already knew him.

Turning to Cannon, she told him they could go into my office to talk. We'd talked about it before he got here, and I had told her she could use it. She knew I wanted to be in there when they did. She had argued against it, but I was adamant. It wasn't that I didn't trust her. I didn't know him, and he wasn't getting in a room alone with my woman. The three of us headed to my office. Once inside, I closed the door and took a stance against the wall close to my desk where they had sat down.

Cannon looked at me then Harlow and shrugged his shoulders. Facing Harlow, he jumped right into why he was here. "Harley, I wanted to talk to you face-to-face not over the phone about this. I just got out a week ago and was getting my things in order. After that I was coming to see you. We always talked about me coming to Hunters Creek when I got out. While I was wrapping things up, I got a call two days ago. A friend I have in Admin called. He called to let me know that in a week, Tucker is going to be out of the Corps. Apparently, he put in his papers and no one knew it was going to happen. I knew you needed to know this asap." He finished worriedly. He took her hand and squeezed it.

At his words I saw Harlow go pale. Her eyes got a little panicked looking and she swayed in her seat. I jumped over to her and grabbed her around the shoulders. Tugging her up out of the chair, I clasped her into my arms. Cannon looked on with worry on his face. "Harlow, honey, who's this Tucker and why are you afraid of him?" I asked her.

She kept her eyes closed for a couple of moments and then opened them. She sighed and pulled back. "I'm okay Terror. It was just a shock. I'm fine now," she replied softly.

Shaking my head, I didn't let her go. "You didn't tell me who he is and why you're afraid. Are you going to tell me, or do I need to get it out of Cannon over there?" I growled.

Sighing, she answered. "Tucker was our commanding officer's Major. He and I had a run in while I was in the Corps and because of this, Cannon knew I would want to know he was getting out." She was trying to be vague, but I knew more than a run in would make her worry about someone, let alone look afraid.

"Tell me all of it." I commanded. She tried to pull away again, but I held fast. She swallowed hard and then I saw tears in her eyes. What in the hell had happened? She took a shaky breath and continued.

"We were out in the field on a mission as usual. He showed up out there as well, which wasn't normal. All of us had met him before of course, but he had never come out in the field like that with us. One night I had watch duty. I was patrolling one of the back corners of our camp. He came up to me and started talking. It was strange but not something out of the realm of possibility. We'd been talking for a little bit when suddenly he grabbed me. I was totally taken by surprise. He put his hand over my mouth and nose cutting off my air. I struggled with him, but without air I was starting to lose consciousness. I felt him disarm me. He then dragged me to an old shack at the back of the camp and he shoved me inside. I got a good breath and started to fight him again. He and I were fighting, and he wasn't able to get control of me like he thought he could, since he wasn't able to surprise me again. He's a big guy. He eventually ripped my top and had me down and was choking me while trying to get my pants off. I was able to get to the knife I had in my boot and I stabbed him in the side. I guess we were making more noise than he thought fighting, because when he yelled out and before he could retaliate, Cannon came busting into the shack. He pulled him away from me, knocked him out, and got our commanding officer."

My guts churned. I wanted to puke. This guy had tried to rape her. What in the fuck was he still doing in the Marines and not in jail? I rubbed her back as she quietly cried. I looked to Cannon and asked him. "Why is this fucker not in jail? He shouldn't still be in the Corps after doing this." Cannon shook his head wearily.

"You're right, he should be in jail. But when it got reported up the chain beyond our commanding officer, we got a visit and orders from upper command. They said it was all a misunderstanding. We were to forget it ever happened and if we talked about it, or pushed it, we would be the ones facing a court martial. We never could figure out what he had on someone to get it swept under the carpet. After it happened, I made sure one of us was always with her. He went back to California, but we didn't trust him not to have someone else do something. She got some weird phone calls after it happened. We talked about it and that's when she decided to get out. She would never feel safe with him in the Corps." He explained.

I was shaking with rage. This was outrageous. I wanted to find him and wrap my hands around his neck and choke him to death, after I tortured him slowly. Once she calmed down a little, I asked her. "Do you want me to get your dad and Demon? They need to know, so they can watch for him there. If you want, I can talk to them alone and you can go back to the house and rest for a while." I offered. She shook her head no and said.

"I need to be the one to tell them. Bring them in here would you, please?" I left them alone to go get them. In the common room, I could see they were still sitting where we'd left them. They had looks of worry on their faces and when they saw my face, they both jumped up and rushed over.

"What the hell is wrong?" Bull growled. I gestured for them to follow me to my office. Inside the room they both went to Harlow, who was now sitting on the couch. Cannon was kneeling down beside the arm of it holding her hand. Again, I felt jealous of him touching her, but I beat that down. Right now, she needed care. Demon and Bull took the two chairs in front of the desk while I sat beside her on the couch. Looking up she sniffed, and you could see her red rimmed eyes.

Her dad grunted and asked. "What the hell is going on?" I decided to not make her repeat what she had told me, so I filled them in on the details. Before I was done, Bull was up pacing the room and by the time I had finished, he put a fist through my wall. Demon jumped up to pull him back. Harlow cried out in protest. Bull got himself under control. I could see Demon was barely holding it together. Her dad came over and hunkered down, taking her face in his hands. "Harley, honey, why didn't you tell us? You kept this inside. I know it had to eat at you. We could've helped you." He rasped.

"I didn't want you to go all crazy. I know you. You'd have gotten in contact with some of your old buddies and found a way to get to him. That would have meant him dead. I would've been fine with that. But it could've come back on you, guys. I couldn't risk you getting in trouble for killing that piece of shit. I hope he's forgotten all about me, but I can't be sure. Cannon was the only one outside of our commanding officer who knew what happened. He encouraged me to get out at the end of my enlistment. He never trusted the creep wouldn't try something again. Also, I was ashamed he almost got the best of me. No way I wanted to tell you guys that." She muttered.

Bull shook his head and hugged her tight. Demon was down on the floor in front of her rubbing her leg in comfort. I found I was no longer jealous of Demon touching her. I understood he truly did see her as a sister. Demon spoke next. "Honey, you're right we wouldn't have let him get away with this, but you should've trusted us to do it, so no one got caught in any backlash. And there's no reason to feel shame. He was someone you wouldn't have been suspicious of to begin with. And if he is a big dude, it would be hard for anyone to counter. Now, we're going to ask for his details and description. We don't need you to go through that. Cannon can tell us. Why don't you let Terror take you to the house?" He gestured to me. I wanted to stay and get the details first hand, but she needed comfort and care more than I needed to stay. The guys would fill me in later. I helped her up and out of my office.

Everyone in the club house saw us and stood when they saw she had been crying and I was supporting her. I shook my head, so they wouldn't stop us or ask questions. I kept going and took her out of the clubhouse over to my house. Once inside and in my bedroom, I helped her strip and get under the covers. I removed my clothes and joined her, pulling her into my arms. She laid there for a long time crying on and off until finally, she fell asleep. I knew one thing. The fucker was going to pay.

Chapter 17: Terror

Several hours later she woke up. At first, she jerked awake and away from me. Once she realized where she was, and who I was, she settled back down. I kissed her softly. "Baby, are you feeling better? Is there anything I can get you? If you're hungry I can get something for you. I just want you to try and relax. If you want, we can talk about this Tucker."

She snuggled closer and shook her head. "No, I'm not hungry. As for getting me anything else, just having you here is what I need. I just want to not think any more about him right now".

I lowered my head and took her mouth. I started it out as a light kiss meant to just give comfort, but it soon grew more heated. Her mouth was devouring mine. I felt her tongue slip between my lips to find mine. Our tongues dueled for a bit. I ran my tongue along her teeth and stroked the inside of her cheek. Our tongues went back to teasing each other. She pulled back before I did. I went to protest, but she then moved down my jaw placing little, nipping kisses. I laid back and let her take control.

Slowly she tortured me with kisses, licks and nips down my neck and over my chest. When she got to my nipples, she teased them with her lips and teeth as well. She lapped at them lightly and then would suddenly take the nub between her teeth and bite down. My nipples grew hard and I could feel my cock growing under the covers. I never knew my nipples were that sensitive. She eased her way to my stomach and traced every one of my abdominal muscles with the tip of her tongue. Licking like a little cat. In between those licks, she kissed and sucked on my skin. It felt so good and just helped to arouse me more.

She raised up and pushed the covers to the foot of the bed. I felt her slide her hand down and take a hold of my throbbing cock. Her small hand stroked up and down my length while the other played with my balls. She massaged my balls between her fingers lightly pulling at the tight sac. Then she moved her head and I could feel her warm breath washing across the broad head of my cock. She wasn't touching it with her mouth, but just her breath was making me harder. Then I felt her tongue lightly tickle across the head. I was weeping pre-cum, so I knew she had to taste it. Last night we hadn't gotten to the stage of her putting her mouth on me. I wanted to see what she would do. She didn't disappoint.

She licked around the broad head several times before she wrapped those plump lips around me and slowly started to slide more and more of my length into her sweet mouth. Once she stopped, I could feel myself lodged almost at the back of her throat. She eased back to where only the tip remained in her mouth and then slid back down again, until I hit the back of her throat. Over and over, she worked my cock with her mouth and tongue. The suction was tight and the teasing of her tongue up the sides and around my sensitive head was paradise. What she couldn't get into her mouth she gripped with her hand and stroked up and down with her hand. All too soon I could feel the cum boiling up in my balls. I pulled her off me and up my chest, where I kissed her mouth. "Baby you have to stop before I fill your mouth with cum. I want to do that, but just not today. Right now, I just need to be in your hot little pussy when I come." I told her urgently.

She laid down on the bed beside me and stretched out. I proceeded to work her body to get her to a fever pitch like she had me. After kissing and fucking her mouth with my tongue, I lavished her breasts with attention. She was so responsive to her nipples being played with and she seemed to like a little pain with her pleasure. Her nipples were standing at attention when I moved down to her pussy. There I licked her clit. She jumped which only spurred me on. I lapped at all the honeyed juices pouring out of her. Her taste was addicting. I teased around her entrance and then would quickly and unexpectedly dart my tongue inside. She was liking it as I could hear her breathing increase and her hand was gripping the back of my head tighter. Increasing the thrusts, while intermittently licking her from bottom to top, where I would suck hard on her clit, I soon brought her to orgasm with her crying out my name.

Once she came, I knew I couldn't wait any longer to be inside of her. I rolled off her. "Get on your hands and knees and on the edge of the bed." I panted. She got up and did so immediately. Goddamn, looking at that ass killed me. One day soon I hoped to be taking her ass. I had to get her used to me and my kind of sex first, but once she was, I'd try to make it mine too. I wanted to own all of her, just like I knew she would own all of me.

I pressed her head down toward the mattress and pulled her hips up and back closer to me. I placed the head of my cock at her entrance and slowly thrust without stopping into her hot, soaking wet pussy. It tried to resist my progress, but I relentlessly pushed forward until I bottomed out. She was so tight. She moaned and I had to lay my head down on her back a minute to control myself. I would come right away if I didn't calm down a little. I pushed her hair to the side where it pooled down around her onto the mattress. I rubbed my hands up and down her sides trying to calm both of us and then stood back up. I slowly pulled back out. Her body was trying to hold onto me like it was afraid I was going to completely leave. After a couple of gentle strokes in and out, I couldn't control it, I had to take her harder. I pulled back and then slammed into her over and over again. The pleasure coursing through my body was unbelievable. She thrust back to meet every one of mine. She was whimpering and moaning.

I slapped her left ass cheek and she tensed up more and looked over her shoulder at me. I could see the heat in her eyes along with the surprise. Her pussy gushed more juices around my cock. Hmm, I guess she liked that. I'd keep that in mind. A little spanking was always fun. I gave her a few more smacks. Every one of them made her hotter and wetter. I felt her pussy start to clench, so I grabbed her hair and pulled her face around to kiss her mouth. I ate at her mouth until she came with a scream, which I captured in my mouth.

I kept moving inside of her throughout her orgasm until it waned. I kept going. I couldn't get enough of her. As much as I wanted to come, I wanted to stay in her more. After about a dozen more strokes, I knew I couldn't hold back any longer. I increased the pace and as I felt my release rush from my body and my cum filled her up, she screamed and came again. It felt like hundreds of mouths were working my cock and sucking every last drop I had. We both collapsed to the mattress exhausted. Once we regained our senses, I picked her up and took her to the shower. There we both leisurely washed each other in between kisses and strokes. Once done and dried off, I took her back to bed to sleep longer.

She slept throughout the night. Early the next morning she woke up looking more rested. After getting dressed, we went to the clubhouse. I could tell she was a little reluctant to go in. I knew we had to put the club on notice about what was happening. Last night while she was asleep, I'd texted Savage to get everyone in for church this morning at ten. It was only nine, but I wanted to get her to eat something, since she hadn't had anything since yesterday afternoon. Entering the clubhouse, I could see a lot of the guys were already here. They looked at her curiously but didn't ask her any questions. It looked like Sherry had gotten here and fixed everyone breakfast. I seated her at a table with her dad, Demon, and a few of the guys, while I went to fix us both a plate.

I came back to the table and set down her plate taking the seat next to her. Bull and Demon caught my eye and raised their brows. I knew they were asking if she was okay. I gave them a slight nod. She was doing better but was far from alright. She was playing with her food and not really eating. I leaned over and said to her. "Baby, you need to eat. Just try and get some food into you, okay?" I stroked her hand. She nodded and took a couple of bites.

We were quiet for the next ten minutes or so, since we were concentrating on eating. Once we were done and the plates cleaned up, I asked where Cannon was? Savage was at our table. He was the one to speak up. "I gave him a room here last night. He got up a little while ago and said he had to run out, but he'd be back soon. It looks like all the guys are here. Do you want to get church started now?" I nodded yes. I placed a kiss on her lips and told her to stay and chat with Sherry. She nodded and said that she would. We all rose and went into church.

Once everyone was seated and the door was closed, I struck the gavel to start our meeting. I decided to tackle this without any delay. "I know everyone is wondering why we're having church again so soon. Also, I know several of you were here yesterday when a friend of Harlow's, Cannon, came to see her and then you saw her so upset. I would've held this meeting last night, but she needed me. Here's the deal." I filled them in on what I found out yesterday. By the end of the recounting of the meeting with Cannon, everyone was pounding the table with their fists, swearing and looking ready to kill. I waited for them to calm down a little.

Menace was the first to speak. "What're all the details on this fucker? We need to know his name, history and what he looks like. If that fucker comes looking for her here, he'll wish he'd never heard her name." I looked to Bull and Demon since they would be the ones to have gotten the information out of Cannon. Bull rose up and paced around the table. His brow was furled with worry and you could see the anger in his eyes.

"What Cannon told us is the man's name is Andrew Tucker. He was stationed out of California as a Major with the Marines. He's originally from South Carolina. Cannon said he would have a dossier on him today with a picture. Also, I thought we could get Smoke on this too. He should be able to dig shit up on this filthy bastard. Once we get all the information, everyone will need to be on alert in case he tracks her down here. We'll be looking for him up at Hunters Creek too. I want to make it plain, if anyone sees him, grab him but don't do anything else. Bring him to the Hole and contact me and Terror. We'll do the same if we catch him in Hunters Creek. I have to wonder if he's done this with any other women in the past. I wouldn't be surprised and all of them were probably threatened too. Harlow is still struggling with this, so I would appreciate it if no one treated her differently than you have been, or ask her questions about this. I don't want her to be more uncomfortable than she is." He explained.

Everyone nodded their heads in agreement. After he finished, we ran through some ideas to be sure both compounds were on alert. Just as we were winding down on the discussion, there was a knock at the door. Hawk opened it and let in Cannon. He walked in and apologized for interrupting. "Sorry, everyone but I thought you'd want this information to discuss in this meeting." In his hand was a folder. He handed it to me. I opened it and inside was a photo and a report.

The photo showed a man in his early forties. He had gray eyes and dark brown receding hair with gray at the temples. His eyes held a hard, sly look. Glancing at the report, it said he was forty-three years old. He was from Charleston, South Carolina. He had no living family. He had been attached to the Marines in California like Bull said. He was six foot one and weighed two hundred and twenty pounds. He would have been hard for any woman to fight off. Even though Harlow was five foot nine, she was probably no more than a hundred and thirty-five pounds.

I slid the report over to Bull and Demon. Once they read it, they passed it along until it had made the circuit around the table. Once everyone had a chance to read it,

I asked Cannon if he had anything else to add. "No, not right now. I have some of my contacts trying to see if they can pinpoint down more on where he is and what he's doing. I plan to stay in the area for a while and wanted to ask you guys to keep me in the loop. I want to help catch this bastard and I have no doubt he'll come after her. I saw his face when he looked at her. He's obsessed. I'd seen him look at her before, but never thought he would do something like he did. She's my friend and I owe her." He stated.

His remark about owing her caught my interest. "Why do you owe her?" I asked. He stared back at me.

"She saved my life specifically twice being our overwatch. If it wasn't for her, I'd be dead. She's someone we all thanked God was covering our backs. In our unit, she was known as the *Angel*, because we thought of her as our guardian angel when she went out on maneuvers with us. There wasn't a better sniper in the Corps than her. Plus, she acted like a sister to all of us. She would do anything for us, and we would do the same for her. She and I didn't tell the other guys what happened to keep them safe, because we knew they'd retaliate. Believe me, I wanted to hunt his fucking ass down like a dog, but she said that would only end up hurting me. However, with him out on the loose, I plan to fill them in. They're all still in but several are talking about getting out when their enlistments are up. She always talked about her dad's MC and how much of a brotherhood it was. It intrigued us as it sounded like what we have in the Corps. I'd actually met Bull and Demon before when I had come home on a leave with her one time."

I was glad to see he was so protective of her and willing to help even if we didn't need it. I wasn't too crazy about him having been home on leave with her before. Had she maybe had more feelings for him than friendship in the past, or maybe him for her? I guess time would tell. But I didn't think she had thought that way about him or she wouldn't have been a virgin. For that I was very grateful.

Picking up the folder, I dismissed the group and asked Bull, Demon, Cannon and the officers to stay. Once everyone else left, I dived in. "We'll keep her here and she'll have no less than two guys with her any time she leaves this compound. Any new information Smoke gets us I'll be sure to share. Cannon, you're more than welcome to stay around and if you want you can stay here at the club, we have a room you can have. When we get him, Bull, I am willing to let you, Demon and anyone else you want out of Hunters Creek have a piece of him. But no one gets to finish him off but me, and I plan to end him after he's suffered. You're her dad, but it's my right as her man to take out retribution. No one does something like this to my woman and gets away with it." I hissed.

I could see Bull wanted to argue he'd end him, but he finally nodded his agreement. Savage, Menace, Ranger, Viper, Blaze, Demon, and Steel all shook their heads in agreement as well. With this said we all filed out of church and into the common room. Harlow was talking to Sherry and a few of the other guys had settled down with her. I could see they were trying to get her to laugh and relax. They were welcoming her with open arms.

We all sat down, and I pulled Harlow snug against my side. She smiled and leaned into me and whispered in my ear. "Did you tell the guys what's going on? I can't tell if you did or not. They don't seem to be acting any differently toward me or asking questions."

I kissed her cheek and told her. "They know what's going on and everyone is on board for catching the bastard if he comes around here. And why would they treat you differently?" She just shrugged and looked at them all. They were all doing a great job hiding their anger. She could tell her dad, Cannon and Demon were mad, but she already knew they were. I saw her take a deep breath and let it out. She relaxed immediately beside me.

Sherry piped up and asked if Harlow was up for more shopping today. I didn't want her to leave the compound, but knew she wouldn't want to be a prisoner. She indicated she would for a little while, but then she wanted to come back and spend time with Cannon and her dad. Since she needed someone with her, I suggested she take Eric and Cannon as their escorts. Cannon readily agreed. It was agreed they would go out for a few hours to check on getting the furniture for the common room shopped for and then they'd be back in the afternoon. I went over to Eric and told him he was to stick to the women like glue. He said he understood and within a half hour, they were out the door and on their way to town.

With them gone, I decided to take a few hours and go over some of the financials with Viper. As our treasurer, he kept us all straight with the various businesses we had. However, there was always things needing my approval and decisions to be weighed in on. Some of them required I take it to the club to vote on, but others I made the decision myself as the president. We were doing very well. Currently we had the garage which not only did regular work, but custom bike work and offered towing services. We had the bar slash restaurant, a construction company, and a tattoo shop. We were looking at adding other businesses, but wasn't sure yet what they would be.

For those of us who had been in the club for a while, we all had nice savings.

Once we wrapped up, I went to my house. There was one chore I wanted to finish before she came back. I went to the far guest room. The one Harlow had set up in on her first night here. It didn't take me long to move all her stuff to my bedroom. I placed her various girly stuff in the master bath and found room in the dresser and closet for her clothes. From now on she was in here with me. After getting this done, I went looking for Bull and Demon. I found them both out at the garage. Ghost and Blaze were working on a custom bike job. At the moment they were working on the framing and I knew the next step would be molding the fender and other body pieces.

Some of the other guys were working on various vehicles brought into the garage. We always had a steady business just in regular mechanic work. Besides some of the members working the garage, we employed other mechanics and employees to help with towing as well. There wasn't enough of us to keep everything going on our own. The good part was it helped our community by providing jobs.

I walked up to them to catch their discussion. Demon was questioning Ghost and Blaze on when they thought they would have the bike done. Ghost responded. "We'll have it done in about four to six weeks we expect. Unless we run into issues getting something. We fabricate our own frames and body pieces but wiring and such we have to order." When they saw I had walked up, they stopped talking to each other and looked at me with expectation.

"What?" I asked. Blaze spoke up.

"Terror man, what're we going to do if that mother

fucker doesn't show his face here or in Hunters Creek? Are we going to let him be?" Without humor I laughed.

"No fucking way. We'll give him time to show and then if he doesn't, we'll track his ass down. One way or the other, he'll be put six foot under where no one will ever find his rapist ass." They all nodded their heads in approval. Before we could dive further into the subject, I heard the front gate open and the car with Harlow and the others pulled back into the lot. I walked over and got to the door before she could open it. I opened it and helped her down. She gave me a small smile, which I could only answer with a kiss to those lush lips. I got lost in kissing her until I heard throats being cleared. Raising my head, I looked around. I saw several faces grinning like asses.

"Fuck you, you jealous assholes." I jeered at them. They just threw back their heads and laughed harder. Someone in the group muttered.

"You got that right, lucky fucker." I put my arm around her and walked us into the clubhouse. Inside everyone took a seat at the bar. Kade started filling orders since he was on bar duty again. He was the main bartender since he was the best at it. Eric went off to probably clean the bathrooms or something. Every one of us had started out as prospects. And as one, you did whatever was asked of you which included bar and clean up duty to name a few. We had four prospects in total right now. Besides Kade and Eric there were Quin and Gage. Gage was at the gate today and Quin was off helping at the construction company until later.

  I sat on a stool and pulled Harlow onto my lap. She didn't resist and I asked her what she wanted to drink. "A water if you have it, otherwise a coke." Kade jumped to get her one, as well as the beer for me. I rubbed her back and asked.

"Is there something else you like to drink that we don't have? I noticed you haven't asked for any alcohol to drink since you've been here. Don't you like to drink liquor?" Before she could say anything, I heard a bark of laughter. Looking over, I saw Demon was laughing and Cannon and Bull were grinning. Demon got his laughter under control.

"Oh, she'll drink, just not often. But look out when she does. She'll drink some asses under the table and God help anyone who gets in her face. She'll kick ass on a regular day, but get her drinking and she'll do it without a second thought." Her dad and Cannon nodded in agreement. She frowned at them.

"I'm not that bad. I just don't like bullshit and my tolerance level is a smidge less when I drink."

"Bullshit," Cannon said. "You're like TNT when someone messes with you or someone who you think needs protected. You recall what happened that time in Kabul when we were in Afghanistan? Remember, you beat the hell out of that Army dude who was terrorizing one of the locals. We thought for sure you'd get the brig for it, but he was too embarrassed to report it and his friends kept their mouths shut." He looked at us and then continued with his story. "She told the guy to stop and he just got in her face. He asked what business it was of a bitch on what he did to a fucking raghead. She went off. Next thing we knew, she'd flipped his ass onto the floor. He got up and the fight was on. He threw punches that never connected. Hers did. She had him out for the count in about five minutes."

"Well, the bastard deserved it." She said innocently.

Hawk spoke up to tease her.

"So, what was he, a hundred-pound weakling?" She smiled and told him sweetly.

"He was about your size." Now, Hawk like most of us was not a little man. He stood six foot two and weighed in at around two hundred pounds of pure muscle. He just laughed at her. She smirked and asked. "What? You don't believe me? I could show you." This made the group perk up. What the hell did she mean she could show him? I shook my head no. Hawk grinned at her harder and said back.

"I'd love to see that, sweetheart." She looked at me in expectation.

"What's that look for? You don't think I'm going to let you fight him, do you?" I growled.

"Sure. Why not? I haven't had a workout since I got here and he's as good as any. Unless you're worried, I'll hurt him. In that case, I can work out with Cannon or Demon." She said matter of fact.

"Work out? Are you telling me you work out by fighting guys?"

"Sometimes. I keep up my skills and when I was in the Corps, it was with Cannon and the other guys in my unit. When at home it's with Demon or one of the other guys there. I've been fighting since I was about eight years old, Terror. I plan to keep it up. If you're not comfortable with me fighting with one of your guys, I'll do it with Demon or Cannon. They know me and know they don't have to hold back."

I didn't like this at all, but also, I knew she had to be comfortable to be herself. If this is what she did, I wanted her to be able to continue. However, I might end up being the one she got to spar with, because I couldn't see myself liking her fighting with other guys. I looked at Demon, Bull and Cannon. They all three were nodding in agreement. I took this to mean she was okay and not overestimating her abilities. "Okay, you decide on one of them, but for today, we'll let Hawk off the hook. Show him and the others what you can do, so they know whether they want you to hurt them or not." I teased. I was taking a jab at the guys.

Amid Hawk's protests, we all got off the bar stools and headed down to the basement. On the way I saw Demon duck into his room. In the basement of the clubhouse, we had our workout room. It took up over half of the basement and had every kind of machine and weight set you could imagine. In addition, we had a ring set up. Several of us liked to box and practice martial arts in it. Sometimes we just went at it to blow off steam.

Demon came into the room and he had changed into shorts. I guess he was going to be her sparring partner. Harlow was dressed in some yoga pants and a tank from her outing. It clung to her every curve and I found I wasn't happy anyone was seeing her body even in clothes. But short of making her wear a sack, which I knew she wouldn't do, and which wouldn't make her any less sexy, I had to bear it. She removed her shoes and asked me to tape her hands up. Were they going to be bare knuckle fighting? I hoped not. Demon had Bull tape up his hands.

They both got in the ring and took a few minutes to stretch. Once they were done with that, they started to test each other. Both of them were moving around and taking steps toward each other and taking light swings and jabs. Suddenly, they got serious. Demon exploded from his side of the ring and swung at Harlow full strength. She ducked his swing and came up under his arm and jabbed him hard in the ribs and then jumped back. He just pranced around a few more steps. She made the next move and swung at his head, he ducked and swept her feet. She stumbled but didn't go all the way down.

For the next twenty minutes, they took turns whipping on each other. They kept fighting with punches, kicks, and other moves. It was obvious they were both using a mixture of boxing, Muay Thai, Krav Maga and wrestling. Every time Demon landed a blow or threw her to the mat, I winced and had to keep myself from jumping in the ring. I hated to see her at risk to be hurt in any way. It didn't matter she obviously knew what she was doing and could take care of herself. She was my woman and that meant I was supposed to defend her. They were not taking it easy on each other.

Suddenly, Harlow took off running and flipped high in the air. Once in the air, she wrapped her legs around his neck, twisting her body around him. She threw her whole body backward and brought him down hard onto the mat, where she wrapped him up in her legs into a choke hold. She had his arm pinned in a locked submission hold. He tried to get out of it and couldn't. He had gotten her down a few times before in holds which she had to work hard to get out of, and she had done the same to him. But this was a new move I hadn't seen either of them do. He wasn't breaking it and I could tell she was going to choke him out. He wasn't relenting and she was squeezing harder. I thought he was going to go the whole way when he finally tapped out. They jumped up and hugged each other. I guess the session was at an end. Thank God! I couldn't stand to see her hit or thrown anymore. Both were sweating but grinning. It'd been a really good workout.

I looked around at my crew. Almost all of the guys had wandered in and were watching. I could see the looks of surprise, shock, and respect on their faces. She'd shown them she had guts and could fight. It made me feel a little better knowing she could defend herself like that. It made me want to see what other moves she had. She'd mentioned before, she had been trained to use knives. We had plastic training ones some of us used. These were in addition to the real throwing knives we had as well. I would have to get her to show us one day what she could do with them. They climbed out of the ring, and I hooked her around the waist. I pulled her to me and gave her a big kiss. She melted into me.

When we broke apart, the rest of the gang was headed toward the stairs. I placed my arm tighter around her waist and headed after them. "Let's get you to the house so you can shower and change. We'll go out tonight and head to the bar for dinner if that's okay with you? I want to check in on them and it's Friday night. They should end up having a good crowd. I want you to see it."

She smiled and said. "That sounds like a plan." As we all made it back to the common room, I called out.

"We're going to the Fallen Angel in a couple of hours for anyone who wants to join us." The group roared in agreement. We parted ways to get ready.

Chapter 18: Harlow

It had been a really good workout. I'd needed one. I could tell Terror hadn't been thrilled with it. But I wanted him to know. I could take care of myself. We reached the house and he followed me up the stairs. I was looking forward to seeing their bar. We had our own back in Hunters Creek, but I liked to see how this one would be different.

I headed toward my room. Terror stopped me outside his bedroom door. "Here, come in my room. All your clothes I moved over to mine while you were gone today. I want you in here with me." I was a little upset he hadn't asked me first, but I didn't want to be in a separate room either. I guess he was feeling the same way if he moved all my stuff into his private space. I decided not to call him out on it.

"Okay."

I entered his bedroom, or I guess it was our bedroom now and headed into the bathroom. I did love this bathroom. I stripped and threw my sweaty clothes in the hamper. I decided a bath would be best so I could soak my muscles after the workout Demon gave me. I turned on the tap. Terror started to take off his clothes. I guess he was going to join me. I hoped it ended in a different kind of workout with him. He helped me into the tub and then stepped in behind me. Once seated, he pulled me back close to his chest.

He took down my hair from the bun I had twisted

it up into at the beginning of my session with Demon. He combed his fingers through it to get out the knots. When he was satisfied all the knots were out, he grabbed the wand that was part of the faucet. I loved it. It was the regular faucet you could then pull out and have a handheld sprayer. He got all my hair wet. I heard him open the lid on a bottle and then felt his fingers massaging shampoo throughout my hair. He had magic fingers. He used his finger tips to work my scalp and give me a great massage along with washing my hair. Once he was done, he rinsed and then did the same with the conditioner. When everything was thoroughly rinsed out, I wrung out as much water as I could and pulled it back up on my head. I used the hair tie he'd removed to get it out of the way.

    I leaned back against his chest and relaxed. He grabbed what I saw was my loofah and then squeezed my body wash on it. He hadn't missed a thing in his moving exercise. The scent of gardenias filled the air. It was one of my favorite scents and always made me relax. He slowly began to wash my back. He moved from it around to my arms and then down my sides to my legs. Once he finished washing my legs, including my feet, he moved back up to my torso. I saw him drop the loofah into the water and he took his soapy hands and began to rub all over my chest.

    The slippery sensation of the soap and his hands made me more sensitive than usual. He ran his hands all over and around my breasts. He cupped them both and gently squeezed. He kept rubbing and squeezing while interspersing it with tweaks to my nipples. They were hard and standing at attention. I hadn't known my breasts would be so sensitive to nipple play. He could almost get me off from this alone sometimes. He kept it up for several minutes while I squirmed and moaned.

He raised his right hand and grasped my jaw, turning my head to the side. His mouth took mine in a deep kiss. His tongue licked at the seam between my lips, his teeth nipped at them and then he pushed his tongue between my lips to get inside my mouth. We kissed for a couple of minutes while his left hand continued to play with my breasts. He kept switching from one to the other. The twisting movement he was doing to my nipples was divine. He broke our kiss and brought his right hand back down to my chest. He then ran both of his hands down my sides to my belly. He rubbed there and played with my belly button, dipping into the little depression. Finally, he made it to my aching pussy. I was so wet from the attention he had already given my body. I wanted to scream.

His fingers parted my pussy lips and eased down to flick my clit. It was hard, distended and begging for attention. He strummed me there making me pant. He kept slipping those magic fingers down my lips and playing around my entrance then back up to tweak my clit. He kept this up for several minutes. I was moving and bucking against his hands. I wanted to feel those fingers inside of me. I finally had to beg. Please baby, I need your fingers inside of me." He chuckled and gave me what I wanted. He pushed in a single finger. I sighed. That felt so good! He moved that finger in and out of me a couple of times and then added a second one. By this time, I was primed, and it only took a few strokes in and out with both of them for me to climax. I threw back my head and yelled my release and his name.

As soon as I came down from my orgasm, he stood and stepped out of the tub. He pulled me out onto the bath mat, dried me and then himself. He swung me up into his arms and carried me to the bed. There he laid me down on my back and pulled my legs open and crawled between them. I felt the broad head of his cock teasing my entrance and then he slid it into my hungry pussy. As always, he felt like he wouldn't fit but he pushed right through my folds steadily, until I felt his pubic bone meet mine. I was so full and stretched to what felt like the max.

Once there he started to stroke in and out. He went deeper and harder with each stroke. I could tell he was excited since he was panting, and he was grunting with every thrust. While he slid in and out again, I felt his hand reach down and stroke my wet slit and rub my clit. This just primed me more. He was pulling back on his stroke when I felt his touch move around to the entrance to my asshole. I tensed. He kissed me and said. "Relax baby, I promise you'll like this. It'll give you more pleasure and that's what I need. One day soon, I want to fuck you in this gorgeous ass, and make you come even harder." I wasn't sure about this, but I was willing to try it.

He kept thrusting in and out a few more times while I worked to relax. Finally, I relaxed, and he eased the tip of his wet finger into my ass. It burned and hurt a little, but I kept trying not to tense up. I was so wet that the juices from my pussy had ran down my ass, so it gave him more lubrication to work with. He continued to ease his finger in a little further until I felt the first sphincter muscle give, then he was in up to what felt like his first knuckle. Once in he pulled back and pushed back in. In rhythm with his cock, he began to fuck my ass with his finger like his cock was doing to my pussy. He was sinking his finger a little further into my ass each time. It did burn and held a bite of pain, but the pleasure sensation was taking over. He was right, it did feel good. This along with the pleasure his cock was giving my pussy had me ready to go off in a matter of minutes.

I tried to hold off to prolong the pleasure, but it was too much. I felt the warmth and tingling start in my toes and run up my legs into my belly. When it hit, my pussy and ass both clenched and I was coming harder than I had ever come before with him. It felt like I would never stop, and I screamed his name. "Declan!" He stroked a couple more times and then came filling my pussy with his hot cum while shouting my name.

He collapsed over me but made sure not to let his whole weight crush me. We panted and gasped for what felt like forever and then he eased out of both my ass and pussy. I rolled to my side and curled up. He kissed my neck and asked me. Aare you okay, baby?" I nodded.

"Yeah, I'm okay. That felt incredible. Are you okay?" He chuckled.

"I'm more than okay. And I'm glad you liked it. So, do you think you'll let me have that ass one day?" I looked at him over my shoulder and grinned.

"I think you may have persuaded me to consider it. Once I got past the burning and pain, it felt really good." He kissed me and patted my ass.

"Let's jump in the shower and rinse off and then we need to get ready to go." I agreed and we got up to get ready for our evening out. Forty-five minutes later we were out the door getting on his bike at the clubhouse. I saw some of the other guys coming out to get on their bikes. Several of the bikes were already gone, so it appeared like almost the whole gang might be there. We eased out the gates and onto the road. In no time at all, we were in town and pulling into the bar. It was still early for the drinking crowd, but the parking lot looked pretty full.

Apparently, the restaurant side did a really good business. Inside, the hostess greeted us and seated us in the back, in a private section which must be reserved for the club. Our waitress ended up being Julie, whom I had met at the barbeque. She said hello to all of us and she and I chatted for a minute. She gave me a quick hug and then took our drink orders and left. There were a lot of orders, so it took a few minutes for her husband, Sam, to get them all filled. Once she had all of the drinks served, we placed our food orders. We all had a great time talking and laughing. Julie kept our drinks filled and we took our time. Before I knew it, the dinner crowd had mostly thinned out and I could see the bar section was filling up. Terror stood and pulled back my chair. I guess we were now going to go into the bar for a while. I could see they had a stage area and a band was in the process of finishing set up. I loved to dance, so tonight looked like it was going to be even better. We weaved through the crowd to the bar. In the bar area, there were several tables and booths. Here there was a couple of huge ones reserved just like there was in the restaurant section. We slid into them.

Chapter 19: Terror

This afternoon, making love to Harlow had been great as always. However, her relaxing to allow me to play with her ass had made it even better. I was serious about having her ass soon. I knew it would bring her a whole different level of pleasure. Every time I had her it just kept getting better. Sex had never been this good with anyone else. I knew it had to be because in this case, I actually cared about the woman, not just about getting the two of us off. Don't get me wrong, I was still thinking about that, but I wanted to be sure she felt all the pleasure she could, regardless of my needs. Watching her feel pleasure only intensified my own.

We finished dinner and had moved into the bar area to the club's booths. Our waitress here wasn't Julie. It was another one named Kim. She was newer but I knew she'd been checking out the guys and trying to get with one of us. We had no problem fucking the bunnies and other women, but we were more cautious starting something with one of our employees. It was never pretty when you were done with a chick, moved on and she wanted something more. Kim hadn't really gotten the message despite all the guys having not taken her up on what she was offering.

She was flirting with the whole table. When she finally made it to Harlow and me, she ignored the fact I had my arm around Harlow and squeezed between Bull and me to lean down in front of me. She was giving me a straight look down her top at her breasts. "What can I get you, Terror?" She throatily asked. I ignored her and asked Harlow what she wanted to drink. Harlow gave her a hard look and ordered a beer with a tequila chaser. I gave Kim my order. She hesitated and then left to go to the bar.

A while later, when Kim got to bringing Harlow and I our drink orders, she again leaned into me and was flirting even harder. I could see Harlow wasn't going to put up with it. She leaned around me toward Kim. "Okay sweetheart, I guess I need to help you out. When a guy doesn't respond to your flirting, it means he's not interested. The whole booth hasn't taken you up on what you're offering, so why don't you run along and bat your eyes at someone else. Get a clue, if they don't respond, then they don't want you. Have a little respect for yourself. Otherwise, you'll get your ass beat one of these days. He's with me, and he's going home with me." Kim just gaped and then gave a squeak and hurried off.

I looked at her. "Babe, you don't have to worry. I would never go there. You're the only one I want. You may have scared her a little too much. We don't want to lose her. She's a good waitress despite her flirting and they're hard to find. Just ignore her."

She glared at me and then responded. "Well better she learns to behave and get her feelings a little hurt, than you lose her when someone kicks her ass. Your choice, but hey, if you want her hanging all over you, I can call her back. I'm sure I can find somewhere else to sit so you two can hang together." She sniped back. I laughed and hugged her tighter to me. She resisted but I wouldn't release my hold on her.

"No need to get upset. I won't let her hang on me again

if she tries. Just calm down." I could see her clinch her jaw. She just shrugged her shoulders and turned to speak to Sherry, who was on the other side of her. I decided to let it go for now, but later we could talk about it. She had nothing to worry about. She was the only woman I wanted. Though to be honest, it did make me secretly happy she was jealous.

A bit later once the band had gotten going and the dance floor was filling up, Sherry asked her if she wanted to go dance. She nodded yes, so I moved in order for her to be able to get out of our booth. Before she walked away, I pulled her to me and laid a hard kiss on her. Pulling back, I looked her in the eyes and told her. "Have fun." She did give me a little smile. Hopefully she was over being miffed at me about Kim.

I sat back down. Kim came back over to our booth to take our refill orders. This time she didn't flirt with any of us. As she left, Savage leaned over. "I guess your woman is a little possessive. Don't give her too much grief about putting Kim in her place. You wouldn't like it if a guy was flirting with her, would you?" I was about to blast him for getting into my business with Harlow, when I thought about what he said. True I wouldn't have liked it, nor would I have ignored a guy coming onto her. I nodded to him to indicate I understood what he was saying.

I sat back and watched the dance floor. Fuck, my woman could move. That sexy as hell body of hers was shimming and shaking like nothing I'd seen. I could see she loved to dance. Watching her was making me hornier than I had been just sitting close to her. But also, I could see a whole lot of other guys in the place watching her. The lust in their eyes was apparent. Now, I couldn't kill them all just for looking even if I wanted to, but God did I want to.

I turned back to the booth when Tiny said something to me. While we were talking, I saw a few of the other guys glance at the dance floor and then at each other with worry on their faces, before they glanced at me and Tiny. I saw Viper open his mouth to say something just as I turned, and that's when I saw it. A couple of guys had joined Sherry and Harlow on the dance floor. I could see the girls both shaking their heads no. The guys didn't seem to want to leave. The girls shook their heads no again and then turned their backs on the guys. The one who had been talking to Sherry shrugged and walked off to a nearby table. His friend didn't. He stood there for a moment watching Harlow. Suddenly, I saw him reach out and grab her by the arm. She spun around to face him. That's all I needed to see. I was up out of the booth and across the floor in a flash. I could feel Tiny and a couple of the guys following me.

As I neared Harlow, I could hear what she was saying. "Listen buddy, I told you I'm not interested in dancing with you or getting a drink. I'm here with someone. Go ask some other woman if she's interested. And keep your damn hands to yourself." He took a step back shocked. Then I saw him get an ugly look on his face.

"Fuck you, bitch. You get up here and shake your ass and then get bitchy when a guy wants a piece of what you're obviously offering? You're nothing but a tease." That was it. I didn't wait for her to respond. I grabbed him by the shoulder and spun him around to face me.

"Why don't you run your mouth to me, you little fuck head." I told him. His eyes got big as he saw me in my cut and then the guys behind me. He started to back up and stuttered.

"S-sorry man. I didn't know she was taken." I shook my head.

"You're a liar. I heard her tell you she was here with someone. Also, it doesn't matter how a woman is dancing, if she says no, then no means no. So, I suggest you leave before I knock your teeth down your fucking throat." He just kept bobbing his head as he backed away. When he got to the edge of the dance floor, he turned and fled to his table where the friend was sitting watching us. They both headed for the door a minute later. I watched to make sure he left.

I turned back to Harlow. She was smirking. "Babe, don't worry he was just flirting. I want you, not him. But you don't want to lose him, do you? He's probably a good customer." She said. She had a twinkle in her eye. The little smart ass. She was getting me back for what I said about Kim. I wrapped her in my arms and crushed her to me.

"Okay, smart ass. Wait until I get this ass home. You made your point. Why don't you two come have another drink with us before you dance more?" I playfully growled. She threw back her head, laughed and followed me to the booth. Tiny came back with Sherry in his arms with the other guys trailing behind us.

We sat down and ordered more drinks. We stayed for a couple of hours. The girls would dance and then sit to take small breaks. We all sat at the booths keeping an eye on them, but no one else bothered them. She did get me to dance a couple of slow dances with her. Holding her in my arms just made me want her more. As it got later, several of the guys started picking up various women in the bar. I knew they'd be spending a little time with them tonight.

In the past, that would have been me. But now I didn't miss it at all. Not when I had Harlow in my bed. Hopefully the rest of them would find a woman one day. Tiny was the only other one of us with an old lady. Him and Sherry had been together since high school and we'd always tormented him. Telling him how sorry we were for him being tied down and pussy whipped. He would always grin and shake his head at us and tell us we didn't know what we were missing. We'd always humored him, but now I knew he was right.

With most of the guys pairing off with their companions for the night, I stood up and took Harlow's hand. I nodded to the guys remaining at the booth and told them I was calling it a night. Tiny and Sherry had left a half an hour ago. I could see when they left, he had plans for her tonight. Just like I had plans for Harlow. Even though I had just had her earlier today, I found I was starving for her. The gang nodded and told us good night. We walked out to the parking lot and got on my bike. Bull and Cannon followed us out. I guess they'd had enough. All of us got on the road. Cannon was riding the bike he had rode to the compound, so I guess he was a rider but not in a club. I was finding I liked him. I'd keep an eye on him and if he did well, I'd see what the club thought of asking him to prospect, if he was interested.

Pulling back up to the gates of the compound, I saw Quin was on gate duty. He saw it was us and opened up. We parked in the lot and swung off our bikes. Bull and Cannon headed into the clubhouse after telling us goodnight. I took Harlow's arm and led her toward my house. She followed and snuggled up under my arm. I planned to spend a few hours tonight loving on my woman. I hope she wasn't too tired from all that dancing.

Once inside, I took off my boots and hers. As soon as they were off, I pushed her into the wall beside the front door. I was so damn hot for her, I couldn't wait. Having her teasing me with her dancing all night, had me on fire. I took her mouth in a fiery kiss as I tugged at her clothes. She seemed as frantic as I was. Harlow was tugging off my tee shirt and then went to work on my jeans, while I divested her of her clothes in between kisses. As soon as I had her naked, I slid my hand down to her pussy to see if she was ready for me. She was soaking wet.

I hoisted her up in my arms. She wrapped me in those long legs and her arms. I probed her entrance, then slammed deep burying my cock in one hard stroke. She gave a small scream. As I pounded in and out of her, she began to thrust back down hard on my aching cock. I kept mapping her body with my hands as she rode me. We were both panting and out of control. I tried to hang on, but she had me too excited. It didn't take long for me to feel my release racing up my legs. Thankfully, she tensed at the same time and her pussy clamped down on my cock, causing me to detonate along with her. My cock kept twitching and jerking as I spilled my cum inside of her. She sobbed as she came.

When I could finally move, I reluctantly let my softening cock slide from her body. I headed toward our bedroom with her still in my arms. Once inside, I took her straight to the shower, so I could clean the two of us up. I planned for this to be the beginning of our night together. As soon as we were clean, I took her to bed. We needed to rest a little bit before the next round started, though the way I was feeling, it wouldn't be long until it did.

The next morning, we got up late. We'd been up

for much of the night between being at the bar and then enjoying each other's bodies after we got home. I had gotten a text from Smoke just a bit ago, telling me he had some information, so I was headed over to the clubhouse. Harlow said she needed to do some laundry, so I left her at the house. As I entered the clubhouse, I saw Smoke waiting. In the corner Demon was playing a game of pool with Ghost. Viper and Savage were talking to Bull, while Steel chatted with Cannon.

Upon seeing me enter, everyone stopped what they were doing and looked from me to Smoke. Gesturing to Smoke to follow me, I headed to my office. I saw Bull following behind him. I could see the rest wanted to come too, but they'd wait until I filled them in on what he had found. Entering my office, the three of us took a seat.

Smoke cleared his throat. "So, yesterday I set up a program on my computer to look for specific data on this Tucker character. You know, things like his social security number, credit card usage, his license plate, his phone records, etc. Also, I did some background checking. He doesn't have anyone I can find that he's really close with. He headed to South Carolina when he got out and he's still there. However, if he's like Cannon said, he won't stay for long. If he uses his credit cards or hits his bank for money, I'll get an alert. I'm using this in hopes he does use one of them when he gets ready to move, so we can track him. I'm trying to find his email account, so I can hack into it and we can monitor him this way too. The one thing which has shown up so far, is he has placed a couple of calls to his old command in California. I'm unable to trace it to a specific person, but I know he made them. It could be he's finishing something off for himself, but it was a number registered to the Administration office."

Bull and I looked at each other. In my gut I knew it had to do with Harlow and not something for him. He was most likely looking for information to track her down. I could see Bull felt the same. We were counting on him making it to Hunters Creek and getting caught there. Bull had already spoken to his VP, Tank, to let everyone in his club know not talk to anyone about Harlow. This included the prospects and bunnies. We didn't want a repeat of someone telling him about her being here like they had with Cannon. I thanked Smoke and he left the office. I felt Bull's eyes on me. I looked across at him. He had a big frown on his face.

"I know it and so do you, that fucker is going to come looking for her. I need to head back to my club tomorrow. Do you think I need to send any more guys this way? We still haven't heard anything from the Bastards, which worries me and then add this on top of it." He grumbled.

"Yes, I agree he'll come looking for her. I think for now we're fine for guys. I have some feelers out, watching for the Bastards to stir. I think they're regrouping right now. We took a big bite out of their club numbers and if they're going to retaliate, they have to get more bodies. That'll take a bit of time. I have those same people keeping their eyes open for any strangers in town. I don't want to take any chances with Harlow."

Bull nodded his head in agreement. He got up and paced a bit. I knew he had something else on his mind. He finally stopped and leaned against my desk. "Terror, I can see you're treating Harlow well and I know you want to keep her safe. I'm really hoping this ends well between the two of you. I never thought about letting her be with a brother. To be honest, I never thought I would like any guy enough to be with my daughter. Just know, she'll challenge you at times and piss you off other times. Her mother was the same way. But I never loved a woman before her or since. She was my everything. I can see Harlow is giving you her all. Don't fuck it up." He said.

I sat up in my chair. "Bull, Harlow has me crazy and loving it. I know she'll be a handful. And I wouldn't want a woman who wasn't able to stand on her own two feet. But I will protect her even if she can protect herself. I know this is way too soon, but I know she has a part of me no one else ever will. I'm more than half in love with her. I promise not to fuck this up." With this said, we shook hands and headed out of my office.

Back in the common room, I saw more of the guys had arrived. It being a Saturday, most would have hung around for the majority of the day. However, today we were having a meeting with an affiliated club, the Pagan Souls, from down in the Cherokee, North Carolina area. I thought it best to get them in the loop on what was happening with the Bastards. Since the Bastards ran their supply lines around their area, it was likely they would start acting up with them. The Souls' President, Agony, had several of his crew coming with him. They would be here around four for the meeting, then we planned to have a little party with them afterward.

Rather than have Sherry and Harlow cook, I had the Fallen Angel's restaurant prepare food. I'd told them a couple of days ago, we'd have guests today. The club bunnies, hang-arounds, and friends of the club were invited as well. I knew the Souls would be looking to unwind. I checked with the prospects to be sure we had enough booze and the clubhouse had the extra rooms ready for our guests. The few of us with houses could put up those who needed it if it was ever necessary. But the clubhouse was huge with dozens of individual bedrooms, plus we had a bunk room with an additional twenty beds. We had done the renovations with an eye toward growth and the need to be able to house all our loved ones if the need arose.

About two-thirty before the Souls came, I went back to the house. Harlow was in the office on her laptop. I didn't disturb her but went toward the kitchen. It was then I smelled the clean, lemony scent in the house. Looking around, I saw she had dusted and mopped the floors. Walking around and inspecting, I saw she had the kitchen and the bathrooms we were using scrubbed and shining. All my clothes were washed and put away. I came back down stairs and gave her a kiss.

"Harlow, babe, you didn't need to clean the house or do my clothes. I usually get one of the club girls to do it."

She gave me a funny look. "I don't mind, and while I'm here, I'd rather do it than have one of them do it." She stated.

I frowned at her *while I'm here remark*. I had news; she was going to be here for the rest of her life. I needed to let her know. "Baby, if you want to do it yourself, fine. But as far as you doing it while you're here, it sounds like you think this is for a few weeks. I have news for you, woman. I have no intention of letting you leave, so just know this is long-term. Now, if you get tired of doing anything, let me know. I'll get it covered." With this said, I ravaged her mouth. Backing her against the wall in my office, I ran my hands up under her top. I could feel her lush breasts under her bra. I pushed it out of the way so I could tug on her nipples. Her nubs got hard right away. She lifted a leg and wrapped it around my waist and ground down on the erection behind the zipper of my jeans. Christ, all it took was one kiss or just looking at her and I was hard and ready to go. She was going to kill me.

Ending the kiss, I rested my forehead on hers. "Babe, I'm sorry but I have to go back to the clubhouse since the Souls will be here soon. We have our meeting at four and then I expect we'll start the party around six. You can come over anytime. Sherry should be there early since Tiny will be in the meeting. You can hang out with her. Hold on to these sexy thoughts and later tonight I'll finish what we started." She grinned and nodded, so I left and went back to the clubhouse. I had an uncomfortable walk back until I got my erection to under control.

Chapter 20: Harlow

I was at the clubhouse. Terror and the guys were in the meeting with the Souls. Dad and Demon had joined them. Out in the common room were the prospects, Cannon, me and Sherry. Since this was a meeting, if any of the Souls had old ladies, they didn't come with them. I was wondering if those who did have one, would partake of the hang-arounds and club bunnies who would be here later. I knew a lot of guys didn't believe in being faithful. It was one of the things I had always hated. But that was between them and their old ladies. If they wanted to put up with it, it wasn't for me to police, though I was known to make comments. Of course, there were women who did the same thing.

About six o'clock the door to church opened and out came the guys and their guests. By this time the bunnies, club friends, and hang-arounds had arrived. The bunnies had stayed away from Sherry and me. This was fine with me. Laci was in that group and she kept giving me shitty looks. A few of the friends who had been to the barbeque I had met, came over and chatted with us. When Terror came out, he was talking to a bear of a man. Terror walked straight to me and threw his arm around my waist. He pulled me to his side and turned me to face the man with him.

"Harlow, this is Agony. He's the president of the Pagan Souls I told you about. Agony, this is Harlow. She's my woman and Bull's daughter." Agony looked me up and down. There wasn't anything offensive in his look. I could see he was curious about me and to be honest, I saw a look of appreciation in his eyes. I wasn't ignorant of the fact many men found me attractive. As long as they weren't crass about it, I was fine to let them look. Agony took my hand and kissed it.

"Hello beautiful lady. What're you doing with this no-good scoundrel? How about you run away with me and leave this one behind?" He purred.? Terror growled and pulled my hand out of Agony's grasp. Agony just threw his head back and roared.

"Listen Agony, you bastard, you try and take my woman and I'll cut your balls off and bury you in the back forty. Also, keep your hands and eyes off what's mine." Terror snarled. I knew he could tell Agony was ribbing him, but I could also tell he didn't want him getting any ideas.

I smiled and told Agony. "Thank you for the offer, but Terror is my kind of scoundrel. Besides, why would I leave him for a bigger one?" This really made him laugh. He winked at me and then told Terror.

"You have a good one here. Make sure you keep her. She'll be good for your ass." With this said, he wandered off to get a beer. Terror gave me a kiss and said he was going to get me a drink. I sat down on one of the couches. Before Terror came back, a man I didn't know came up and sat down beside me. I was looking at dad in the corner laughing with someone, so I didn't really pay attention to the guy. All of a sudden, I felt a hand on my knee. I looked down and the guy next to me had his hand there rubbing it up and down my thigh. He leaned in and licked his lips.

"Hey gorgeous. What do you say, we go find somewhere quiet to get to know each other better?" I was a little stunned. As I scrambled to get my thoughts together to blast him, I saw Terror coming. By the look on his face, he was not amused. When he reached the couch, he hauled the guy up by his collar and punched him in the face. The guy looked surprised, but I have to say, he stayed on his feet. He looked at Terror and yelled.

"What the fuck, Terror? Why're you hitting me? You got first dibs or something? Fine, I'll wait until you're done then have my turn with this fine piece of ass." The room had gotten quiet and everyone seemed to be watching the show. Terror snarled and grabbed him by the throat.

"I'll tell you what's the matter. You had your fucking hand on my woman. There's no having a go at her when I'm done! Now, I suggest if you don't want me to feed my fist down your throat and my boot up your ass, that you leave her alone and get out of my sight." He looked around at the others in the room. "To be clear to anyone who isn't aware, this is Harlow. She's my woman and Bull's daughter. Keep your fucking hands off her." I saw several of the guys look surprised at his claim. I guess no one expected Terror to be claiming a woman. I could see Laci with a sour look on her face.

Terror took the seat where the other guy had been sitting. He handed me my drink he'd sat down before grabbing and hitting the guy. He threw his arm around my shoulders. I leaned into him. "Thank you, baby, but I was about to set him straight." He shrugged and said.

"Well now everyone is straight." He then nuzzled his lips behind my ear and nibbled there. He knew this drove me wild. Deciding to play with him, I crawled up on his lap and licked and nibbled on his ear lobe. I knew that drove him crazy. Suddenly, he had his hands on either side of my face and was devouring my mouth. As I was about to run out of air, he lifted his head. Around the room I could hear the catcalls and whistles. He gave me one of those smirks I loved and eased back to take a drink of his beer. I ground down on his crotch feeling the erection he was sporting, gave him a wink and sat back down beside him to sip my drink.

The evening was shaping up to be a fun one. We mingled and chatted with almost everyone. There were too many names to recall. At least with the Souls, they had on cuts with their names. An hour or so later, I excused myself to go to the bathroom. When I came back out, I could see Laci had slunk her way over to Terror while I was gone. Just as I got within earshot, she reached out and touched his arm. He glanced behind him and seeing who it was, shrugged off her touch. "Laci, get your hands off me. What do you want?" He asked with a pissed look on his face. She smiled and fluttered her eyelashes.

"Oh, Terror honey, I just wanted to spend some time with you tonight. You always liked to spend time with me," she cooed. He shook his head at her.

"I don't want to spend time with you tonight or any other night. You know I'm with Harlow. Why would you think I'd want you? With Harlow, I don't need or want anyone else." When she heard this, she got a look of thunder on her face. She then noticed I'd come up on them. The look of hate she threw me was unbelievable. She turned and stomped off.

I stepped into his line of vision. He smiled and took my hand. I snuggled up beside him. I laughed and told him. "I can't leave you alone for a second. Do I need to get my name tattooed on you, so other women stay away?" He grinned.

"Only if you let me put my name on you, so the guys know to stay the fuck away from you too." When the guys around him heard us, they busted out laughing. One of them looked at Terror and said.

"You're so gone man." Terror just smiled. The remainder of the night stayed drama free. Everyone seemed to have a good time. I saw guys starting to hook up with the women. Most of them weren't shy. They were kissing and making out very scandalously in front of anyone who may have looked. I saw a few of them go outside and others down the hall. I wasn't innocent to how wild and uninhibited it could get at a club party, so nothing shocked me. In fact, even though they tried to not do it back home when I was present, I'd seen some of the guys outright having sex before. I guess Terror didn't want me to see that tonight or he was just anxious to go. Because once this all started in earnest, he said goodbye quickly and we headed toward the door. I was ready to spend some time with my man in bed anyway.

We reached the house and went in the front door. As soon as the door closed, he pushed me up against the wall and kissed me. As always, he consumed me. Our mouths were frantic, and we were ripping off each other's clothes desperate to feel skin just like we had been last night. Once we were naked, he ran his hand down my belly to my pussy. I was already dripping wet for him. To tell the truth, I'd been wet most of the night. Just looking at him got me so horny. Feeling my wetness, he rasped in my ear. "Baby, I need to take you now. I can't wait any longer. You've driven me nuts all night. Wrap your legs around my waist and hang onto my neck."

I placed my hands around his neck, and he hoisted me in the air, so I could wrap my legs around him. He kept one hand under my ass for support and with the other he took his cock in hand. He rubbed it all over my pussy coating it in my juices. He then notched it at my entrance and slammed full into me with one stroke. I screamed and my head fell back against the wall. Fuck, he felt bigger than usual! He was sucking on my neck and moving in me like a piston. It only took about five minutes for me to be ready to climax. I tightened my fingers around his neck as I felt the rush start. He was panting in my ear. Just as I let go and came yelling, I heard his grunt and moan. I could feel his cum splashing inside of me. He kept stroking until we both stopped shuddering. Giving me a kiss on the mouth, he let me legs down and supported me until he was sure I could stand on my own. Once both of us were steady, he grabbed my hand and led me upstairs to our room. Not a bad way to end the evening at all. This man was stealing my heart. I only hoped he felt the same way.

Chapter 21: Terror

It had been a week since the meeting and party with the Souls. Bull had gone back to Hunters Creek. Things were going well. Harlow and I were enjoying ourselves. The sex was off the hook. I couldn't get enough of her. We were having it at least a couple times a day, sometimes more. Just yesterday I took her on my desk in my office at the clubhouse. I couldn't remember what she came in to ask. I'd just gone crazy and had to have her that instant. Now I couldn't look at the desk without seeing her spread out there. She was still helping Sherry with the remodel. Cannon was around and come to find it out, he was a really good mechanic. So, he'd been helping us out in the garage.

No one had any word on this Tucker fellow. Smoke said he still showed his purchases as occurring in South Carolina. To help fill her time when not helping Sherry, Harlow had taken over helping Viper with all the paperwork involved with the various businesses. He'd needed help for a while but hadn't asked for any. Harlow kind of pushed in and took over a portion of it. Apparently, she helped out her dad's club the same way. I was finding she was very business minded and had good ideas on new businesses we could get started.

Needing a break, I wandered outside to go to the garage. I heard loud voices coming from the side of the clubhouse. Walking around it to investigate, I saw a bunch of the guys in a circle in the yard. Curious as to what they were watching, I pushed through them. In front of the group was Cannon and Harlow. They were dressed for exercise. In each of their hands was a practice knife. I guess the time had come to show the guys what she knew about knife fighting. I felt a nudge to my left arm. I looked over at Demon. He had a huge smile on his face. "You came just in time, Terror. Harlow is getting in her practice then we're going to practice throwing at targets."

I watched as the two in the middle squared off. Just like with the other fighting, Harlow turned out to be an expert. She was quick and precise. While Cannon got in some good hits, she got in as many if not more on him. Each had welts they'd remember for a while. After they tired of this, they decided it was time to throw real knives at targets. Kade fetched the throwing knives while Quin set up the targets. For this match, Harlow asked who all wanted to compete. Several of the guys said yes. They decided the best out of fifteen throws would be the winner.

There were only three target areas for throwing knives and there were ten all together wanting to throw. Harlow said for all the guys to go first and then she would go last. That got a lot of kidding from the guys about her not chickening out once she saw how good they were. She laughed at them and told them to do their best. Now, all of us were decent and a few of the guys, like Steel and Hawk, were really good. Cannon was one of the others going up against her.

After the nine guys threw, it was down to Steel being the best out of them. He'd hit the center circle on all but one of the fifteen throws. One had landed just outside the center circle. It was now Harlow's turn. She stepped up and calmly focused on the target. Almost faster than you could blink, she was hurling one knife after another at her target. You could hear each thump as it found its mark. When she was done, there were fifteen knives in the center circle. Jesus Christ, she was amazing. All the guys were looking slack jawed. Harlow just smiled innocently at them. Looking at the others first, Steel then looked at Harlow. "Okay, you showed us what you could do in a fight and with a knife, how about we find something else out," he asked?

"What did you have in mind?" Harlow inquired.

"How about we go out to the shooting range and see who the better sniper is, you or Demon. We heard it was a toss-up on who was better. Let's see." He egged her on. She looked at Demon, who nodded his head in agreement. She then caught my eye. I winked to let her know I was okay with it. I had to admit, I was curious myself. I knew both of them had brought their sniper rifles with them. He went to his room to get his, while she went to the house to get her rifle. Once both of them were back, we headed out to the range we had at the back of the property.

Again, the prospects set up the targets. However, this time it was not at the usual hundred meters out. Since they were both using sniper rifles, the targets were placed a thousand meters out. These targets we couldn't see at that distance without a scope. Each one of them would take five shots. For the second time today, they agreed whomever made the most in or near the center of the target wins. They had set up two targets, so they could both shoot at the same time. Opening their cases, they pulled out their rifles. There is nothing like looking at a sniper rifle. Demon had a Barrett M95. I could see on the side of Harlow's Savage 111 long range 338 La Pua;

someone had painted wings and in script had the words *Guardian Angel*. They got set up and comfortable at the table. Everyone was quiet. Suddenly, the first of the ten total shots rang out.

Once the shooting was over, Quin went to get Demon's target while Kade grabbed Harlow's. Bringing them back to the long table, we compared the holes. Of course, every shot hit the target and within the body outlined on it. Some areas were worth seven points, getting higher in number the closer one got to the center chest and of course, the head. They had agreed to try for only center mass shots at the beginning of the match. Demon scored forty-nine out of fifty, as one of his shots hit just outside the center body ring worth ten points. Looking at Harlow's she scored a perfect fifty out of fifty. I'll be damned! They had been serious about how good both of them were. I had never known anyone to come close to Demon. All the guys were congratulating her and expressing their awe.

After she had packed up her rifle and had gotten all her congratulations, I pulled her into my arms. "Baby, that was awesome! Remind me not to ever piss you off enough to take a shot at me." I joked. She grinned and gave me a kiss. Then she told me.

"Don't do anything to piss me off that much then you won't have to worry." I carried her case for her as we all headed back to the main clubhouse. When we got there, I could see Smoke was standing outside. He hadn't been one of the ones to go out to the range. He walked over to me. I could see he had a serious look on his face. Taking him aside I asked what was up.

"I was over at the construction site to check on the internet issue they were having. It looks like someone broke into the foreman's trailer last night. A bunch of it has been wrecked. Now, for the site itself we hire a guard. He said he didn't see or hear anyone. But the guard also walks the whole site. If it was more than one person and the guard was on the far back part of the site, someone could have done it." Smoke said with a frown on his face. I agreed with his thinking. The question was it just some random kids looking for something to do or was this the Bastards?

Today was church day so we would discuss it as a group. Looking at the time, I decided we had time for lunch before the meeting. We'd pushed it to the afternoon rather than in the morning because Ghost had to recert his CPR this morning. He was a trained paramedic and had been a corpsman in the Navy. Inside we found all kinds of things for sandwiches, since yesterday the grocery run had been made. Everyone piled into the clubhouse and made themselves some lunch. I saw Harlow had made herself a salad from some of the salad fixings she had gotten yesterday. I went up to her. "Harlow, are you sure that's going to be enough? You don't eat enough babe." I told her.

She laughed. "Terror, this is fine. I had breakfast this morning and I'm not that hungry. Keep in mind I don't need as much as you guys. Also, I'm not working it off like I used to do. Believe me if I'm hungry, I'll eat. I'm not one of those women who starves herself." I nodded my okay but I still worried about her. She seemed to be preoccupied and not eating a lot. We'd had a lot of great times together over the last couple of weeks, but I knew she was stressed. This Tucker guy was weighing on her mind.

In fact, Demon, Cannon, Bull and I had spoken

about it yesterday. We had a conference call to check in and Demon raised it. He said he could tell it was on her mind and this made all of us just angrier and more frustrated. I didn't want her to have to worry about anything or anyone. A few times I had awoken in the night to find her awake. She said she was fine, but it still had me worried. I couldn't help but think, if it wasn't this Tucker ordeal bothering her, was she second guessing being with me? God, I hoped not. I already knew I wouldn't know how to handle it if she decided she didn't want to be with me.

After lunch and cleanup which the prospects did, it was time for church. The whole crew was here which was the case most of the time. Upon a rare occasion, a few might not be able to make it. However, they knew if I said it was mandatory, they had to be there. Lately we had been making all of them mandatory with the Bastards and Tucker businesses.

We got settled in and the meeting was underway. We went through a rundown of the monthly profits for each of the businesses. Also, we discussed a poker run we were doing in a month. It would be to raise money for the local hospital. There were still several things which needed finalized. We had the run laid out. We were selling tickets at all our businesses, as well as set up on our website to sell them and take donations. There would be food at each stop, along with entertainment of a band at the final stop, where the winning hand would be determined. The winner would get fifty percent of the poker run entry money. The band had volunteered its time, so no cost there. Several businesses were supplying the food and drinks. It should turn out to be a good run.

After talking this through, I brought up the break

in at the construction site. It was a commercial one we were doing for a local business in town. Luckily, nothing on the actual build had been touched, but that didn't mean it couldn't happen. We decided to put two guards on every night rather than one. This would allow one to always be on the front part of the site, while the other patrolled the back half. Hawk raised the question on all our minds. "Do we know if it was kids or maybe the Bastards?"

I shook my head. "We have no idea. It looked to be petty vandalism which to me says it wasn't the Bastards. They'd be looking to hurt us in some way and not just make a mess. I've been keeping in contact with my resources. They all say they aren't hearing a peep about the Bastards. However, I don't want to chance it's them or someone more serious, so the double guards will start immediately. Ranger, you work out the rotation and make sure everyone is aware of it." Ranger nodded his head. As Sergeant at Arms, he regularly took care of details like this for the club.

Player from the Hunters Creek chapter asked. "Has anyone gotten any news on that creep, Tucker?" I shook my head.

"Nothing. Smoke says all his purchases show he's still in South Carolina around the Charleston area. But I'm not letting down my guard. He'll come for her eventually, so be ready."

Player spoke up again. "I know we're here to help with the Bastards and Tucker. Just wondering if you're going to be growing your club more and maybe patching in any of the prospects or taking on new ones? If so, I have someone who might be interested in prospecting with you. He's a childhood friend's little brother. His name is Adam and he lives around this area rather than Hunters

Creek."

We had been thinking about growing and Kade had been a prospect for ten months. He had been doing great. Also, I liked Cannon, so I decided to get the guys thoughts. "I'd like us to consider if we should patch in Kade. I want everyone to think and then we'll vote in a couple of weeks. As for bringing in new blood, I think it's a good idea. Player, have this Adam come around to our next party and let us meet him and see. Speaking of prospects, I wanted to ask you guys what you think of Cannon? Do you like him and think he'd make a good Warrior? I'm thinking of seeing if he would be interested. I have no idea if he already had things in the works since he got out of the Marines, but he sure seems to be willing to stick around as long as needed to help and he jumps right in. He's one helluva mechanic too."

I saw numerous nods agreeing to the proposed patching of Kade, checking out this Adam guy and offering Cannon a prospect spot. "So, all of those in favor of asking Cannon to prospect with us, say aye." Of course, the Hunters Creek members didn't have a vote, but everyone else in my chapter voted yes. Good, I'd talk to him after church. The remainder of the meeting consisted of just odds and ends in updates and then we were done.

When we got back out to the common room, I saw Cannon at the pool table with Gage. I went over to them. Seeing me coming they stopped their game. Both expectantly looked at me. "Hey Cannon, can I talk to you outside for a minute?" He nodded putting down his pool cue. We went out the door and I walked over to the playground area. We took a seat on a bench set near the swings.

"Cannon, I don't know what your plans are after this shit with Tucker is over. But you've been doing a great job helping us at the garage and in general. I know Harlow trusts you which means a lot. We're wondering if you would be interested in prospecting with the club. It usually takes about a year before one is patched in or not. I really wouldn't expect you not to be able to make it. It just depends on if you're interested. What do you think? Are you interested in becoming a Warrior?"

"I actually didn't have any solid plans after getting out of the Corps. I thought I might work for a garage somewhere. I have to be honest, Harlow talked about the club to some of us, and it has always intrigued me. I thought about checking out the Hunters Creek chapter when I got out. I'd love to prospect with the Warriors and since it looks like Harlow is going to be here and not in Hunters Creek, your offer makes it perfect. I want to be close to where she is. I'd love to prospect with the Warriors," he replied.

I was glad to hear it. I knew him and Harlow were close and with him around I'd never have to worry about someone to help keep her safe. I told him. "That sounds great. Welcome to the Warriors." We both stood up and I gave him a back slap. We headed back into the clubhouse. When we got in the door, I nodded to Savage so he would know Cannon had accepted. Savage came over and handed me a cut. It had the word *Prospect* on the back. If he made it to be a patched member, the top rocker saying Archangel's Warriors, the club's emblem and the bottom rocker saying Dublin Falls, TN would be added. On the front would be his road name once it was determined. I presented the cut to him and the crowd started cheering and congratulating him. After the roar died down and the drinks started, I turned to see Harlow entering the clubhouse. Quin was trailing behind her. Him and Kade had been out today with her.

Chapter 22: Harlow

Quin, Kade, and I walked into the clubhouse to find the guys were celebrating something. I walked over and gave Terror a hug and a kiss. As always, the kiss wasn't a simple peck on the lips. The man could kiss. He took over my mind when he kissed me and made me forget where we were, let alone if anyone else was around us. Finally breaking apart to catch our breath, I asked him what I'd missed.

"What're you guys so happy about?" I asked.

"We're celebrating a new prospect. Cannon just agreed to join the club to see if he can hack it." Shit, that was the best news! I loved Cannon to death, and he would make an awesome Warrior. I had always hoped him and a few of the other guys in our unit would someday join. I talked about the club over the years and knew it intrigued them.

"Fantastic! I'm so happy he said yes. I knew he was interested in all the things I would tell him over the years about the club." I moved over to the bar where Cannon was drinking with some of the guys. Seeing me coming, he sat down his beer. I grabbed him in a hug and gave him a kiss on the cheek. He smiled and hugged me back. I could see he was very happy with his decision. "Congrats Cannon! You're going to be so happy you made this choice. Now just prepare yourself for shit duty for the next year." I teased him. This got a big laugh out of the guys and a sheepish grin out of Cannon. Terror came over and clasped Cannon on the shoulder. "No worries prospect, we'll be nice and wait until tomorrow to start abusing you. So, enjoy tonight," he joked. This raised a cheer from the guys. As everyone had another drink, I decided to have a drink with them. I asked for a shot of tequila. I wasn't much of a beer drinker, but I could drink wine and hard liquor. Usually, I preferred tequila and whiskey. Downing the shot, I stood with Terror and joked with the guys. After about an hour or so, I decided to go back to the house for a bit. The guys all had decided to go out to the bar tonight to continue the celebration, and I wanted a chance to get cleaned up from being out today.

I told Terror I was going to the house and would be back soon. He nodded. It had been really hot today, so I thought a shower would be nice. Back at the house, I turned on the shower and stripped. I pulled my hair into a bun on the top of my head to keep it out of the water. It was too much to wash and have to tame that crazy mess. Stepping in, I felt the lukewarm water hit my body. Ah! That felt great. Closing my eyes, I lathered up my face with my face soap. I was rinsing it off when I felt a breeze and then hands touch my body. I gasped in surprise.

I heard Terror's chuckle. "It's just me, baby. Why would you be surprised? You had to know if you were going to take a shower, I'd be joining you. I'd hate to miss an opportunity to look at this gorgeous body." He teased. I opened my eyes and leaned back into him. I could feel his taut muscles rubbing along my body and his erection growing against my ass.

"Baby, I thought you might stay there with the guys. I'd never complain about you joining me." I turned around to face him. I ran my hands up his chest to around his neck and pulled him down for a kiss. This time I took command of his mouth. I licked around the edge of both his lips and interspersed the licks with flicks of my tongue at the seam between them. I grasped his bottom lip between my teeth and pulled. Once I had it, I nibbled and sucked on it. I then pushed my tongue inside to wrestle his. After a couple of minutes of this, I broke away from his mouth. I ran my hands down his chest to his nipples where I played with each of them. Twisting and rolling them just like he liked to do to mine. They both became hard nubs. I then licked and sucked on them.

As I was teasing his nipples, I was outlining each muscle of his six pack and circling his belly button with my fingers. I could tell he was liking it since his cock was now fully erect. Breaking away from his chest, I dropped to my knees. I kissed the head of his cock. I could taste the pre-cum that was weeping from his slit. I licked it off of my lips. I loved the salty, musky taste of him. I wanted more. I bent forward and took the head of his thick cock into my mouth. At first, I just concentrated on licking all around the head and playing with the underside of it. While I was doing this, I worked the rest of his cock and balls with both hands.

He was starting to thrust into my mouth, so I removed my hands and took as much of him as I could. I made sure to suck as tightly as I could too. I slowly started to bob up and down on his erection licking the head every time I came back up. Then I felt his hand in my hair. He grasped it tightly but not enough to really hurt. He started to push me up and down his cock faster. His hips were thrusting more, and I could hear the grunts he was making. He definitely liked what I was doing to him.

Before I knew what was happening, he pulled out of my mouth and pulled me to my feet. He turned me around and put my hands on the tiled shower wall.

"Harlow, I want you to put your hands right there. Lean forward for me and hold on." He rasped in my ear. I did as he commanded. I felt the head of his cock at my entrance and then he was slowly pushing his length into my wet pussy. He was going super slow and it was torture. God, he felt so amazing. I could feel every vein on his big cock. When he bottomed out, he touched my cervix. I moaned. He slowly pulled back until just the head of his cock was still inside. Back and forth he continued his slow torture. I came in no time. I tightened down on his cock and felt like I could have squeezed him in two. The waves kept coming and I kept squeezing until I felt faint.

Once I came down off my high and started to relax, he picked up his pace. He was now fucking me faster and harder. Each stroke was better than the last. In a matter of minutes, I was feeling another orgasm coming on. When I went over the edge this time, he went with me. He was jerking inside of me while he groaned and panted in my ear. We both rested for several minutes, before he pulled out of me. He quickly washed me and then himself. Turning off the water, we got out and dried off.

He patted me on the ass and told me. "Get ready. I'll meet you at the clubhouse." He got dressed in a tight, black tee shirt, faded jeans, his cut and pair of black riding boots. As always, he looked so sexy. Before he left the bedroom, he gave me a kiss and added. "Thank you for the best shower I've ever had, baby." He grinned as he left the room. It had been the best shower of my life as well.

I wanted to look even sexier tonight. Not only were we celebrating, but I wanted to be sure to drive Terror wild. I curled my hair and left it to hang below my ass. I did my makeup with a dark, smoky eye and bold red lips. For clothes, since I knew we were going on the bike, I stuck with pants. They were a pair of black jeans that hugged my body like a second skin. The underwear under the jeans was a pair of red boy shorts made of stretchy lace. I decided to wear a halter top. It had a deep 'V' in the back which ran down to my waist. No bra with this one. In the front, it had a scoop neck which hinted at my cleavage. It was the same color red as my lipstick. I wore a gold bracelet on my left wrist, a three-tiered gold necklace that hung between my breasts and gold hoops in my ears. I finished it off with black heeled boots and my leather jacket. I quickly sprayed on perfume, pocketing my ID and my lipstick. I was ready for the evening.

    I turned out the lights, headed out the door and over to the clubhouse. When I got inside, I could see everyone seemed to be ready to go. Finding Terror in the crowd, I went over to him. He saw me coming. His eyes were devouring me, and I could see heat in his eyes. I guess I picked the right outfit to wear! When I reached him, he grabbed me by the ass and pulled me tight against him. He gave me a hot kiss and whispered. "Why don't we stay here tonight and celebrate by ourselves?"

    I laughed and shook my head. "No, we need to celebrate with Cannon and then later, if you still want to celebrate just the two of us, we can do that." He sighed dramatically and then agreed. Getting all the guys rounded up, we headed out to the bikes and to the bar.

    We spent the night dancing, drinking and having a great time at the bar. I could tell everyone had a lot of fun. Once the evening was over, Terror took me home. There we celebrated just the two of us and he blew my mind as usual. What a great night!

Chapter 23: Terror

It had been two weeks since Cannon had joined the Warriors as a prospect. Bull was down again for a couple of days to see Harlow. Today, we were hanging out at the garage. Harlow had gone into town to get groceries with Gage and Eric. The guys were just finishing up on a car they had been working on for the last few days. The back ordered parts had come in. We heard the rev of a car coming fast down the road. Looking out toward the front gate, we saw the SUV Harlow had gone out in. It pulled through the gate and whipped into a parking spot fast. That was not the way any of them normally drove, so we hurried over to them.

I got to the car and before I could open the door, Eric jumped out and ran around to the passenger side. He had a look of worry on his face. What in the hell happened? He jerked open the passenger door at the same time, Gage jumped out of the back seat. It was then I noticed they had blood on their shirts.

Harlow stepped down out of the SUV and turned toward us. She looked shaken and I saw she had blood on her. I rushed over and grabbed her. "Where are you hurt? What happened?" I yelled. I was hugging her to me and trying not to hyperventilate. Pushing her away, I patted her over to see where she was bleeding from. She shook her head at me.

"I'm fine. I didn't get hurt. This isn't my blood." She

soothed. Upon hearing that it wasn't her blood, I was able to take a breath. I looked over to Eric and Gage.

"What the fuck happened," I growled. Gage was the one to answer.

"We were coming out of the store and getting the groceries in the car. Out of nowhere, this van pulled up beside us and the side door opened. Two guys jumped out and grabbed Harlow. They were dragging her to get her into the van. We jumped them and started to fight. While we were fighting them, the driver got out and took over trying to get her in their van. We got our two subdued and that's when the one who had a hold of Harlow started to yell. He had blood coming out of a wound on his thigh. We were attracting a lot of attention. People were coming over, so they all jumped in the van and took off."

I looked at Harlow. "Is the blood on you from the guy who had a hold of you? What caused his wound?" She looked at all of us calmly.

"When he grabbed me, I was able to get his knife away from my neck and I stabbed the bastard in the leg. He was distracted by what was going on with the other two guys and the prospects. It stunned him enough to get him to let go of me."

Jesus Christ he'd had a knife to her neck! I could have lost her. "Do you have any idea who it was?" I asked wildly. They all shook their heads no. Eric spoke up.

"I did get a license plate number for the van and the make and model." Well, that was one piece of good news. Holding her close, I told him to go into the clubhouse with Smoke and give him the details, so he could run the information. Bull was now pulling Harlow away from me and into his arms. Once he'd assured himself, she was unharmed, he let go. I told them I was taking her to get cleaned up and we would be back at the clubhouse in a little bit. He reluctantly nodded and then allowed me to lead her away.

In our bathroom, I helped her strip off her bloody clothes. She seemed to be calm, but I wasn't sure if it was because she really was, or if she was in shock. I helped her into the shower. She quickly washed off and got out. After she was dried, I took her to lie down on the bed.

"Babe, how're you feeling? Can I get you anything?" I whispered to her as I held her against my chest and rubbed her back.

"I'm fine, Declan. It was a surprise is all. They were so quick and honestly, I didn't expect someone to try something like that in a busy parking lot. What were they thinking? Also, whoever they were, they had no idea I would fight back. The guy I stabbed was stunned when I did it."

"What the fuck were you thinking to fight with some guy with a knife to your throat?" I half yelled. "He could've slit your throat and you'd be dead."

She eased away from me and frowned. "What did you expect me to do? Let them take me? They probably would've killed me anyway and the prospects too. I did what I've been trained to do. I'm not some helpless woman who faints and waits for a man to rescue her. Would you rather I let them take me?" She snarled back.

I thought about what she said. She was right. It was just my fear talking. I pulled her resisting body close again. "No, I wouldn't rather you went with them. I'm sorry I yelled. This scared me. What would I do if something happened to you? I thought with two guys you'd be safe. I guessed wrong. I need to be able to keep you safe." I tenderly kissed her.

Hearing this she sighed and relaxed into my arms. We stayed this way for about fifteen minutes. She finally stirred. "We need to get back to the clubhouse before dad and the rest of the guys storm in here. They're not a patient bunch." She joked. She was right, we needed to go talk to them and see if Smoke had found out anything. She got dressed and we went back to the clubhouse.

Inside it was a somber mood. All eyes swung to us when we came in the door. Bull, Cannon, and Demon were the first to get to us. All three took turns hugging her and asking if she was okay. Once that was over with, Bull rested his stormy gaze on me. "What the hell? I thought she was covered."

Before I could respond, Harlow did. "Dad, they did have me covered. They were dealing with two of the guys when the third jumped into the mix. I was able to get away from him on my own, just like you taught me. It is no one's fault. Let's concentrate on figuring out who it was. I didn't recognize any of the voices and they had on masks."

He sighed but didn't say anything else. Smoke came out of the hall where his room was. His room was set up with computers and surveillance camera monitors. He was our resident tech guru. Looking at him, no one would think he would have a clue what to do with a computer. Like all of us, he was over six foot, and he had brown, wavy shoulder length hair and green eyes. He sported a goatee like some of us. His thick arms were tattooed with random tattoos all over them.

He was frowning when he joined the group surrounding me and Harlow. I knew it wasn't good news. "Hey Pres, I ran the plate numbers for the van. The van was reported stolen yesterday in Knoxville. I'm hacking into various video feeds around town to see if we can get an idea where they went. Or if we're lucky, a visual on their faces without the masks. This may take a while. I'll let you know if I find out anything."

It wasn't what I wanted to hear, but it was out of our hands. I needed to have church right away, so me and the guys could talk it over. I led Harlow over to the couch and got her seated. Giving her a kiss, I told her. "Babe, we need to have church right now. You stay here and relax. I'll be back as soon as possible. If you want anything let Quin know. He's at the bar." She nodded and sat back. I whistled to the room and yelled, "church now!"

Most of the guys were here, so it was close to full attendance. We all sat down, with the Hunters Creek crew joining us. Even though Cannon was a prospect, since he had been in on helping protect Harlow from the beginning, I allowed him to attend the meeting. Prospects weren't generally involved in church.

I looked at all of them. Every face held looks of anger and frustration. Also, there was worry. I wearily shook my head. "I have no idea who they were. It most likely would be someone with the Bastards, but this doesn't feel like their style. I could see the Bastards rolling up in force on their bikes and taking her. I would hope they were smarter than to do it in broad daylight in a crowded parking lot."

Bull leaned forward. "What about this Tucker shit? Do you think it had anything to do with him?"

I shrugged. "I have no idea. How would he know to look for her here? Smoke has kept tabs on his bank account, and nothing indicates he's left South Carolina, so he couldn't have been one of the ones in the van. And Harlow said she didn't recognize any of the voices and she would know his voice. He could have hired someone to grab her, but again how would he know to come here?" There were numerous murmurs and curses from around the table. Everyone was on edge. Demon spoke up. "So, what do we do now? It's likely they may try again to get her. Having two guys with her wasn't enough. I'd say make her stay in the compound, but we all know she's going to buck that idea."

He was correct and even though I wanted to forbid her to leave the compound, she'd have my balls if I did.

"Until we know more, I want to add a patched brother or Cannon with her, in addition to the two prospects, any time she leaves the compound. I'll go with her as much as possible, so as not to mess with your schedules too much." I looked at Tiny. "Tiny, I know Sherry and Harlow have almost finished the work here at the clubhouse. Until this is resolved, they can postpone doing the rest. I'd like to keep Sherry from going out with her too. This is to keep her safe as well." He nodded his head in agreement. Now the girls might not like it, but I know if I told Harlow it was for Sherry's protection, she'd agree to it.

Turning to Smoke I told him. "Let me know right away if you get anything on the van or those three guys. Keep your eyes peeled when you're all out," I told them. Smoke chimed in.

"It was an older dark blue van. It had blacked out windows and the side mirror on the passenger side was cracked." Apparently one of the guys had given him more details, while I had Harlow at the house. With this settled, we all ended the meeting and returned to the common room. Harlow was still sitting on the couch. Her dad and I went over to her.

"Sweetheart, why don't you go lie down for a little

bit? Later we'll have some dinner. The guys and I'll cook something on the grill. No need for you to cook." I told her. She looked from me to her dad.

"What did you all decide in the meeting," she asked.

"We want you to limit leaving the compound. Now, this doesn't mean you can't leave at all, just consolidate trips and only go if you really need to. For right now, to make sure Sherry is safe, we don't want her to go out with you. You both can spend all the time you want here. In addition, when you do go out, you'll have three of us with you. Two prospects and a patched member or Cannon. I'll be with you as much as I can. Please let us do it this way. Hopefully it won't take long to find these guys and eliminate the risk." I explained.

I could see she wasn't happy with the restriction but also, she understood. She wearily nodded. Bull helped her to her feet. "Go with Terror to the house for a bit and rest. We can talk more later." She hugged him and took my hand. Once back to my house, she took off her shoes and I helped her under the covers on the bed. I laid down beside her and molded her to my side. For a long time, she laid there with her eyes open but not talking. Finally, she closed her eyes and I heard her breathing even out. I continued to think. No one was going to take her away from me. I would kill anyone and everyone who threatened her. She was mine and I planned for her to be with me for the long haul.

Chapter 24: Harlow

It had been three days since the attempt to kidnap me. Smoke hadn't had any luck finding the van or identifying the men. This had Terror in a perpetual bad mood. My dad stayed a couple extra days but then had to get back. Even though Tank could handle things as his VP, there were things which needed his attention. I hadn't been out of the compound and to be honest, it was driving me crazy.

Today, I was doing some finishing touches for the poker run happening at the end of next week. We were going to have some prizes to give away for a silent auction as well. That meant I needed to get the prizes. Sherry and I had decided on those with input from the guys. Terror had decided a majority of the crew would go along to buy them. This meant Sherry would be allowed to go as well, with Tiny glued to her side.

We were all lined up to head out. The prospects were bringing the SUV to carry the prizes. I was riding with Terror and the rest of the guys were on their bikes. Sherry was on the back of Tiny's bike. Our first stop was at the electronics store. We were going to auction off a forty-inch television and a gaming console. The Warriors had a connection at the store, who was going to let them have them at wholesale price. Once we finished there, it was off to our next stop.

The guys all had ideas on what to get, but they

were all geared toward what a man might like. Us girls had convinced them we had to get a few things kids and women would like too. So, our next stop was the spa. There we purchased a spa package. The next place was to get a gift certificate at a boutique in town which sold fabulous and unique women's clothing. Sherry and I had shopped there one day, and we loved it.

Another gift idea from the guys was to have a gun to be auctioned off. At the gun store, we got a Glock 19 handgun. Since most of the guys served, we could get a Glock at "blue label" price, which was only open to active and retired law enforcement officers and military. Ranger had been medically retired from the Army, so he was able to get it for this lower price. Our final stop was at the toy store. We put together a basket of various toys for summer play at the pool.

We'd finished off and were all hungry. The group decided to go to the Fallen Angel. The guys had been super alert all day. I could tell they were leery of someone coming at me, but honestly, with this big of a group, someone would have to be crazy to try anything. When we all filed into the restaurant, the hostess seated us in the Warrior's private area.

Our waitress this time wasn't Kim. It was a new girl and her name tag said her name was Janessa. She was a gorgeous little thing. She stood about five foot three I would say. She had light blond hair down to the middle of her back. Her blond hair was a mixture of white, yellow, and golden strands that shone in the sun. Her face was a perfect oval topped by the bluest eyes I had ever seen. She smiled at all of us. She was nice and joked with us. But she had an underlying reserve I wondered about. I noticed Savage couldn't take his eyes off of her. She had taken his order and there was no way she couldn't see his interest. I saw her blush and stammer a little bit. She hurried away as soon as she finished getting our orders.

I looked down the table to Savage. He was still watching her. I nudged Terror and nodded my head toward Savage. He looked at him and then followed to where he was looking. Seeing Janessa, he laughed and whispered to me. "My brother may have just joined the one woman only group. If the way he's looking at her is an indication, he'll be pursuing her. And looking at her, she's not an easy conquest."

I had to agree. I didn't see Janessa as someone who was looking for a casual hook up. So, if Savage wasn't looking to be with one woman, he'd better forget it. "I think you're right. You might want to warn him. She's not going to fall into his bed only to have him roll out and go to the next woman." He just smirked.

The restaurant and bar area were filling up since it was moving into evening time. At the table closest to our area, a group of four guys sat down. They were talking loudly, and it was obvious they'd had several drinks before they took a seat. Janessa brought us our drinks and told us our food would be out soon. She went to the table with the four guys next. They were flirting heavily with her, but in a much more obnoxious way than the Warriors had. She was looking very uncomfortable, but kept her composure and got their orders.

I could see Savage was watching them. He had a pissed look on his face. I hoped those guys kept it under control. If not, there was likely to be a fight tonight. I excused myself to go to the bathroom. After I finished, I saw Janessa on my way back to the table. I stopped to talk to her for a minute.

"Hi Janessa. I wanted to introduce myself. My name is Harlow. I see you're new here. Please, be assured the Warriors I'm with are a good bunch of guys. Don't let their flirting bother you." I told her.

She smiled sweetly at me. "Thank you. Nice to meet you too, Harlow. I've only been in town for a couple of weeks and started this job a couple of days ago. This helps me with my expenses while I finish school. And the Warriors didn't bother me with their flirting. I know they own this place and I've heard nothing but good things about the club."

"That's great. I'd love to hear about your schooling, but I know you're busy. Why don't you and I get together one day next week and chat? Let me give you my number." I scribbled my cell number on her order pad. She smiled wider and nodded.

"I'd like that. I'll call you to see when it would be a good time." She got called to pick up an order. Before I got back to our table, I stopped to say hello to Lisa and Sam at the bar. Continuing on to the booth, I passed the table with the four guys at the same time Janessa stopped to ask if they needed anything else. The blond guy who was the apparent leader and the most obnoxious, grabbed her arm and tugged her onto his lap. We were both surprised. I stopped and looked at him. I was about to tell him to let her go, when I felt a hand snake around my waist and pull me toward their table. One of the other guys thought he would try the same thing with me! I snapped my elbow back and caught him right in the nose. I heard the crack as it broke. He howled and dropped his arm from my waist to grab his nose with both hands.

I'd stepped forward to get Janessa away from the other creep, when Terror and Savage, along with a couple of the other Warriors appeared. Terror came straight for the guy who had grabbed me. Even though I had taken care of him, this wasn't enough for Terror. He jerked him up from his chair and slammed his head into the table. The guy just moaned louder. Terror gritted out between his teeth. "Never fucking touch my woman again, asshole. You do and I'll kill you." The guy said nothing, just kept nodding his head yes, as blood ran down his face.

I looked over to see what was happening with the other guy who had grabbed Janessa. While I was dealing with my guy, I had overheard the blond speaking to her. He said gruffly. "Come on sweetheart, you know you want some of this. I'll give you a real good ride. Why don't you sit here and feel the cock I'm going to give you?"

Now that I could look, I saw Savage was in his face. He had pulled Janessa out of the guy's lap. She appeared to be shaken. Her face was pale, and her hands were shaking. Savage had such a look of fury on his face. He grabbed the guy and dragged him out of his chair and over to the nearby wall. There he lifted him by the neck up the wall. The guy was sputtering, and his face was turning red. Savage shook him like a rag doll. "Don't you ever touch her again. Never come in here again either. If you see her on the street, go the other way. If I find out you or your buddies bother her in any way, you're all going find yourself planted six feet under. Understand me?" He shook him once more and then let him down. The guy rasped out.

"Okay, no problem, dude," and he scurried over to his friends. All four stood up and one of them threw money on the table. They left in a hurry. Savage walked over to Janessa and took her by the arm. He walked her toward the back of the restaurant where I knew there was an office.

They disappeared into it. I wanted to follow to see if she was all right, but decided Savage had it under control. We headed back to our table. The restaurant had gotten quiet as everyone in there had watched the show. Terror merely nodded at those he passed, then helped me back in my seat. The table was slow to resume talking. Everyone was thinking about those creeps. Terror took my hand and asked me. "Baby, are you okay? Did he hurt you when he pulled you?"

I shook my head. "No, he didn't hurt me. Thank you for coming over even though I had him under control. Do you think Janessa is going to be okay? She looked pretty shook up."

He looked back toward the office and then at me. "I think she'll be fine. Savage will make sure of it. I'll let Sam know to put something extra in her check for putting up with that shit. Not only does he bartend the place, he also acts as the assistant manager." About that time, I saw Janessa and Savage come back from the office. She appeared calmer and he had his hand on her elbow. He left her after saying something in her ear and came back to our table. He took his seat with a frown on his face.

"Is Janessa okay, Savage?" I asked anxiously. He glanced at her and then at me.

"She'll be okay. He just really startled her and then she couldn't break his hold. I told her she needs to learn some self-defense moves. I'd told her I'd be glad to teach her. She was a little hesitant." He grimaced.

"I talked to her earlier about us getting together for coffee and a chat. She seems nice and she's new in town, so probably has no friends. How about if she does, I talk to her and maybe she'll let me teach her?" I suggested. He mulled the thought over for a moment and then smiled.

"That would be great, Harlow. Thanks for trying to get to know her. Let me know when you set up to meet." I could tell he was really interested in her. For the remainder of the evening, she continued to serve us and her other customers with a smile. She would look at Savage with a look of puzzlement from time to time. He kept his eyes on her the whole evening. When we were done, we decided to head back to the clubhouse. As we were leaving, Savage came up to Terror.

"I'm going to hang around here until she gets off work. Just in case those assholes decide to come back or wait for her in the parking lot. I'll see you later." Terror nodded his head in agreement and squeezed his shoulder. The rest of us got on the bikes to head back. It certainly looked like Savage was interested in Janessa. I couldn't wait to see what happened with them.

Chapter 25: Terror

It had been two days since the restaurant fight. Harlow seemed unphased by it. I still got pissed when I thought about it. Why did some guys think it was okay to manhandle women? Yes, I had flirted with a lot of women, but you don't lay a hand on one unless you got the signal saying they are open to it. And even then, if they tell you no, you back the hell off! Janessa and Harlow sure as hell hadn't given them any such sign. My brother, Savage, had gone to the restaurant the next night when she worked. I think he must have gotten her schedule off of Sam. He was quieter than usual. He was interested in her, I could tell.

Today, I decided to take Harlow on a ride, just the two of us. There was this great lake on some property I owned further out in the country. I had gotten some food Sherry put together for me and had it in my saddle bags. I was going to surprise her with a picnic. I reassured the others; we'd be fine on our own. We had been riding for about an hour when I turned off onto this overgrown lane. After riding about a mile in, I parked the bike under the trees. Getting off, I removed the items in the saddle bags and a blanket. Harlow had a surprised look on her face.

"Baby, you looked surprised. I thought we'd have a picnic. There's a beautiful lake right through these trees. It's quiet and private. We can enjoy and take our time.

Come on, follow me." I turned and led her through the trees. On the other side, it opened into lush, green hills and a lovely blue lake with crystal clear water. On the bank, I spread out the blanket. Harlow sat down and began to take out the items Sherry had prepared for us. In the bag, we had a bottle of red wine, which I knew Harlow liked. I was more of a beer or whiskey drinker, but I could deal with wine. Also, we had thick ham sandwiches with cheese and tomato, pasta salad and fresh fruit salad. To finish off, there was a couple of slices of chocolate cake.

I could tell by her face, Harlow was happy. We chose to eat first. After we finished, we laid on the blanket just talking and looking at the sky. After a bit, I asked her if she wanted to swim. She frowned. "Declan, I don't have a bathing suit and whoever owns this could come along at any time. I don't want to get us in more trouble for being here." She explained. I laughed.

"Harlow, I own this land, so no worries about the owner coming along and running us off. As for not having a bathing suit, it's private, so no one else will come here. We can go swimming in our birthday suits." I enticed her. She got a momentary look of surprise on her face.

"Really, you own it? Well, what're you waiting for?" She jumped up and started to pull her clothes off. I watched her as she revealed her lush body. The one I couldn't get enough of. She was down to her pants before I started working on my boots. She finished undressing first of course, but I couldn't have missed seeing her strip. Once I was naked, we walked to the water's edge. She dipped her toes in. I knew it was still a little cool even though it was July. I gathered her in my arms and slowly walked into the lake, immersing us both a little at a time.

By the time I had it up to my shoulders, it felt warm. I had to hold her up since she couldn't touch the bottom in this spot. I kept her pressed to me and bent my head to give her a kiss. I explored her mouth while the refreshing water lapped against our skin.

    Eventually we came up for air. We swam around for a while, splashing and racing each other. I hadn't relaxed and played like this since I was a kid. Eventually we ended up tiring out, so we decided to lay on the blanket again. Once down on the blanket, letting the sun dry us off, I poured her more wine. When she sat down her glass, I yanked her to me and laid her down. Hovering over top of her, I kissed her forehead and down her nose to her chin. She had a little stubborn chin that she liked to jut out when she was pissed. I nibbled her neck and over to her right ear, where I licked and sucked on her earlobe. Placing a kiss behind her ear, I felt her shudder. She always liked to be touched there.

    She was running her hands up and down my sides, up to my shoulders and all over my chest. She kept petting and tweaking my nipples as I kissed her. This led to me moving down to her breasts. She had such full and perfectly rounded breasts. They overflowed my hands. I squeezed each one and then rubbed my thumbs over those sweet nipples. They were hard and begging for attention. I took them between my thumb and forefinger to tweak them. Hearing her ragged breathing, I twisted them a little harder. Her hips rose off the blanket. My woman liked it a little rough. I wanted to see if she would go along with something new today.

    Easing down her body, I came to her beautiful, bare pussy. It was begging me to taste it. I could smell her floral scent with a hint of musk teasing my nose. I pulled her thighs apart and nuzzled my face into her folds. I zeroed in on her clit and sucked until it was hard. Flicking it with the tip of my tongue every once in a while. She was already glistening with her excitement. My licking just made her wetter. I lapped up her sweet juices, swiping my tongue back and forth from her entrance to her clit and back. Every so often, I would stab my tongue into her pussy and circle her opening.

She was panting and moaning now. Her hips wouldn't stay still, and she was begging. "Please Declan, I need to come baby. Please stop teasing me."

I smiled and continued my attack. I ran my forefinger through her juices and slid it down to her puckered back hole. She tensed for a moment and then relaxed. I was able to work my finger into her ass much quicker than last time we'd done this. Once in, I continued to fuck her ass with my finger while I licked her pussy and fucked her pussy with two other fingers. I could feel her body tensing and releasing. She was close. I sped up my movements and she clenched down on my fingers in both her holes. She came with a deep, strangled moan.

I eased her down from her orgasm. I was rock hard and dripping pre-cum. God, she was so gorgeous when she got off. I told her to roll onto her belly. She did so without a word. I raised her ass and eased my cock into her tight pussy. She was so hot and wet. Her pussy pulled my cock greedily inside her. I started out with slow strokes even though I wanted to pound into her. She was working up to another orgasm right away. I leaned down and gently bit the spot between her neck and her shoulder. She jumped. I licked the spot to soothe the sting. She moaned and looked over her shoulder at me with so much heat in her eyes. I whispered. "Do you trust me, baby?"

She nodded at me. With her indication that she did trust me, I reached over to my cut and pulled a small bottle out of the pocket. I'd prepared today just in case she would agree. I had plans to introduce her to something new. I placed some lube at the entrance of her asshole. I worked it in with my finger until she was nice and slick. Pulling my finger from her ass, I pulled her ass up higher. I pressed her head to the blanket. She was watching me over one shoulder, curious to see what I was doing.

I slowly slid my cock out of her pussy and placed the head at the entrance to her asshole. I squeezed a little more lube on my cock. She looked worried and tensed. "Declan, honey, I don't know about this. Your cock is so big, it's going to hurt a lot."

I smiled. "Baby, relax, we'll take it slow and I promise it'll fit and you'll enjoy it. Trust me. If you hate it, I'll stop and I'll never ask you to do it again. Will you let me try?"

She looked at me for a minute and then nodded. "I trust you."

With those words my heart clenched. I eased just the head of my cock into her ass. She was tense but I could tell she was trying to relax. The head of my cock was much broader than a couple of fingers, which is all she'd had up her ass. "Push out," I told her. This helped her to take a bit more in. I planned to get her some toys. A butt plug was on the list. We could have so much fun with it and she would get more pleasure.

I used my other hand to play with her breasts and pussy to help distract her and keep her aroused. I would push in another inch then stop to allow her time to adjust. It was killing me, since she felt so fucking good, but

I wanted her to enjoy it and want to do it again. I loved fucking her pussy, but I enjoyed anal as well and wanted to be able to experience it with her. After several minutes of working in and out, I had all eight and a half inches of my cock buried in her snug ass. She felt even tighter than her pussy, which was the tightest thing I had ever felt. I groaned. She had asked a couple times for me to slow down when it burned and hurt a little too much. But each time she'd indicated after a minute or so, she was ready for more.

I slowly withdrew until just the head remained inside. Then I pushed back in slowly again. Fuck, she felt wonderful! I kept gently stroking in and out while playing with her clit. Soon, she was pushing back when I was pushing in and her body had picked up speed. She was moaning constantly and was saying. "That feels so good, baby. So good." That excited the hell out of me. Suddenly, I couldn't stand it anymore. I slapped her left ass cheek which caused her to tense. Her ass squeezed down on my cock. I grabbed her hair and pulled her head back. Leaning over I kissed her mouth as I fucked her ass. I was going harder and deeper with every thrust. She was asking for me to give her more. "Declan, fuck me harder, go deeper, I need it. Oh God, please don't stop. I didn't know it would feel like this."

Sweat poured off both of us. I could feel my orgasm building in my lower back, and it was coming around to my cock. "Fuck, baby, you feel so good. I'm gonna come." I groaned. I sped up and slammed into her three more times. One the last thrust, I stilled and felt her whole-body shudder as her ass squeezed my cock hard. I shot my cum deep into her tight, little hole. I yelled out her name. I could feel my cock jerking hard and the warmth of my load filling her snug ass. Once she stopped squeezing and I stopped jerking, I slowly and carefully eased out of her. That was the best anal sex I'd ever had in my life.

Lying beside her, I rubbed her arm. She was laying on her stomach with her eyes closed. Her eyes fluttered open and she leaned over to kiss me. After she was done, I told her. "Baby, thank you for trusting me. Did you like it, or do you never want to do it again?"

She laughed. "I think you could tell I liked it. I thought my orgasm and begging for more would've been a clue. Yes, we can definitely do it again. I loved it, just like I love everything you do to my body. I trust you completely." Her words made me feel so good. I gave her a kiss.

"Harlow, you can always trust me, and babe, that was the best anal sex of my life. Every time with you is the best. I don't know what I did to deserve you, but thank God I did. Baby, I love you." This was the first time I had told her I loved her. I looked into her eyes waiting to see how she would respond. I'd never told a woman I loved her. I always thought that was something special and not something you just said to any woman.

She got a huge smile on her face. Her eyes were glowing. She whispered back. "I love you too, Declan Moran." She then gave me a deep kiss. We kissed for several more minutes. After stopping for air, we took a nap. We woke up about an hour later and took another dip in the lake, before drying off and packing up. It was getting close to dusk when we left and headed back to the compound.

I couldn't help but smile the whole ride back. I was enjoying the feel of her arms around me. We were about ten miles from the compound, when a truck coming from the other direction, suddenly veered into our lane. I quickly jerked the bike to the right which put us in the gravel and debris alongside the road. The front tire started to lose traction and skid out from under us. I tried to wrestle it under control, but it was too late. We went down in a skid and ended up in the ditch.

The truck kept going. It never even slowed down. I eased my left leg out from under my bike. I could feel the road rash down my entire left side. It hurt like a bitch. But that had to wait, I needed to find out how Harlow was. I saw her laying a little further over in the ditch. I hobbled over to her yelling. "Harlow, are you alright? Talk to me, baby. I need to know you're okay." I reached her to see her eyes were closed and she was bleeding from a gash on her forehead. My heart seized and I couldn't catch my breath. Was she dead? Please God, let her be alright!

I shook her lightly since I didn't know the extent of her injuries. She didn't open her eyes. I could see her chest rising and falling now, so I knew she was alive. I called 911 and then I placed a call to Savage. I told him we'd had an accident and where we were. He said they were on their way. I waited for someone to come and tried to get her to wake up. It was obvious she had road rash like I did, but I didn't know about internal injuries. I could hear the roar of bikes not too much later. Where in the fuck was the goddamn ambulance?

Savage and what looked like the whole club pulled in. Bull was the first one off his bike, with the others not far behind. He ran over and dropped to his knees. "Harley, sweetheart, it's dad, you need to wake up honey. Come on, wake up." He pleaded. I could see the fear on his face, which had to match what was on mine. She remained motionless.

Ghost slid in beside him. He had corpsman experience and volunteered, when needed, as a paramedic with the Dublin Falls emergency team. He'd brought his medic bag. He pulled out a penlight and lifted her eyelids to check her pupils. He didn't remove her helmet. I knew it was because he was worried, she might have a neck injury. He then pulled out a stethoscope and BP cuff to check her heart rate and blood pressure. He ran his hands up and down her arms, ribs, and legs gently squeezing. Obviously feeling to see if he could feel a break. About that time, I heard the sirens. In a couple of minutes, the ambulance pulled in and the paramedics jumped out.

They knew Ghost of course, and greeted him. He then started to rattle off his assessment. "We have a twenty-four-year-old female. She went down on the bike approximately twenty minutes ago. She has remained unconscious since the wreck. Her pupils are equal and reactive to light. Her heart rate is seventy-six and her BP is one twenty over eighty. She has extensive road rash down her left side. I hadn't had a chance to remove her clothes to see if she has other visible injuries. There's a gash to her forehead. I checked her arms, ribs and legs and felt no obvious breaks." As he finished his assessment, they took over. Ghost then turned to me. "Let me check you out while they work on her."

I shook my head. "No, I'm okay. She's the one who needs help. Other than road rash, I feel fine." I assured him. I kept my eyes glued to Harlow. Please God, let her be okay. It was all I kept repeating to myself over and over in my head. She had to be alright. I couldn't live without her. Savage and Bull leaned down to me.

"What happened? Why'd you go off the road?" Bull tersely asked. I explained to them what happened and also the description of the truck. Even though it happened fast, I had trained myself in the Army to watch for and recall details. Sometimes it saved your life. It had been a big half ton, red Ford pickup with the extended wheels. By this time, the sheriff had arrived. Since it was outside of town, it was in their jurisdiction. They were loading Harlow in the ambulance. They told me to ride along since I needed attention as well. I told the sheriff to come to the hospital and I would give him my statement. He didn't question it and said he would be there. We could talk after I got checked out. The ride to the hospital felt like it took forever. I was getting more scared by the minute. What if she didn't wake up? Why in the hell had that truck moved into our lane? It was no accident. I saw it driving fine until we appeared then it whipped into our lane on purpose. Someone was going to pay.

Once we reached the ER, they rushed Harlow back into the exam area. I followed them even though a nurse was trying to get me in a wheelchair. In the exam rooms, I insisted we be in beds next to each other. They reluctantly agreed. Ghost had come back with us and told them it was best if they just did it. They wouldn't leave the curtain open while they examined her, but I knew Ghost would stay on top of them and update me. A doctor and nurse were now talking to me and performing their exam. It irritated me. They checked me out and only saw road rash. I told them I hadn't hit my head and didn't have a headache. Other than the road rash hurting, I had no other pain. The doctor still wanted to have some x-rays done and maybe a CAT scan. I reluctantly agreed, but I told them not until they finished with Harlow.

I could hear bits and pieces of what her doctor and nurse were saying about Harlow. I heard one of them say she might have a brain injury. Another questioned if she was internally bleeding. My stomach seized and I wanted to puke. I could hear more muttering but no distinct words. I was about to get off my bed to see what was happening, when Ghost came around the curtain.

"Listen, Pres they need to take her for some tests. They are going to x-ray her, do an MRI and possibly a CAT scan. These are just precautions to make sure nothing is broken or internally bleeding, as well as ruling out a brain injury. It takes time, so try and be patient and let them treat you. They know to give us an update as soon as they know anything." He explained.

I reluctantly laid back on the bed. I would try to be patient, but I needed to get out of this bed soon. They came after they took Harlow and had me get my x-rays and CAT scan. Everything came back fine. I really had only sustained the road rash, which a nurse was scrubbing with some shit that stung like a bitch. They'd given me some meds to help with the pain, but it felt like I was on fire. They had to use a brush to get the gravel, ground in dirt, and other debris out of my skin. The nurse was scrubbing so hard in some of the areas, she was rocking my body on the exam table. While the nurse was scrubbing, I looked down at what she was doing. The whole area she'd already scrubbed looked like it was bleeding. I found myself sweating from the intensity of the fire moving through my body. When she was done, she applied these almost rubbery looking bandages to my road rash area which was cool and soothing. I asked her what kind of bandages they were, and she said they had silver nitrate in them. She assured me after a few bandage changes with these, the road rash would be healed. I'd never know I had had it. Once the torture was over,

I drifted for a bit. A little while later, the sheriff came in and took my statement. He said they would put out a BOLO (be on the lookout) to the local and county police on the truck. I knew my guys would be searching too. Now, if only they would come back and tell me Harlow was awake and alright.

Chapter 26: Harlow

I felt like I was swimming in a dark pool. I was slowly making my way to the surface. I could hear something that sounded like a constant, annoying beeping. I sped up my swimming. As I became more aware, I could see light even though my eyes were closed. I tried so hard to open them, but they seemed to weigh a ton. Then I noticed someone was holding my hand. That hand felt familiar. As I struggled to make sense of what was going on, the hand squeezed mine and then I heard a voice. His voice.

"Harlow, baby, please. You need to wake up right now. I'm going to lose my fucking mind if you don't. The doctors say you have a concussion but no other brain injury. They're not sure why you're not awake. Come on baby, I need you. I love you. You have to be okay." Terror whispered. I could hear the worry and fear in his voice.

Why did I have a concussion? I could feel my body and it was hurting all over. The left side hurt the worst and burned. I tried to move my arm, but it stayed where it was. Was I paralyzed? Please God not that! I struggled more and was able to lightly squeeze his hand. He jumped.

"Babe, you can hear me! Now open your eyes. I need to see those gorgeous violet eyes of yours. You know the nurses have been checking your pupils and all of them remark on how beautiful and unusual they are. Please wake up."

I heard movement, like someone else had entered the room. Then I felt a hand on my face. I smelled my dad's cologne. "Hey baby girl, you need to wake up. You've rested enough, now it's time to get up. You're killing all of us. The hospital is about to kick us all out because their waiting room is filled with bikers. You have the Dublin Falls and Hunters Creek guys here. We love you. We need you to wake up." He ordered.

I really had to wake up. I gave it one last try putting my whole effort into it. My eyelids slowly rose. I had to blink because the light was so bright. I saw my dad looking down at me. The chair at the side of the bed scraped across the floor and then I was looking up at Terror. Both of them looked haggard and had lines of worry around their eyes and mouths. I wanted to reach up and wipe those looks away, but I still couldn't lift my arms.

"Thank God," Terror whispered. He was kissing me like he would never get to again. Once he stopped and leaned back, my dad bent down and gave me a kiss on the cheek. He had tears in his eyes like Terror. These two big, strong men were in tears. What had happened?

I saw Terror push a button on the bed and a voice came over a speaker asking if she could help us. Terror told her I was awake. Within a few minutes, I had a couple of nurses and a doctor in my room. They had dad and Terror leave even though I wanted them to stay. The doctor and nurses spent the next twenty minutes poking, prodding and in general annoying me. They finally must have been satisfied since they decided to leave. They ordered me to rest. I asked them to send my dad and Terror back to my room.

Both of them were in the door within seconds.

Dad took the chair on the right side of the bed and Terror the one on the left. Each of my hands was being swallowed up by their big ones. Terror started first. "Baby, do you remember what happened?" I frowned. I didn't remember. I concentrated hard and then I saw an image of a big, red truck and then remembered feeling pain.

"I remember a red truck and feeling pain but that's all. Did it hit us?"

"Yes, there was a truck. It didn't hit us, but it swerved into our lane. We hit debris on the side of the road and went down on the bike. I'm so fucking sorry I couldn't keep from going down. I would never do anything to hurt you. Do you remember where we went before the wreck?"

I thought back and then recalled us going to the lake, the picnic and then making love with Terror. I blushed and nodded to him. He smiled, winked and said. "I'm glad you didn't forget that. I know I won't."

I looked at my dad. He had a curious look on his face but didn't ask what we meant, thank goodness! Dad then spoke up. "The police are looking for the truck and so is the club. It wasn't an accident, honey. The driver intentionally ran the two of you off the road. Not sure why he didn't stop, but he must have thought the wreck had done you both in. You just need to rest and get better so we can take you home."

I thought that sounded really good. I was suddenly feeling very tired. I yawned. Dad said he was going to go let the guys know I was awake and how I was doing. Terror remained in his chair holding my hand. I drifted off secure in the knowledge he was with me and nothing bad would happen.

It was dark when I woke up the next time. Terror

was snoozing in the chair where he had been when I fell asleep. Had he even moved? He looked exhausted. He needed to go get some rest. I saw in the other chair that my dad hadn't come back. Instead, Demon was there. He was reading a book. I moved to adjust myself in the bed since my butt hurt and he looked up. Seeing I was awake, he stood and leaned over the bedrail.

"Hello beautiful. It's good to see those pretty eyes. How're you feeling? Do you need anything? The nurse said to use this machine if you needed pain meds. You're beat to hell and have to be feeling it." He whispered. I saw the relief in his eyes.

"I'm fine, Luca. I do hurt, but I'm not sure if I should take any pain meds. You know how I hate to take any kind of medication since it makes me loopy." I told him. I rarely called him by his real name, but it seemed right that I did this time.

"You need to keep on top of your pain, so press this button right here." I heard Terror say. Our talking must have woken him up. He went ahead and showed me which button he meant, and he pushed it for me. Meds were released into my IV. I could feel it almost immediately. He then went on to explain I could push this every hour if I needed it. The nurse had said not to worry about taking too much. It was time-controlled and if I tried to push it too soon, it wouldn't administer more medication. That was good to know.

I touched his face. "Declan, babe, you went down too. You have to be in pain. What injuries do you have?" This time I was more lucid and was thinking about his injuries. Shouldn't he be in a hospital bed too? Why was he sitting here rather than resting at the house if he didn't need to be in the hospital? I got restless thinking about it.

"Now settle. I'm fine. They did give me pain pills which I'll take if needed. I got a road rash down my left side, which hurt like hell when they cleaned it. You were lucky, they cleaned your road rash while you were out. You have a concussion, a small gash on your head along with the rash, but thankfully nothing else. You've been out and wouldn't wake up for a whole day and had us worried to death." He finished with a big frown on his face.

Wow, I had lost a whole day. I recalled what they told me earlier about the truck. Observing both of them I asked, "did they find the truck?"

Terror gave a negative shake of his head. "No, they haven't found it yet. I have Smoke looking for it through his cameras and contacts. I doubt the police would think to use cameras. Right now, we're trying to figure out who it was. It may have been the Bastards, but this doesn't seem their style. It might be the same guys who tried to grab you before. But why try to kill you, when last time they seemed bent on taking you?" He considered.

It did worry me that we didn't know who was behind it. However, we had things to do. The poker run was in five days and I had to be there for it. It was too important for the club and the community. I wiggled up in the bed. Damn that hurt! "Did the doctors say when I could go home?"

"You just woke up a couple of hours ago! They want to monitor you to be sure everything is okay. Doc did say if everything checked out, you could go home tomorrow evening at the earliest. Try to rest and we'll see." Terror chided.

I wasn't happy to stay, but I would do what the doctor ordered. I wanted out of here and back in our bed.

I nodded my head, so he knew I understood. He kept rubbing my arm. Demon gave me a kiss on the cheek. "I'm going to go, babe. Some of the others are anxious to see you. Are you okay if they come in one at a time?"

"Yeah, that's fine. I'd like to see them. It'll help pass the time until they spring me from this place." He laughed and left. Terror still had such a look of worry on his face that I told him to come closer. He bent down and I laid a passionate kiss on him. He quickly took over the kiss and devoured me like he hadn't seen me in years and was starved. A throat being cleared brought us back. Standing in the door was Cannon.

Seeing he had our attention; he came the rest of the way into the room and over to my side. He gave me a kiss on the cheek like Demon had. I could tell Terror wasn't crazy about other guys kissing me, even if it was on the cheek and strictly as friends. He'd have to get used to it because I tended to be affectionate with those I knew and liked.

"You look better than you did. You have some color in your cheeks. Before you were white as a ghost. I thought we were going to have to tranquilize your dad, Demon, and Terror," he joked. Terror just gave him a shitty look and grunted. "I wasn't that bad."

"Sure, you weren't. The nurses were hiding when they saw one of you three coming." Cannon laughed.

"I can't imagine them hiding. If they did it's because they saw the whole gang and thought, you were going to trash the joint. You guys can look terrifying." I told them. At that they both laughed. Cannon spent a little bit of time just chatting and then left. Over the next few hours, I saw every one of the Dublin Creek guys, including the prospects, Sherry, then over half the guys from dad's club.

It made me feel so good they all cared that much about me. Those thoughts must have been on my face when the last one left, because Terror bent down and whispered in my ear. "Everyone loves you, baby. How couldn't they?" He placed a soft kiss on my lips, and I drifted off to sleep.

The next day passed much like the day before. I had visitors in between the doctors and nurses doing their checks and tests. They decided to make me spend one more night, so I didn't get discharged until ten a.m. the following day. I was wheeled out of the hospital in a wheelchair. They wouldn't let me walk. At the entrance, was the club's SUV. Terror helped me up and got me buckled into the passenger seat. As he got in behind the wheel, I heard the rev of bikes. Looking behind us, I saw at least ten bikes lined up. I guess we were getting an escort home. I was glad because I was nervous about whoever was after me trying something again. I looked at Terror. He winked and we got on the road. When we got back to the house, I was going to get him to take a nap with me. He looked exhausted. I would tie him down if I had to. Hmm. Kinky. Maybe we could try that one day when I was feeling better.

Chapter 27: Terror

She was home. I was so glad to see her out of the hospital and in my bed. She still looked beat up and was moving really slow. She was in pain but trying to push through it. I might end up having to make her rest. I felt exhausted and my road rash hurt. But there was no way I could've left her in the hospital and gone home to sleep. Even with all the club there, it was my job to watch over her. She was mine and I protected what was mine. This thought made me pissed off. I hadn't protected her and that was eating away at me. I knew realistically I couldn't have foreseen that truck running us off the road, but it still rankled me. Whoever it was, they were going to pay when I found them, and we were going to find them. It was only a matter of time.

When we got home, I hustled her into bed. First though, she insisted on a shower. She said she needed to get the hospital smell off of her. I helped her to remove her dressings before I removed mine. Once in the shower, I carefully washed her. She told me she could do it herself, but I didn't want to chance her falling. Besides, any chance to touch her body I would take. I got pleasure from just looking at her and touching her. Sex didn't always have to be the outcome.

Once we were done and our bandages reapplied, she insisted I take a nap with her. I wanted to go and check if Smoke had found anything. However, I knew if he had, he would come tell me immediately. I slid under the covers with her. I spooned her body and rested one of my arms across her waist. I cupped her breast. She quickly went to sleep, and I felt myself slip away not long after she did.

I woke up and looked at the clock. Wow, we had been asleep for six hours. I eased back out from under her. Sometime during the nap, she'd practically crawled on top of me. She was still out. I quietly put on my clothes. I left her with her cell phone right by the bed and a note to call me when she woke up. Also, I told her one of the guys would be downstairs if she needed anything. Hopefully I would be back before she woke up. This was just in case I wasn't. When I got to the clubhouse, I pulled Kade aside and asked him to go and wait at my house in the living room. I wanted someone there as well in case something happened. Call me paranoid, but I wasn't taking any chances with Harlow.

The majority of the club members from Hunters Creek were still hanging around the clubhouse. They all started asking me how Harlow was. They were truly worried about her. She had grown up in the Hunters Creek club, so it made sense they felt that way. I was surprised at how much she had won over my club in the less than two months she'd been here. It was like she had always been a part of us. I planned to make sure she stayed with us forever. I told them she was doing better but still sleeping. The worry eased on many of their faces. Demon, Bull, and Cannon still looked very worried. I saw Smoke coming out of the back. He strolled immediately over to me.

"Hey, Terror. How's Harlow?" He anxiously asked. I repeated what I'd already told the others. "Just to let you know, I've found what I think is the truck. It showed up on a camera in Maryville. I ran the license plate, but it shows as plates for a Dodge Charger, so they're obviously stolen plates. I am checking the DMV records for anyone owning this type of truck in Tennessee, Kentucky, or North Carolina. That way we can try and rule people out. Unfortunately, I can't make out the face of the driver. I have a program running which may clean the image up for us. We'll just need to give it time. Let me know if Harlow needs anything."

I clapped him on the back in appreciation. "Thanks Smoke, for the update and all the work you're doing. Harlow seems to not need anything. She's just resting but I do appreciate the offer."

"No problem. I'm glad to help. Harlow is one of ours. We protect what's ours. She's good for you man." He grinned and then walked off to talk to Hawk and Hammer. Bull slid in beside me.

"Do you think it was the Bastards? Because they're the obvious choice, but to me this doesn't feel like their kind of deal. Riding up on you and gunning you down, sure. Running you off the road and not even stopping to check to see if your dead doesn't. I'm wondering if it has something to do with that Tucker asshole? He could've hired someone to do it and stayed in South Carolina to keep his hands clean."

I thought about what Bull said. I agreed about the Bastards. As for Tucker, that was a possibility. I wanted to have church, so I called over Savage. He sauntered over. "What do you need Pres," he asked?

"Send out a text to all the guys not here. Tell them I want to have church within the hour. It looks like there are only a few of them missing. Let everyone else know to stick around for it. I want the Hunters Creek guys to attend as well." He nodded and walked off, already typing away on his phone. I turned back to Bull.

"We'll discuss your idea in church. Right now, I left Harlow sleeping. Kade is at the house in case she wakes up and needs anything. I want her to get as much rest as she can, so she can heal. I have to tell you, it scared me to death when we went down, and she wouldn't wake up. I thought I'd lost her. I have to be sure she's protected."

He grinned. "Yeah, you've got it bad. I felt the same way about her momma. Anything putting her in danger drove me crazy. We'll find the ones responsible; I promise. Let's get a drink."

I followed him to the bar and got a beer. It was around five in the afternoon. Demon and Cannon came to join us. We all sat and silently drank our beers deep in thought. Before I knew it, an hour had gone by. I stood and called everyone to church. The last of the guys missing had come in ten minutes ago. We all went to the meeting room and took our seats.

"Okay, I know everyone is more than aware of what went down a couple of days ago. Bull and I were talking about it. As much as we'd like to lay this at the door of the Bastards, we don't think they did this. It doesn't match their style of doing things. Shooting us, yes; running us off the road and keep going, no. Bull brought up the idea, could it be this Tucker bastard? He may still be in South Carolina, but he could've hired someone else to do it for him. I want your thoughts. We have to figure this out, because I can't stand to have her in danger."

Several of the guys were nodding their heads. I could see they hadn't thought of it being anyone but the Bastards. However, the thought had merit. Smoke was sitting there with his laptop. He almost always brought it to church in case there was anything we needed to look up right away. He was clicking away on his keyboard. I let them discuss the possibility for a few minutes. Finally, Smoke looked up.

"Pres, if he's behind this, then he's being smart about it. If he paid someone, there's no indication of it in his bank account. I'm monitoring his phone records, and no unusual calls showed up to new numbers. He seems to call the same set of people. But I can't rule out that he hasn't found another way such as another person's phone or a burner phone. He could have had cash available to pay someone. I agree this doesn't sound like the Bastards. What do you want to do?"

That was the question. We had the poker run in a few days. Until it was over, we couldn't send a group to check on him in person. However, I didn't want to wait. Then I thought of something. "Let's call Agony with the Pagan Souls. They have a chapter close to Charleston. I believe. Maybe they can send someone down to check him out. After the poker run, we'll dig into him ourselves. I'm not crazy with letting him hang out there waiting to see if he comes after her." They all seemed in agreement. I pulled out my cell phone and called Agony right there.

"What's up Terror?" He asked when he answered.

"Agony, I need some help and I hope you guys can assist."

"Sure, tell me whatcha need."

"We wondered if your chapter of the Souls down around Charleston, South Carolina could go and check out a fucker for us. He's someone we believe either is, or will be, coming after Harlow. She was under his command in the Marines. We've had two attempts on her. The first one, they tried to grab her in the parking lot of the grocery store. The second one, a truck ran us off the road a couple of days ago when we were out on the bike. It was no accident." I told him.

"What the fuck! Are you two alright?"

"Yeah, I got road rash, she got the same but also a gash on her head, a concussion and was unconscious for a day. I just got her home this morning. We don't think this is the Bastards way of coming after us."

"I agree with you about the Bastards. I'll call the president of the Charleston chapter and have them check him out. They're on a run, however, they're due back in a couple of days. Send me the information on this asshole. I hope Harlow gets better soon. Let me know if you need anything else."

Thanking him, I signed off the call. I felt better now that someone would be checking in on him soon. Since we were all together, we ran through everything for the poker run. It seemed like Harlow and Sherry had finished getting things set up. It was in four more days. We were going to station at least two members at each stop to be there to prevent trouble and to help out. There would be five stops total. Best poker hand wins. There would be light snacks and drinks at the first four stops while the bulk of the food would be at the final stop. This was where the band would be. Also, we would auction off those prizes at the final stop. It looked like it was going to be a good turnout based upon advance sales. I knew more people would sign up the day of the ride. With all that squared away, we broke up the meeting. I was anxious to go check on Harlow. I was exiting the clubhouse when my phone rang. I saw that it was Kade. I hurried to answer it. "What's wrong?"

"Nothing's wrong, Pres. I just wanted to let you

know I heard her moving around. I asked her through the door if she needed anything and she said no. But I think she's in a lot of pain. I could hear it in her voice."

"I'm almost there. Give me a second." I hurried across the remainder of the lot and up the steps. I jerked the door open. Kade was standing in the entry waiting for me. I gave him a chin lift in thanks. He asked. "Do you want me to go get something to eat? She has to be hungry." He offered.

I thought about it. He was right. She hadn't eaten since breakfast and taking those pain pills on an empty stomach wasn't a good idea. I asked him to go to the Italian place in town Harlow liked. I told him to order lasagna, alfredo pasta with breadsticks and salad. That should do the trick. We'd had food from there a couple of weeks ago and she'd loved it. After I thanked him, he headed out.

I took the stairs two at a time. I knocked on the bedroom door and entered. She was stiffly sitting on the edge of the bed. She glanced up quickly when I entered. She gave me a slight smile. She had on a nightgown now. She must had put one on. I could tell she was trying to hide the pain. Bullshit, she was going to take those meds. I walked over and sat down beside her.

"Baby, you need to take your meds. Don't argue about it. I can see you're in pain. You'll heal quicker if you can rest. Kade ran out to get us some food from the Italian place. He'll be back within a half hour. Why don't we get you in the tub to soak and by the time you're done with your bath, he'll be here with the food. You can take a pain pill then. You don't want to take those on an empty stomach."

I was surprised when she didn't give me any resistance. I knew that had to mean she was in a lot of pain. I helped her to the bathroom. While she used the toilet, I started to run her a tub of water. I made sure to put a generous amount of Epsom salts in it. Though it might sting her road rash, the road rash had scabbed over already. The Epsom salt would help with those sore muscles. We'd play it by ear. Once she was done, I helped her over to the tub and removed her gown and bandages. She had some bright purple and blue spots on her body. I had the same. I decided to get in with her. We both got into the hot water. It felt great. I relaxed back with her between my legs.

We just sat quietly enjoying the hot water and the relaxation it brought. The Epsom salts didn't seem to bother the road rash at all. After about twenty minutes, we got out and toweled off. She didn't want to be back in her pajamas, so I helped her get into shorts and one of my tee shirts. She swam in the shirt, but I loved seeing her in my clothes. I got her situated, raised up with pillows so she could relax. I turned on the television in the bedroom. We settled on an old rerun of a custom bike building show. I was lucky she liked the bike show as much as I did. About ten minutes later, I got a text from Kade saying he was back with our food and at the door. I went down to let him in. I thanked him then he headed over to the clubhouse. In the kitchen, I pulled out plates and silverware and got both of us a plate of food. I carried them up to the bedroom.

She got a few bites in her before I insisted on her taking a pain pill. We didn't talk, just ate and relaxed watching the show. She did comment that she thought the guys could do as good or better job on a custom bike as the guys on the show. I had to agree. She didn't eat much, but insisted she was full. I'd try to get more in her later.

I took our plates back to the kitchen and cleaned up the mess. I heard a knock at the front door when I was on my way back upstairs. I answered it to find Bull, Cannon, and Demon all standing on my doorstep.

I greeted them. "Hey guys. I expect you want to see Harlow. She's upstairs in the bedroom. Why don't you relax in the living room and I'll go get her? She took a pain pill just a bit ago, so hopefully she's feeling a little better." They agreed and took a seat while I headed up.

I entered the bedroom. She asked me who I was talking to. I told her who was downstairs. She was more than willing to go down to see them. I insisted she only go down for a little while, since I didn't want her to overdo it. She just gave me an adorable frown. I kissed her hard then helped her down the stairs and to the living room.

All three of them stood when she came in. They took turns gently hugging her and asking how she was. When they were all done, we sat down. I pulled her into the oversized chair to sit with me. Demon and Cannon took the sofa and Bull the love seat.

"Baby girl, can I get you anything? Have you eaten? I can go get something. You need to keep your strength up." Bull said.

"No dad, I don't need anything. Terror has been taking real good care of me. He had Kade go get me food. As a matter of fact, I know there are a bunch of leftovers. Why don't you guys get some. It's Italian." I nodded and told them where to find the plates and utensils. They all went and grabbed some.

Once they were all reseated, Demon spoke. "Harley, seriously, how are you feeling, babe? You have to be sore. Make sure you stay on top of your pain. We hate like hell you have to go through this. You need to let us know if you need anything."

She smiled. Then she looked at me and back to them. "Okay, enough talking about me. Who do you think did this? I don't think it was the Bastards. You guys have to have thoughts." That was my woman. Right to the point. I wanted to keep her out of it, but I knew that wasn't going to happen. I broke the silence.

"Baby, we don't think it was the Bastards either. We're having the Souls down in South Carolina checking on that asshole, Tucker. We want to see if he may have hired someone to come after you. That's where we're at right now. I wish I had more. Just know we're on it."

I could see she was thinking about what I said. She nodded her head and sighed. "What about the poker run? Is there anything I need to follow up on before Saturday? I want to be sure it's a success."

"Everything is set. We talked it over in church today. All there is to do is man the stations on Saturday. If you're feeling better, maybe you can come for a little bit." When I finished, she sat up straight and gave me a peeved look. "

I plan on going Saturday and I'll decide how long I'll stay! I appreciate you wanting to take care of me, but I'm an adult. I'll decide when I've had enough. I spent a lot of time on this. I want to see how it goes." She snipped. She had a frown on her face and heat in her eyes.

I couldn't resist as usual. I grabbed the nape of her neck and pulled her in for a kiss. She tasted so good. I licked at her mouth until she let me in. I was lost in her when I heard Bull speak. "Can you stop devouring my daughter like you're going to rip her clothes off in front of me? Shit man, this isn't something a dad wants to see." He groused. We broke apart laughing. They stayed for over an hour and we just chatted and had a good time. I saw her yawn a couple of times. Apparently, so had the guys. Demon stood up and was the first to say they needed to go.

Within five minutes, all three had said goodbye, hugged her, slapped me on the shoulder and left. I helped her back upstairs where she laid down and was out like a light within five minutes. I stayed awake for a few more hours. I couldn't stop thinking about the wreck. Was Tucker behind it? God help him if he was. I turned out the light and wrapped her in my arms. She sighed in her sleep and snuggled into me. This was the best way to sleep.

Chapter 28: Harlow

The day of the poker run was a sunny one. The temp was in the high eighties which was unusual for July. To add to it, the humidity was lower which was perfect. That was going to make for a great day to ride. I was stationed at the final stop. Terror insisted he stay with me, along with several of the guys not manning the other stops. The turnout was fabulous. To ride each person had to pay fifty dollars with an additional rider costing ten more dollars. A lot of the riders had passengers. It was a steep price but because it was for the hospital, we wanted to make as much as possible. People seemed willing to pay the amount. In all, we ended up with two hundred and fifty riders and one hundred seventy-five passengers. This brought us in at just under thirteen thousand dollars. The winner would get half the money. In addition, there were straight donations. We would total those, the auction profits and sales of the food at the end of the night.

  The riders were starting to trickle in at the last stop. Everyone was enjoying the food and drinks. In an hour the band would be setting up to play. Kids were running around and having fun. We held it at the large park on the edge of Dublin Falls. There was a huge playground area for the kids to play on. In addition, there were shelter buildings to set up food in and bathrooms. A plus in my mind. No one liked to use port-a-potties. It was perfect.

Terror made sure I stayed close to him. A couple of hours later, the last rider had made it.

As evening approached, the auction items were raffled off. The band had gotten started and many people were dancing. I'd gotten Terror to slow dance with me which was a surprise. He didn't want me to do anything even a little bit strenuous. He kept asking if I felt okay. I reassured him I was fine. I'd been sitting for most of the day, since none of them would let me do anything. I was watching the band when I saw Laci over by the food stands. She was staring at Terror as usual. She hadn't been around the club lately, now that I thought about it. She must have gotten the message he was off limits. She saw me looking at her and turned away. Oh well, she could look, just not touch.

I was talking to a couple of people from the local businesses who had offered their services for free. Two prospects were standing with me, since Terror had been called away to check on something. Dad, Demon, and Cannon were busy with one of the vendors who was having trouble. All of a sudden, someone started yelling about a fire in one of the buildings on the far end of the park. I saw Terror along with some other Warriors run off to check it out. I could see flames from where I was standing, so it was pretty advanced. Others were trying to keep people calm. No one wanted to cause more panic.

The prospects and I were watching when Laci ran up. She had a look of fright on her face. She grabbed Gage and Eric's arms. "I need your help! Two little kids are missing. We don't know if they're over near the fire or not. Please help me look. The parents went over there to look." She gestured to another area of the park with more playground equipment. It was getting dark and harder to see. All three of us took off with her.

We'd just rounded the corner of one of the buildings, when I felt someone grab me and clasp a hand over my mouth. I saw Eric and Gage go down as two guys knocked them in the head. I struggled, but weakly since the guy holding me had a cloth over my mouth. It smelled funny. I was getting drowsy and weak. As my eyes fell shut, I saw Laci smile and heard her say. "Now Terror will be mine." My last thought before I fell unconscious was of Terror and how much I loved him. The blackness overtook me.

I woke up what seemed like hours later. I was in a building in what looked like some kind of basement. I was in a chair with my arms tied behind my back and my ankles tied to the chair legs. Whoever tied me had done a good job. I listened to see if I could hear anything. All I heard was silence. I wondered how long I'd been out. Where had they taken me? Did Terror know I was gone yet? How would they find me?

My head ached. They must have used chloroform to knock me out. Was it the Bastards? I hoped Eric and Gage were alright. They had been hit pretty hard. Thinking of Laci, I had to give her credit, she'd played us perfectly. Using lost kids was guaranteed to get our attention. When I got out of here, I was going to beat that bitch within an inch of her life! Did she really think with me gone? Terror would turn to her? I knew him and my dad had to be going crazy.

It looked like it might be a long night. I looked around the basement to see if there was anything I could use to get loose. Unfortunately, there was nothing. I'd bide my time and when the time was right, I'd get the fuck out of here. I'd just found Terror and there was no way

I was going to lose him. I tried to relax to conserve my energy.

Several hours later I was aroused from a light nap, when the basement door was opened. Down the steps came someone I did recognize. It was that fucking creep, Tucker. I should've known he was behind this. He strutted over to me with a big smile on his face. God, I hated this slimy bastard!

"Well, hello, Harlow. It's so good to see you again. Did you have a nice nap?" I just ignored him and stared him down.

"I see you're as stubborn as ever. I told you we'd meet again someday. You caused me a lot of grief. It was because of you that I was forced to put in my papers. Apparently, someone tattled to the wrong person in the chain of command. I don't know why you lied about what happened. We both know you wanted me and was just playing hard to get. Well, we're alone this time, so no need to worry about anyone interrupting us. We're going to have such a good time."

He made my skin crawl. The bastard was delusional. He thought I wanted him and had only been trying to play hard to get? He was going to rape me that day out in the desert. How he could think fighting him was playing hard to get, I had no idea. I did know one thing. I would fight him until my last breath. He wasn't going to rape me. He came over and ran his finger along my jawline. I held back my shudder. I didn't want to give anything away to him. He enjoyed toying with people. I wasn't going to give him the satisfaction.

"My new friend, Laci, sure came through. She told me you would be there today and came up with the idea on how to get you away from your bodyguards. You've been a lot of trouble. First at the store, when my guys tried to get you and those asshole bikers stopped them. I admit I was pissed after that and thought about just getting rid of you. That's why I had one of them watching the biker's clubhouse for you to leave. It was our lucky day when you left with just the one biker."

He grabbed my chin hard. "That's the kind of fucker you let touch you, a scum of the earth biker? Well, you don't have to worry about him. You and I are going far away from all that biker trash." He raged. He stepped back and then continued speaking calmly again. "My guy just waited until he saw you coming back, and it was easy to run you off the road. However, the dumb ass didn't stop to be sure you were dead. After I found out you were both still alive, I knew I shouldn't have tried to kill you. We can have such a good life together. All I have to do is get you away from those bikers who are messing with your mind. You'll see, we'll be so happy." He smiled. He was crazy! He believed what he was saying.

I tried to keep my mouth shut, but I couldn't. "You're crazy, Tucker. There's no way I would want to be with you. Those bikers will look for me and when they come for me, you'll wish you'd stayed the hell away from me." I spat at him.

He pulled back his hand and slapped me. My head whipped to the side. Pain exploded down my cheek and jaw. I knew he would hit me. I had to get him angry enough to lose his control, so he wasn't clearly thinking. But not let him get so mad, he killed me. It would be the only way to get a chance to get out of here. He struggled to get back in control. Finally, I saw the smile come back on his face.

"That's okay my dear. I'll let you have some time

to think and realize you do belong with me. I'll see you later." He walked to the basement door and left. At least I had a reprieve. Just how long of one, I had no idea. Please God let them find me soon.

Chapter 29: Terror

We had gotten the fire out in the building. As we returned to the main area, I saw Eric and Gage racing toward me. I ran over to them. "What's wrong?" I could see blood running down both their faces. Gage spoke up first. By this time Bull and several others had joined us.

"After you guys went to help with the fire, Laci came and got us. She said someone needed help finding their lost kids. We went with Harlow and followed her. When we went around one of the buildings, both of us were jumped and knocked out. We came to and Harlow is gone along with Laci. We looked around some and didn't see them at all." He said worriedly. I could see he was waiting for me to blow.

"What the fuck!" I screamed. "She's gone? Did you get a look at who hit you?" How long ago did this happen?" I was rattling off questions as my mind tried to grasp the fact she was gone.

Eric spoke up. "It was about twenty minutes ago. We never saw the guys who hit us. Just Laci."

I swung around and gave the command for the guys to spread out and look for Harlow. I hoped she had just gone for help, but in my gut, I knew that wasn't it. The guys all scattered. Within ten minutes all of them were back. Everyone was shaking their heads no. Rage boiled through my gut. I swung and hit Eric and then decked Gage. "You'd better pray we find her safe and sound. Otherwise, you're dead. That's my fucking old lady!"

I paced away to get myself under control. They didn't deserve my anger. Bull joined me. He placed his hand on my shoulder. "We'll find her. We just need to think. We need to think where around here it is likely someone would take her?"

"I don't know. What if they didn't keep her around here and took her farther away?" I could feel the bile in my throat. All the things that could be happening to her, rolled around in my mind.

"You can't think like that, Terror. We have to think positive. We all refuse to allow her to be taken from us. Let's head back to the compound and get to work." Bull admonished. He was right. We had to think positive. I would find her and get her back. We rounded up the club and headed back to the compound. Once there, we met in church.

"I was thinking where she could've been taken." Hawk said. "I think Laci is key to us finding out where. If nothing else, she can tell us who took her since it looks like she helped them. Amber is the closest to her out of the girls. Let's get her in here." He was right. Amber was closest to Laci and I had seen her in the common room when we all came in. I sent him out to find her.

Amber hesitantly followed Hawk into the room. Her eyes roamed around the table. She was scared to death. A club bunny had never been pulled into church. I told her to have a seat. She reluctantly sat down. "Amber, we need some information and you're the one to give it to us. We need to know if you've been talking to Laci lately. Do you know what she's been up to and where she might be found?" I asked her.

She swallowed and her gaze jumped from face to face. At my glower, she spoke. "She's not been hanging with me much anymore, since the last time you told her to leave you alone. I know she was pissed about Harlow and kept ranting you'd come back to her. A couple of weeks ago, she got all happy. She said it was just a matter of time before she had you back and Harlow was out of the picture. I don't know what she meant. She was so convinced she was going to be with you. I knew that was never going to happen, even if Harlow hadn't come along."

"Did she say if she had been hanging out with anyone new? Do you know where she might be if she's not at home?"

She shook her head. "She didn't tell me the name of anyone new. If she isn't home, there's one place she might be. Her family has an old cabin out in the woods off of Gopher Canyon. I can show you on a map. She took me out there one time when we wanted to get away. If she's not there, then I have no idea. I'm sorry." She had tears in her eyes.

I reassured her and got Smoke to get us a map. She looked at it and pointed out where the cabin was. We thanked her and told her to hang around. Once she was out of the room, we got our plan together. Everyone made sure to suit up with extra ammunition. I planned to find Harlow and God help anyone who got in my way. Within fifteen minutes we were on the road.

We decided not to take the bikes, this way Laci wouldn't hear us coming. We all piled into various vehicles. We stopped about a half mile down the road from where the cabin was located and walked the rest of the way. It was dark and I could see a faint light on in a cabin window. I sent some of the guys to the backside of the place. The rest remained in front with me. I kicked in the door to find Laci sitting in a chair in the living room. She screamed in surprise when the door came crashing open. She tried to run for the back door, but Savage and the guys with him came through it. She was trapped. She froze and looked between us. She took a scared look at my face. I could see the moment when she decided to brazen it out.

"Terror, what a surprise! You guys scared me. What're you all doing here?" She coyly asked? She stepped up to me and ran her hand up my arm. Did she think I was this stupid? I grabbed her arm and shoved her in a chair. She gasped.

"Laci don't try that shit with me. You know why we're here. Now you're going to tell us who those men were with you. The ones who took Harlow. And you're going to tell us now." I roared. She cringed back in the chair. I heard her whimper. She tried to play dumb.

"I have no idea what you're talking about. There were no men with me. I haven't seen Harlow."

I grabbed her by the throat. "Listen bitch, I don't hurt or kill women as a rule. But in your case, I'll make an exception. Tell me what you know or so help me God, I'll strangle you right now."

She gasped, trying to breathe around the hand I had squeezing her neck. I eased back. She coughed and cleared her throat. "A man approached me a couple of weeks ago. Said his woman had run off and was shacking up with some biker. He told me her name and that he knew I hung out with you guys. He promised me money if I helped to get her back. So, I took it and gave him information when I heard it."

"What did he look like and did he give you a

name?" She denied he gave her a name but her description fit Tucker. Son of a bitch, he had been the one! Now we had to find him and Harlow. "Do you know where he hangs out?"

"No, I don't. I mostly hung out with the three guys he had working for him here," she denied.

"Think! Did you ever meet them anywhere?" She cringed more. I could see she knew I was serious. Finally, she said hesitantly.

"One time they met me at this old house outside of town. It was on the west side. It's an old farmhouse about ten miles out. I could show you where it is." I pulled out the map Amber had marked for us and had her show us where this old house was. Once she did, I had Hammer, Gage and Eric take her back to the clubhouse. I wasn't finished with her yet. She cried, begged, and yelled out how much she loved me as they took her away. I shut all her bullshit out of my mind. All that mattered at this moment was finding Harlow. We all got back in the other vehicles and headed to the west side of town. Again, we parked down the road from the house.

We quietly moved in on the place. It was an old cottage. The place was practically falling down. We could see a faint glow in the window, just like we had at Laci's cabin. We followed the same game plan as we had at her place. When we came through the door, a guy jumped up with a bottle of beer in his hand. He was watching porn on the television. Before he could grab the gun on the coffee table, we had him subdued and sitting on the couch. He stared at all of us with a pissed look in his eyes.

"You're going to tell us where Tucker has taken my woman, Harlow." I growled at him. He smirked and shrugged.

"I don't know a Tucker or a Harlow. You must have me mixed up with someone else." I hit him right in the mouth. His head reared back, and blood began to pour out.

"Let's try this again. Where's Tucker and Harlow?" He kept up his innocent act for about ten minutes. By that time, he had been beaten black and blue and had some broken bones. It had been a few hours since she was taken. I needed him to tell me what he knew. I looked at Bull. "Why don't you show him your knife, Bull?"

Bull pulled out a wicked knife he always carried. He was known for his knife skills and I knew he wanted a piece of this asshole. He cut the guy's shirt down the front. The guy's eyes grew wide. Bull made the first cut on his chest. He yelled out. Bull kept making precise cuts all over his chest and abdomen. He finally broke down begging us not to cut him anymore.

"Him and the others took her to a place he has out toward Chattanooga. He had us rent it for him. He just came in last night. That's where he should be. I don't think they would have left yet." He groaned out.

"We need to know the exact address." I growled. He nodded and gave us the address. I called Smoke. He'd stayed back at the clubhouse to coordinate and be on hand for such things as this. I gave him the address. He had it pulled up with notes on the surrounding area in less than ten minutes. I had a couple of the guys take this one back to the clubhouse as well. We got on the road to Ooltewah. It was a town north of Chattanooga on I- 75. There were a lot of places out in the country there. One of those was where Tucker had rented a place.

It took us an hour to get there. The whole way I kept praying, let us be in time. I couldn't live without my soul. And my soul was exactly what Harlow was. She had all of me and without her, I would never be complete again. We took the road toward the address we were given. We passed one other house about two miles from the one we were looking for. These were big properties with lots of acreage. You could keep someone out here and they could scream, and no one would ever hear them.

We stopped like we had done two other times tonight, away from the house. Everyone checked their guns again to be sure they were good to go. Smoke had texted some more information on the house. It had a front and back door, but also on one side there was a cellar door. He had access to satellite data. How he got this information so fast, I didn't ask. All I knew was it was due to his past work for the government. We were splitting into three groups to breach all three exits at the same time. I had a feeling he may have her in the basement. So, I decided to lead that group. Bull was leading the group going in the back door and Demon was leading the one going in the front door. Cannon chose to go with Demon. My group reached the cellar door. I counted off and signaled to Demon and Bull via text when to breach. I busted down those cellar doors. The sight that greeted me made me go insane.

Chapter 30: Harlow

Tucker left me alone for a couple of hours. When he came back, he had a swagger to his step. This fucker really thought he was going to get away with this! I waited for my moment. He came over and laid his nasty mouth on mine. He tried to push his tongue into my mouth, but I kept my lips closed tight. He ground his mouth hard against mine and I could taste blood where my teeth cut the inside of my lips. I jerked my head away.

This only seemed to make him angry. He grabbed my hair and jerked my head back. "You'll do what I say, bitch. I'll train you to enjoy what I do to you. Now open your fucking mouth!" He yelled. He shifted back toward my mouth and I head butted him. I heard his nose crack. Blood began to pour down his face. He roared in rage. He pulled back his fist and hit me in the eye. I saw stars. He hit me a few more times, but this time in the stomach. I doubled over as far as I could while being tied to the chair.

He stomped away and stood for a minute breathing hard. He reached up and I heard him snap his nose back into place. I had news for him, that was the least of the injuries I planned to give him. The first time he had taken me by surprise out in the desert. When he had approached me, I thought nothing of a commanding officer stopping to chat. It was a little weird he was up so late, but there were officers who were like that. This time I was ready for the motherfucker.

He came back to me and stared at me. I held his gaze. He snarled and backhanded me in the face. Then I felt him grab the front of my top. He ripped it from neck to waist. My chest was now exposed and only covered by my bra. I had a front clasp bra on today. He reached up and unsnapped it. My breasts were now out for him to see. He leered before he reached out and roughly grabbed my left breast. He squeezed it until I cried out. He then did the same to the right one. He kept twisting and pulling at my breasts. It hurt bad but I refused to make any more sounds.

He finally tired of this and stepped back. I saw him eyeing me and a spot over on the floor. An old mattress had been left in the basement. I could see the exact moment he decided to rape me there. He pulled out a knife and cut my feet loose. He kept my hands tied behind my back and jerked me to my feet. I tried to kick his legs out from under him, but he was too quick. He dragged me to the mattress and threw me down. Luckily, I landed on my side. He stood over me removing his shirt and kicking off his shoes.

"I'll show you what a real man feels like between your legs. When I'm done with you, you'll never want another man." He sneered. He bent down and I kicked him in the crotch. He doubled over and roared out in pain. While he was doubled over, I wiggled and got my ass and legs between my arms, so I could get my hands in front of me. This would give me more of an advantage, even if they were tied. Thank goodness I was very flexible, and I had practiced this very move many times. It was something the guys at the club told me to know how to do just in case. Was I glad I listened!

He got his breath back and kicked me in the ribs

several times. I tried to curl up and protect them as much as possible, but he still was able to make contact. When he was done, I was sure I had cracked, if not broken ribs. I was having a hard time catching my breath. He grabbed my legs and pinned them to the floor. He ground his mouth against mine again. This time I opened my mouth. I could sense his feeling of triumph. He stuck his tongue in my mouth and I bit down hard on it. He screamed and pulled away. More blood ran down his face. He grabbed my neck and started to choke me. I thought he was going to kill me. However, he gained control again before I passed out. He threw me away from him and I rolled off the mattress onto the dirty, hard cement floor.

He grabbed his knife again and crouched over me. "You'll pay for that you whore!" He sliced a cut down my belly on the right side. Then he did another matching one on the left. They burned. I could feel the warm blood running from the wounds. Luckily, they seemed to be rather shallow. Where was Terror? Would they find me in time? I decided that if they didn't, I was going to make him kill me before he had the chance to rape me. There was no way I was going out of this world with him having been inside of me. Terror was the only one who would ever have that pleasure. I just would keep fighting him until he got so enraged, he killed me.

He held the knife to my throat while he wrestled the snap and zipper of my jeans open. Removing the knife from my throat, he held my bound hands and used the knife to cut my jeans and panties away. I was now totally exposed to him. He leered down at my body. I could see the lust raging in his eyes. He no longer looked human. He laid the knife off to the side where I couldn't reach it and began working his pants off. Jesus, please don't let this happen!

I tried to get away, but he had me at a disadvantage and without free use of my hands I couldn't. But I put up a hell of a fight. It took him several minutes to subdue me again. Once he had his pants off, I could see his engorged cock. He was so excited at the thought of raping me. I tried to kick out at him while keeping my legs closed. He put his weight on them and pried my thighs apart. I bucked and tried to throw him off, but he just laughed. He had my legs open and he was probing my entrance with the head of his cock. I wanted to puke. I pulled my hands loose from his grip and swung at his head with all my might. I connected with his temple. He was momentarily stunned. I twisted to the side trying to reach the knife. Just as I was almost to it, I heard the door to the basement explode open.

I looked over my shoulder and saw Terror and some of the guys. He spotted us and I saw a terrible rage transform his face. Tucker was naked and still between my legs. Thankfully, he hadn't been able to penetrate me due to the strike to his temple. I grabbed the knife and swiped it across his face. He screamed and reared back on his heels. Terror reached him and jerked him away from me, throwing him across the room. Viper came over to me. He cut my hands loose and pulled off his shirt to cover me. I couldn't stop shivering. I watched Terror go insane. At the same time, I heard several pairs of boots stomping down the stairs. Apparently, Terror had brought more of the club with him.

Chapter 31: Terror

As I breached the basement, I saw Harlow on a dirty mattress on the floor. She was naked and Tucker was hunched over her with his body between her thighs. He was naked too. I yelled in rage, sprinting across the floor. Just as I got to him, she swiped across his face with a knife. He yelled and I grabbed him. I flung him as far away from her as I could. He'd fucking touched my woman! I could see in that quick glance, she was beaten, bleeding, and tied. I wasn't sure if we had gotten here in time or if he'd already raped her. He was a dead man either way. As I went after him, I vaguely saw Viper cutting her loose and putting his shirt on her. Bull, Demon, Cannon and most of the other guys broke into the basement from upstairs. I saw them freeze when they saw the state of Harlow.

I grabbed a hold of him and jerked him to his feet. I pounded away at his face. I was going to smash in his face and splatter his brains all over the place. Through my rage, I heard Bull. "Terror, you need to stop. We'll make him pay, but right now Harlow needs you. Come on son, go to her. We'll take him back with us to the compound. We already got the two guys who were upstairs. Rein it in."

How could he be so calm? Didn't he see what he'd done to her? I dropped Tucker, and turned to face Bull. Then I saw his eyes. He was far from calm. He wanted this fucker to die as much as I did. But he was right, I needed to take care of Harlow first. I turned to Savage and Ranger. "Get this fucker out of my sight. Take him back to the compound." They nodded and roughly jerked him up off the floor where he had fallen. Savage punched him in the gut and Ranger smashed his fist into his face. He was a bloody mess and was whimpering and begging. He would beg a lot more before we were through with him.

I walked slowly over to Harlow, where she was huddled up in Demon's arms. Her poor face was a mess. Her right eye was swollen shut. Her mouth was busted, and she had bruises all over her face. I could see finger marks around her throat. Her hands were bruised, and she had blood coming through the shirt on her stomach. Blood was running down her legs and more bruises were starting to appear on her thighs.

I gently took her in my arms hugging her to me. She was shaking and then I heard a sob break loose. "Shh baby, I got you. Come on let's get out of here. Everything is going to be okay. Let me take care of you." I picked her up in my arms and carried her out of there. A few of the guys stayed behind. We didn't know what kind of DNA we might have left, so they were going to make sure this place burned to the ground. I hoped the real owners had insurance.

I took her up the stairs and out to the SUV. I got in the back seat with her and held her on my lap. Her dad got in the back with us. Demon drove while Cannon road shotgun. Everyone was quiet. The only sound was her ragged breathing and sobs she would let out every once in a while. She was killing me. As we got closer to home, I told Demon to head for the hospital. She needed to be checked out. This got a response out of her.

She jerked up into a sitting position. "No, I don't

want to go to the hospital. I've had enough of that place. Take me to the clubhouse."

"Harlow, babe, you need someone to check you out. You're bleeding and could have internal injuries."

She adamantly shook her head no. "I have bruises, a couple of cuts and probably cracked or broken ribs. Since I can breathe, I don't think the ribs have punctured my lungs. All they would do for those is wrap them anyway. Ghost can take a look at me if you want. But no hospital!" She was starting to get more upset. I decided to concede to her wishes and see what Ghost had to say. If he thought she needed to go, then she would go, even if I had to take her kicking and screaming.

"Okay, we'll go to the clubhouse. Now just relax and try to sleep."

She did sit back in my arms, but I could feel the tension still in her body. She stayed awake. We pulled into the compound and right outside my house an hour later. Demon had texted Ghost to meet us at the house. I took her straight out of the SUV and inside to our bedroom. Before I could lay her down on the bed, she yelled for someone to throw something on it to keep from ruining the comforter. I told them. "Fuck the comforter," and laid her down.

Ghost was already there with his medical bag. He asked everyone to step out. I sat down to stay. He looked at me. "Terror, you need to let me check her over. I have to ask her something and it might be easier if you're not in here. I know she's your old lady. I promise to take real good care of her and get you back in here as soon as possible." I could see the worry in his eyes. He didn't want me to lose it in front of Harlow. She was hanging on by a thread. I reluctantly left the room. We all paced the hall waiting for his examination to be over. Bull stood with his head hanging down. He had a look of absolute agony on his face. Cannon and Demon didn't look much better.

I clasped Bull on the shoulder. "She'll be alright. No matter what happened she'll be okay." I knew I was telling him what I wanted to hear. I was worried. What if she wasn't ever the same? Did he rape her? Did he do other things we didn't know about in those hours he'd had her? How could I ever look her in the eyes again? I'd failed to keep her safe. I hung my head and closed my eyes. About twenty agonizing minutes later, Ghost came out of the room. We all anxiously crowded him to hear what he had to say.

"She has the obvious bruising. While her face looks bad, I don't think anything is broken. He did crack some ribs and I bound those up for her. It'll take several weeks for those to heal. There were two shallow knife cuts on her stomach. I stitched them up. They probably won't even scar."

I swallowed and then asked what I knew we all wanted to know. "Did he rape her?"

Ghost shook his head. "No. From what she said, he was about to penetrate her when you busted in. She wouldn't let me check for any tears or trauma, so we have to assume she's telling the truth. She's going to need to talk to someone even if he didn't rape her. She's been through hell."

We all breathed a sigh of relief. We followed him back into the bedroom. She was lying on the bed staring at the wall. When we entered, she looked over at us. At first, she seemed unable to focus on any one of us. Then she seemed to realize who it was. Her dad sat down on the edge of the bed and gave her a gentle hug. "Baby girl, I'm so glad we found you. Everything is going to be alright. Just take your time and rest." She nodded at him.

Next, Demon hugged and gave her a kiss. Cannon did the same. After they all had a chance to comfort her, they excused themselves. Ghost went with them. I eased down on the bed and laid beside her. She was just watching me. I ran my hands through her hair. "Baby, I'm so glad we found you. I don't know what I would do without you. I'm so sorry I fucking failed you. I told you that you would be safe, and he still got to you. Will you ever be able to forgive me," I asked with a knot in my stomach. What if she said she couldn't forgive me?

She jerked in surprise. She raised up on her elbow. "What makes you think you failed me? You didn't fail me. You rescued me. No one could've imagined Laci would have helped him. Also, you had him being monitored in South Carolina. There's nothing to forgive." She ran her hand over my jaw. I sighed. I leaned over and gently kissed her on her sore mouth. She laid her head down on my shoulder and I wrapped her in my arms. We stayed this way for a while. Then I had to ask her what happened in that basement. She took a fortifying breath and told me the story. My heart stopped when she told me she had decided to make him mad enough to kill her. I couldn't have lived with that. When she finished, I was truly amazed. My woman was one strong ass woman! She had fought like a tiger. I kissed her again.

I had asked her if he had raped her and she reassured me no, we'd made it there in time. I held her until she drifted off to sleep. I knew everyone was anxious for an update. I sent a text to Bull and let them know we would have church in the morning at nine. In the meantime, they needed to keep our guests on ice. We would be handling them later.

She woke twice during the night screaming. I held her and soothed her back to sleep. I woke around seven the next morning. She was sound asleep, so I got up and went downstairs. I fixed her some breakfast. Also, I texted Kade to be at my house by 8:45, so I could go to church and she could have someone with her. She seemed the closest to Kade out of the prospects.

I took her a tray up to the bedroom. I had made some bacon, eggs, toast and orange juice. She was just stirring when I came in. I sat the tray on the dresser. "Do you need to go to the bathroom, baby?" She nodded. I helped her up and into the bathroom. Once she was done, she washed her hands and face. I told her after breakfast I would help her get a bath. I knew she had to be craving one.

I helped her get situated in the bed and gave her the tray. While she ate, I cleaned up the room. In the bathroom, I found the pain pills the doctor had prescribed her after the wreck. I took her out one. She had to be hurting. She took it without protest confirming I was right.

She ate some of everything, but still not as much as I would've liked. I took the tray away after she was done. Then I helped her back to the bathroom. I knew with her stitches she shouldn't immerse them in water for a few days, therefore, I got the shower going. I helped her out of her clothes and into the shower. Much like what I had done after the wreck, I got her cleaned up and washed her hair. Back in the bedroom, I dressed her in a pair of low waisted shorts so they wouldn't rub on her cuts. I put her in another one of my tee shirts. Before she laid back down, I quickly stripped the bed and put clean sheets and a cover on it. I tucked her in.

"Harlow, I need to go to the clubhouse for a little bit. I'm going to have Kade come over to stay with you while I'm gone. If you need anything just text him. He'll be downstairs. You have his number in your phone. As soon as we get done, I'll come right back." I could see she was hesitant to be left, but I had no other choice. I didn't want her sitting in the clubhouse. She needed to rest. She finally nodded her head in agreement. I gave her a gentle kiss. I knew the inside of her mouth was sore from her teeth cutting the inside of her lips. I softly lapped at them. When I was done, I made sure she had water, the remote to the television, and her cell phone. I took the tray down to the kitchen. I would clean this up later. I heard a knock at the door.

Kade was on the porch. I had him come in and explained what I had told Harlow. He said not to worry, he'd keep an eye on her. I left for the clubhouse. The sooner we got started, the sooner I could get back to her. Entering the common room, I could see everyone was here. Everyone was somber. Sherry was there and had tears in her eyes. She came over and gave me a hug. I thought about seeing if Harlow wanted company. I shot off a quick text to her. She responded right away and said yes. I told Sherry, and she happily scurried away.

I called everyone else into church. The whole crew was restless. We were all trying hard to stay in our seats. I started off the meeting by giving them the overall details. Murder was in all their eyes. Savage piped up." What're we going to do with Laci, Tucker and those other three guys?"

I glared. "What do you think? We're going to kill those fuckers Tucker hired as well as him. As for Laci, you know I don't like to beat or kill women. What do you suggest we do with her? She can't be let off the hook scotch free. She can't stay around here."

Tiny spoke up. "How do you feel about another woman doing the beat down?" That was a good idea. I had no problem with it, but Harlow was out of commission for a while.

"I think it's a good idea. We'll have to keep her locked up until Harlow is better. She's in no position to kick her ass right now." The other guys laughed and said they thought it was a great idea too. We decided to keep her under wraps until Harlow was feeling better. That was unless Harlow had another idea on how to punish her. Then we moved onto the others.

"As for the three Tucker hired, I say we just kill them and get rid of the bodies. We can beat the hell out of them first. They need to suffer some. If we let them live, they'll do something like this again. We'd be doing the world a favor killing them. Tucker is the one I want to see suffer. We'll keep his ass and torture him for a bit. Then we'll get rid of him." I coldly told them. I had no pity for any of them. Those three took money to hurt and then kill her. Tucker was going to rape her. He would die the slowest and hardest out of the four.

No one disagreed with the plan. I decided to let the guys have fun with the three hired hands. But when it came to Tucker, he belonged to Bull and me. I struck the gavel to signal the meeting was at an end. It was time to get back to Harlow. As I headed toward the door, Bull caught up with me. "Harlow is going to ask what you plan to do with all these guys. What're you going to tell her?"

Typically, we wouldn't tell a woman about club business. However, this did directly involve Harlow and I knew she wouldn't take being told not to worry about it.

I told him, "I'm going to tell her what we plan to do. I feel it's the right thing. If she has other thoughts, I'll listen to what they are." He smiled.

"Good idea. I'll come over later and see how she's doing." He walked over to Demon and Cannon. I continued back to the house. As soon as I got there, Kade left. He said Sherry had left about ten minutes ago. Harlow hadn't needed anything, and he'd checked a couple of times. I went into the kitchen and found he had cleaned up for me. I definitely would be nominating him in the next few weeks to be patched in. I didn't think anyone would object, so I had Savage order his cut already. I went upstairs.

She was resting in the bed and watching some cooking show when I came in. She turned off the television. I sat down and told her what she had missed last night between Laci and getting the other guys. When I finished, she was silent for a while. She looked at me with trepidation. What was she afraid of?

"I want to ask something?" I told her anything. "I do want to be the one who kicks Laci's ass, so thank you. What else I want is to be there when you take care of Tucker for good."

I didn't want her to see that. I started to protest but stopped when she held up her hand. "The only way I'm ever going to be able to feel safe, is by seeing, with my own eyes, him put down. I need this, Declan. Please let me have this." She was half begging. I couldn't say no. I understood where she was coming from as well. I broke down and agreed. She hugged me and we wrapped ourselves around each other. I spent the rest of the day taking care of her and having her dad and a few others visit. By evening she was exhausted, and I got her to take

more pain meds before she fell asleep. I had told Bull her request. We would be holding off on taking care of Tucker until she was feeling better.
• •

Chapter 32: Harlow

It had been three weeks since the ordeal with Tucker. I was healing well. My ribs would hurt if I didn't watch how I moved sometimes. All the bruising and other injuries were healed. Today, I planned to have the come to Jesus talk with Laci. Terror wanted me to wait longer, but I didn't want to. I wanted her out of our lives now. They had been keeping her in one of the cells out in the Hole. This was a building on the back part of the property specifically set up for this kind of thing. Tucker was kept in one of the other cells. They had taken care of the three other guys. I didn't ask what they had done with them. I didn't care.

They brought Laci to the clubhouse and down to the gym in the basement. She looked like hell. They'd given her food and water but that was about it. Her eyes were sunken into her head with dark circles under them. When she saw me waiting there, she stopped and tried to get out the door. The guys laughed and just shoved her toward me. I walked up to her. She refused to look me in the eyes.

I hunkered down until I could see her eyes. "Laci, you're lucky none of the guys really believe in killing a woman, otherwise, you'd be dead. Also, they don't believe in a man beating a woman." She got a hopeful look in her eyes. I dashed that hope. "However, they have no problem with another woman beating the hell out of you. Today,

I'm going to teach you to never betray another person again and to never covet what isn't yours to have. You'll be allowed to defend yourself. Now get your ass in that ring. We're settling this. Once we're done, you have a day to get all your shit and leave town. If we ever hear of you being around any chapter of the Warriors or one of their affiliates, you'll be eliminated permanently."

She flinched but looking around, she saw she had no way out. She slowly got in the ring. I slid in behind her. I stood still to allow her to take the first shot. At first, she didn't look like she would do it. But when I didn't hit her, she looked a little cocky. She threw the first punch. It wasn't an impressive one. I easily ducked. From there on out, I systematically beat her all over her body. I made sure to not do permanent damage, but left her with plenty of visible injuries that would hurt for a long time. After I was done, Eric and Quin carried her out of the ring. They would be taking her back to her place to pack and would make sure she left town by tomorrow at the latest. The rest of the guys laughed and told me to never get pissed at them enough to try that on them. She hadn't landed a single punch.

With Laci out of the way, it was time to talk to Terror about finishing with Tucker. I wanted this to be the final clean sweep. I wanted to get on with our lives. Having him hanging around, made me unable to do it. I pulled him to the side. "Baby, I want us to take care of Tucker today as well." I could see he was going to try and talk me out of it. I stopped his protests. "No, honey, I need for this to be over. I know you, dad, and probably Demon and Cannon have been torturing him over the last three weeks. It's time to finish him. You already know why I have to be there. Please, let's get this over with. And as much as I know you want to strike the last blow; I need us to do it together."

He really didn't like that. But I wasn't going to back down. He must have seen it in my eyes. He reluctantly nodded and said to give him a little time to set up. An hour later we were on our way to the Hole. The whole club was following us. Someone had pulled Tucker out of his cell and into the big common area. He was hanging by his arms from a chain hooked into the ceiling. He was unrecognizable. His face was beaten and looked like raw hamburger meat. Every inch of his body looked like it was covered in cuts and bruises. He looked up. When he saw Terror and me, he began to moan. We came to stand in front of him. I got up close to his face.

"You filthy, raping bastard. You'll never be able to hurt another woman ever again. Today, we are going to put you out of your misery. I hope you rot in hell." I spat. He merely looked at me with dead eyes. I walked over to the table where the guys had various instruments of torture. I picked up a knife and Terror did as well. Back in front of Tucker, we stood. While I had the urge to torture him myself, I knew I needed to just end it. I wouldn't let him be a part of this world. We looked into each other's eyes. Terror nodded and counted from one to three. On three we both cut Tucker. I stabbed him in the crotch and Terror slit his throat. He made a high-pitched gurgling sound and we listened while he took his last breaths. I'd killed people before in the Corps. I'd never gotten satisfaction out of it. It had been my job. With Tucker, I got satisfaction. Once he had stopped breathing, I handed the knife over to Hawk. Terror told the guys to take care of the mess and we walked out of the building.

The whole way back to the house, we remained

silent. Once back at the house, we headed straight to the shower. When we were done, I pulled Terror to me. I kissed him with everything I had in me. Over the last three weeks, he'd been so caring and gentle. He held me at night, but never made any moves to make love to me. A part of me wondered if he didn't want me after what happened with Tucker. I hadn't gotten the nerve to ask him. But I was tired of waiting. I pulled him with me to the bed and pushed him down. He fell back and I crawled on top of him. He grabbed my hands and stopped me exploring. "No baby, you need to rest," he said.

I jerked back. I was pissed. If he didn't want me, then fine. I got off the bed and started to throw on some clean clothes. He got up and came over to me. "Where are you going"? I whipped around.

"If you don't want me anymore because of what Tucker did, then be man enough to tell me. Stop using the excuse I need to rest or to heal. I'm going to find dad. I think it's time to go home to Hunters Creek." I stomped out the door and headed down the hall. Fuck this! If he didn't want me, I wouldn't beg or stay here.

I'd made it to the top of the stairs before I was grabbed and thrown over his shoulder. He marched back to the bedroom and lowered me to the mattress. Before I could get up, he had me pinned on the bed. He had my hands secured by one of his above my head and his legs had mine pinned. He was glaring down at me.

"You think I don't want you? You think what Tucker did has changed how I feel about you? You've lost your mind! There is nothing in this world that would ever change how I feel about you woman. I fucking love you. Even if he'd raped you, I'd never stop wanting you or loving you." He growled and then took my lips in a searing kiss. I moaned as he took over my mouth.

He broke the kiss and started to tug my clothes off. He pulled my shirt up over my head and launched it across the room. My panties and shorts soon followed. I had been in a hurry and I'd forgotten to put on a bra. As soon as I was naked, he cupped my breast and started sucking and nipping my nipples. I felt my pussy get wet. It seemed like it had been forever since he had touched me like this.

His hand slid down to my pussy while he was ravishing my breasts. He slipped a finger between my folds. He found my clit and worked it over and over. He ground the heel of his hand into my clit while sinking two fingers into my pussy. God, that felt so good! I bucked in his hand. He kept relentlessly kissing, sucking. and kneading my breasts and my neck. While he continued to play with my soaking wet pussy. I was just on the brink of an orgasm when he pulled back. He crawled up my body and straddled my chest. His knees were on either side of my face.

"Open up. I want you to suck my cock." He ordered. His eyes were glazed with lust. I could see his cock was red and angry looking. Pre-cum was oozing out of his slit. I opened my mouth and swallowed him. He stretched my mouth to the limits. He was pushing me to take him deeper. He never hurt me or went too far, but he challenged me to take as much as I could. I played with his balls and sucked and lapped his cock. I could tell he was getting closer to an orgasm because he was grunting as he slid in and out of my mouth.

After several minutes of this, he pulled back and slid down my body. Once there he lapped at my pussy juices spilling out and running down my thighs. He sucked like a starving man. It only took a few licks and sucks for me to go over the edge. I screamed as I came. I didn't have time to even catch my breath, before he was slamming his cock in my pussy. He went all the way in with just one stroke. I screamed more. Fuck, that felt wonderful! He pounded away inside of me never letting up. He looked almost crazed. He hammered in and out of me like a piston. Pushing me higher and higher. I could feel another orgasm coming. Suddenly, the tingling was racing up my legs from my feet. It reached my pussy and centered there. I came yelling again. I was thrashing my head all over the bed. He was killing me. He had never been this out of control before. I loved it!

He abruptly pulled out of my pussy and flipped me over onto my belly. He yanked me to my knees and then I felt his cock at the entrance to my ass. He slowly pushed his slick, engorged cock into my tight ass. God, he felt bigger than he ever had. Once he was fully seated, he began to plow his cock in and out of me. I could hardly catch my breath. I could feel a third orgasm coming on already. I could hear him panting and groaning.

Suddenly, he pulled all the way back until only the tip remained in my ass. He paused. I felt him take a deep breath, and then he slammed back inside of me. That was all it took. I came screaming and crying for a third time. He cursed, grunted and then I felt him spilling his hot cum in my ass. He kept moving until his cock stopped jerking and my pussy stopped milking his cock. We both collapsed on the bed. I was so dazed I wasn't sure where I was. He pushed my hair off my neck and kissed me behind my ear. He panted. "Does that feel like I don't want you? Never think that again, baby. I always want you. I always will. I love you woman. Will you marry me?"

I couldn't believe he had asked me this in the

middle of me trying to regain my senses. He had just blown my mind with the best sex ever and now he was asking me to marry him! I couldn't talk yet, so I just nodded yes. He eased his softening cock out of my ass and rolled off the bed. He reached into his nightstand and pulled out a small box. He crawled back on the bed beside me and opened it. Inside was a gorgeous emerald cut diamond in a platinum band. It had small baguette diamonds all around it. It had to be at least one and a half carats worth of diamonds. He slid it on my left ring finger and kissed my lips. Then he pulled me into his arms.

"You've just made me the happiest man alive. Thank you, Temptress. I love you." I caressed his face.

"I love you too and you've made me the happiest woman alive." We fell asleep holding each other. I woke up a couple of hours later. He was smiling at me when I opened my eyes.

"Do you still have any doubts I want or love you?" He teasingly asked. I shook my head no. I had no doubts this man loved me as much as I loved him. My tender pussy and slightly sore ass were reminders. I pulled him to me and kissed him.

"No Declan, I have no doubts. I love you so much. But you can tell me again, the way you did a while ago, any time you want." I teased him back. He threw back his head and laughed. He stood up and smacked my ass.

"Get a move on woman. We need to go tell everyone the good news." I got up and we both hit the shower. After getting out and ready, we headed to the clubhouse. Walking in, everyone seemed to be in a good mood. I walked up to dad. Before I could say anything, Terror was yelling. "Quiet everyone. We need your attention." Everyone got silent. He grinned and raised my left hand with his ring on it. "I asked Harlow to marry me and she said yes!" He shouted. Everyone cheered and was congratulating us. I saw him nod to Savage and he left the room. Dad grabbed my attention. He was staring hard at Terror. What was wrong?

Dad came over and got up close to Terror. "What makes you think I'd let you marry my daughter?" The room got quiet. Terror just smiled.

"Bull, you're going to let me marry your daughter, because you know there's no one else in the world who will love her more than I do. She has every single piece of me. I'll do anything and everything in my power to make her happy. I can't see myself having children with anyone else but her. That's why you're going to allow me to marry your daughter." He told him confidently.

Dad waited a minute and then broke out into a huge smile. He hugged me and Terror. He congratulated us as well. We were all laughing when Savage came back in the room and handed Terror a box. Terror gave the box to me and told me to open it. I was curious. I opened the flat box. Inside was a leather cut. Pulling it out I read the back. It said *Property of Terror*. On the front I saw my road name. In script it said *Temptress.* Terror leaned down and whispered in my ear. "You're always my temptress, baby." He gave me another kiss. We spent the rest of the evening celebrating with our friends and family. It was the perfect ending to a horrible ordeal and the beginning of the rest of our lives.

• •

Epilogue:

It was our wedding day. It had been three months since Terror had asked me to marry him. I hadn't wanted to have a big church wedding. I just wanted us to have our friends and family celebrate with us. There had been some debate on where we would get married. After back and forth between dad and Terror, we settled on having it at the lake where Terror had taken me the day, he'd first told me he loved me. My Hunters Creek family traveled the four hours to the site. Most were staying at the club for a few days.

We chose to do it at sunset. Everyone had chipped in to help. There were chairs set up facing the lake with an aisle down the middle. An arbor had been raised in front of the chairs for us to say our vows. It was covered in flowers. Sherry was my matron of honor. Menace stood up as Terror's best man. Dad of course was giving me away. I decided a suit or tux was not the way to go. I wanted Terror to be comfortable. We decided him and the rest of the men would wear black jeans, their boots, with a long-sleeved white button down, collared shirt. Over top the shirt they would have on their cuts.

Sherry had picked out a short strapless turquoise gown with lace trim. Turquoise and cream were my colors. I did go the more traditional route with an actual bridal gown. But that was it. It was all lace over a nude underlay. The neckline formed a deep 'V' in the front which showed off my cleavage to advantage. The back was cut to the base of my spine exposing my whole back down to almost the top of my ass crack. The length went to the floor, but up the left leg, it had a slit which came almost to my hip. It hugged my body like a glove. I had curled my hair and pulled half of it up in the back and let the rest cascade down my back to my ass. I had a diamond choker around my neck with a matching bracelet and chandelier earrings. My shoes were open-toed crystal sling backs with a small heel, since I needed to walk across uneven ground. Dad was going to escort me to the aisle on his Harley. My bouquet was made up of the same flowers around the arbor. There were cream roses and lilies with turquoise orchids.

One of dad's members, Bear, was officiating. A small tent had been set up for the bridal party, just on the other side of the woods from the lake. Sherry left first with Tiny driving her on his bike. Dad came to get me. He had tears in his eyes. "Baby girl, you look beautiful. I wish your mom could've been here to see you today. Here is something for your big day." He handed me a box. Opening it, inside I found a beautiful diamond and sapphire bracelet. It was stunning. I told him thank you breathlessly. He helped me put it on and gave me a hug and kiss. Outside he helped me on his bike. We rode the path through the woods to the aisle.

Demon stood ready to help me off. Dad then got off the bike and walked me down the aisle while Demon took his seat. Terror was staring at me in awe. When I reached him, he took me from my dad with a chin lift. He whispered, "you look so beautiful, you take my breath away."

We stood just staring into each other's eyes as the

minister spoke his words. When it came time to exchange vows, we recited the ones we had written. Terror said his first. "Harlow, today I take you as my wife. You are the keeper of not only my heart but of my soul. I love you without end. I never thought I would find someone like you, nor could I have ever imagined loving someone as much as I love you. As we walk through the remainder of this life together, I promise to love you more every day, to take care of you in every way. I will take care of you in the good and the bad. I will cherish you and put no one before you. I will be faithful and never let you doubt that you have my heart, mind and soul. I love you."

As he finished his vows, he slipped the wedding band on my finger. It was platinum with intricate Celtic scrollwork. It was my turn to say my vows to him. "Declan, today I take you as my husband. You are my knight, my love and the keeper of my heart and soul. I love you without end. You were a gift that I never could have imagined receiving in my life. You make me feel things I've never felt. As we continue on this journey, I promise to love you more every day, to take care of you in every way. No matter what comes, good or bad, I'll be there. I will put no one before you and I will always be faithful. You have my heart, mind and soul. I love you."

I slipped a bigger band matching the one he had placed on me, on his finger. We both turned to the minister. He finished by blessing our union and pronounced us man and wife. Hearing this, Terror bent me over his arm and proceeded to kiss me senseless. The whoops and hoots of the crowd finally penetrated our minds. He stood me back up laughing. I could feel my face was a little red. The minister was just smiling at both of us. Facing the crowd, Bear announced us to the gathered crowd as Mr.

and Mrs. Terror and Temptress. Terror led me down the aisle and to his bike which was waiting. Hiking my dress up, I got on the bike with help from Sherry. To the cheers of everyone, we rode off. Time for the reception.

We had shut down the restaurant for the night so we could have the reception there. We had hired the band that played there one night when we went dancing. As the evening progressed, I saw Janessa. She and I had become friends over the last three months. She was still a bit shy and reserved. I was learning more about her a little at a time. Seeing her, I looked around to see where Savage was. He was over in the corner staring at her. I knew he had some kind of feelings for her. He was always watching her when she was around. He'd been to the bar several times when she was working because she had mentioned it.

When I asked her about going out with him, she would blush and change the subject. I could see the interest in her eyes, but wasn't sure why she was hesitant to go out with him. Did she think he was like most bikers, and only wanted a piece of ass? Before Terror, I used to think that way. But something in Savage's eyes told me he wasn't thinking this with her. I knew so far; he hadn't gotten her to agree to go out. However, he hadn't given up. She looked stunning in her pale blue cocktail dress. Her hair was pulled back in an elegant twist. His eyes were eating her up. I couldn't shake the feeling Janessa was hiding something. I hoped the two of them got together. I thought they were perfect for each other. I guess time would tell.

Turning I saw my husband looking at me from across the dance floor. He'd been talking to my dad. Catching my eye, he gave me a sexy smile. He left my dad and glided over to me. Wrapping his arms around me, he whispered. "Are you ready to go home, Mrs. Moran? Your husband is hungry to taste his wife."

My panties got instantly damp. I had been ready since I saw him at the altar. Kissing his lips, I whispered. "I've been ready, what've you been waiting for Mr. Moran?" He laughed and then swung me up into his arms. We practically ran out the door and to his bike. Thank God it was a short ride to the house. Our guests could continue the party without us. Honestly, I knew most of them were surprised we'd lasted as long as we had.

He carried me up the porch steps and over the threshold. I guess he was a little old fashioned in some other ways. Once in the door, he had me up the stairs and in our room in a flash. Someone had decorated it while we were gone. Around the room were lots of candles which threw soft light throughout the room. On the bed were red rose petals. He gave me a gentle kiss then turned me around. His hands worked their way down my dress undoing all those tiny buttons. He kissed my back every time more skin was revealed. When he got done, the dress pooled at my feet. Stepping out of it, I turned and reached up to help him remove his cut and shirt.

I ran my hands up his bare chest to his neck. I stood on my tiptoes to reach his earlobe. I took it into my mouth to suck. I licked my way across his jaw and placed a slow, nibbling kiss on his mouth. While I was busy doing this, he ran his hands up my back and undid my bra letting it fall to the floor. His hands were now playing with my breasts. He was caressing them and pinching my nipples.

Pushing him to sit on the couch at the foot of the bed, I sank down and undid the laces on his biker boots. He removed them and I pulled off his socks. Rising back up, I stepped out of my heels, which left me in my thigh high hose held up by my garters. My silk white satin panties covered my pussy.

He picked me up and carried me over to lay on the bed. Once there, he unhooked my garters and slowly pulled my stockings off. He removed them slowly with his teeth placing little kisses as he went. Once he had them and my garters off, he ran his hands up my legs to my thighs. There he pulled my thighs apart and lowered his head to my wet center. He stopped and drew in a deep breath. He'd once told me he loved the smell of my arousal. After easing my panties off, he lowered his head to me. One hand pulled my pussy lips apart, so he could see my clit and my juices.

He proceeded to tease me to the brink of insanity with his licks up and down my center. His stabs with his tongue into my core were delicious torture. When I was beyond half-crazy with lust, he added his fingers to my pussy. He stroked and made sure he hit my G-spot over and over. After several minutes of this, I couldn't contain myself. I felt the rush of tingling race up my legs to my pussy. I came shaking and yelling, "Declan."

He raised his head and sucked my juices from his fingers. Then he stood up and removed his pants. His hard, engorged cock sprang free to stand at attention. It begged me to touch it. I leaned up and took him in my hand. I felt a shudder run through his body. His eyes were so heated it almost made me burst into flames. I couldn't believe I made him feel like this. I stroked up and down is cock several times. I had leaned further up to take him in my mouth when he stopped me. "Baby, I can't take you putting your mouth on me. If you do, I'll shoot my load right now. Later you can give me that gorgeous mouth of yours. Right now, I need to be inside you."

I pouted but laid back on the bed. He quickly crawled up my length. Once there he placed his mouth on mine. The kiss was a passionate one. He bit down on my bottom lip and when I gasped, he speared his tongue into my mouth. I could taste myself on his tongue. That just made me burn hotter. Tongues dueling, we kissed each other over and over. Slowly breaking away, he fisted his cock and brought it to my opening. He pushed in slowly looking like he was savoring the feel of every inch. Soon, he was seated fully in my hot, soaking wet pussy. I was so full, and he felt wonderful.

He started out stroking in and out slowly, but that only lasted for a few strokes. Exhaling deeply, he picked up the rhythm. The strokes became faster and harder. He was making my whole body catch on fire. His breath was getting more and more ragged and I could hear his groans. It was during one of his deepest thrusts that I came again without warning. The sensation just raced over me like a wave. I gripped his shoulders, my nails biting into his skin. I threw back my head and wailed out my release. "God Declan, I love you!" I screamed.

I didn't get a chance to come down from my high before he thrust a few more times. Then he groaned and grunted. "Harlow, baby, I fucking love you." He kept moving inside of me until my spasms stopped and his cock stopped jerking, filling my pussy with his cum. He fell on top of me and I wrapped my arms around him. We laid there holding each other and easing back down. When we finally recovered, he rolled off of me. He gently swept my hair out of my face. He had such a tender look on his face. He smiled and spoke. "I do love you more than anything in the world, my Temptress." I smiled back and said to him.

"I love you more than anything in the world too, my Terror." As we drifted off, I thought of all the wonderful things yet to come for us and our Warrior family.

• •
**The End until Archangels' Warriors
Book 2: Savage's Princess**

About The Author

Ciara St James

I'm a sassy Libra bookaholic who has been reading just about anything I could get my hands on, since I was six years old. I love the written word and numerous genres, but romance has always been a favorite!

I grew up in Rural southeastern Ohio in a village of 4000 people. Then I married and went to San Diego where the population was several million, quite the change I can tell you!

Today, I live in beautiful TN. And I'm ruled by two pugs who try to get me to stop writing and be their sofa.

2019 I took the plunge and quit my nursing management job to dedicate my time to writing. It had been a life long dream. I find I like all romance but have a particular love for romances in all its forms. My biggest dream would be to have others read and receive joy from my books as I have from several of my favorite authors!

Books In This Series

Dublin Falls Archangel's Warriors MC

Terror's Temptress

Savage's Princess

Steel & Hammer's Hellcat

Menace's Siren

Ranger's Enchantress

Ghost's Beauty

Viper's Vixen

Printed in Great Britain
by Amazon